# A GOOD MOTHER

MICHELLE DUNNE

Storm
PUBLISHING

Ebook ISBN: 978-1-80508-528-7
Paperback ISBN: 978-1-80508-530-0

Cover design: Blacksheep
Cover images: Shutterstock

Published by Storm Publishing.
For further information, visit:
www.stormpublishing.co

ALSO BY MICHELLE DUNNE

*The Hotel Maid*

*This book is dedicated to mothers everywhere, especially my own.
For you, Ann McNamara*

*There is no way to be a perfect mother,*
*And a million ways to be a good one.*
—Jill Churchill

# PROLOGUE

The lights from the rescue boats danced across the black water, each sweep bringing Jen Blake closer to the moment her world would end. She could feel it. Whatever it was that made her human, was withering inside her, as the scene before her played out. Boats of all shapes and sizes, manned by people she'd never met, moved slowly on the now calm river, collectively illuminating the night sky. It might have looked nice, mesmerising even, to a passerby, if they knew no different. But Jen's body convulsed with the cold. Her jeans and hooded top were waterlogged, and silt from the dirty river clung to her soaking wet skin.

'Over here!' A voice rang out in the distance.

Jen's entire body slackened as everyone's attention was drawn to the silhouette of a man, waving his arms in the air. The beam from his torch cut through the darkness, signalling to anyone nearby. He was half standing, half hunching on one of the rigid inflatable boats farther along the river, not too far from the shore. Beside him, another man was on his knees, his torso disappearing over the side. Their urgent voices carried through the cold night air, but their words did not. They didn't need to.

People started to move towards them, but Jen couldn't. Her feet sank down into the shale beneath her, and whatever strength her legs once held, evaporated. Someone's arms wrapped around her as she was about to fall, and for a moment she thought it might be Dale. But he went stumbling past, with loose, mossy stones giving way under his tired feet as he tried to run. He saw nothing, only the RIB up ahead, the men leaning over the side of it and the diver in the water beneath them. Right then was when she wished for death to come. But for *her*. She screamed and begged for death to return, and to take her instead. Take anyone else out of this world, but not her child. Not her beautiful Alex.

Of all people, it was Lia Higgins who was holding Jen up now, while she watched strangers in high visibility clothing, hauling the limp body of her daughter out of the river. Lia was the one whose shaking arms Jen screamed into, while the shoulders of the many volunteers around them seemed to sag in unison, as they watched the men on the boat shaking their heads at one another.

Jen fell to the ground and Lia dropped down beside her. Lia cried like it was her own daughter being raced towards a waiting ambulance, while Jen sobbed towards the night sky. Lia tightened her grip, anchoring her to the earth.

'Oh, Jen.'

Jen squeezed the woman tightly and curled into a ball, as Dale's anguished shout cut through all the other noise. It was a sound that none of them would ever be able to un-hear.

'No, Alex! No, no, no... my baby!' He cried more quietly then, as his voice started to disintegrate.

'I'm sorry, Alex,' Jen keened. 'I'm so sorry, baby.'

# ONE

## JEN

*Three months earlier*

'Did you know that during World War Two, the American army got together with Walt Disney to design a gas mask that looked like Mickey Mouse?'

'What? Why would they do that?' Jen asked, hastily wrapping a plain cheese sandwich in tinfoil for Alex's school lunch, while mentally running through her own day. The bread was two days old, but it would have to do.

Alex shrugged. Her dark hair framed her face, highlighting her bright eyes and the slight smile playing at her lips. A familiar ache bloomed in Jen's chest as she watched her daughter. That surge of love that still caught her off guard sometimes. It seemed like only yesterday that she was packing her baby's snacks for preschool. How was she already a St Brendan's girl? Her mind flashed back to her own school days at St Brendan's, some memories making her smile, others making her wince. But Alex seemed happy there.

'So that kids wouldn't be afraid of them,' she continued. 'Gas attacks were quite normal back then, as you can imagine.'

'Oh.' Jen smiled and ran her fingers through Alex's hair, planting a quick kiss on top of her head before she had a chance to object.

'Hey! Watch the hair.'

'It looks gorgeous.' Jen smiled. She'd used Jen's straightening iron on it, which was new. Alex wasn't the type of girl who stressed about how she looked, usually. She was a messy ponytail and baggy T-shirt kind of a girl. But today, in addition to her styled hair, she had mascara on, and a subtle tint on her lips. Jen frowned when she noticed her make-up and looked quizzically at her.

'What?'

'Nothing.' Jen smiled. 'You look lovely.'

'Is it illegal to break away from the ponytail, or something?' Alex's smile vanished now as she shoved her hair self-consciously behind her ears.

'Whoa, look at you!' Dale came into the kitchen wearing a V-neck jumper over a shirt and tie complete with grey sweatpants, tucked into brown socks. 'Who is he then?' he chuckled.

Alex flushed red and grabbed a hair tie from the counter. She roughly pulled her hair back into a low ponytail. For some reason she was embarrassed, but she deflected like she always did. 'Dad, I'm absolutely mortified for you.' She looked him up and down with a grimace.

There used to be a time when Jen and Alex talked about everything. They'd curl up on Alex's bed, reading stories and talking about her day. Back then she knew everything about her daughter and her friends. But then Alex became a teenager, Dale lost his management job at the multi-national where he'd worked for ten years, forcing Jen to go full time at a job that she now hated. Their lives had changed irrevocably. After a torturous year on the dole, he now held a much lower position at a cheese factory, so as a family, they hardly saw each other now, let alone talked late into the night. If Alex had a crush, then Jen had no idea who it might be.

'Hey! Don't knock it, kid,' Dale bounced back. 'I get to work from home today on account of the fact that the boss is away.' He picked up Jen's cooling coffee, took a tentative sip and nodded his approval. Then he brought it with him to the table where he proceeded to drink the rest of it. He always did that, and it was just one of the things that bugged Jen far more than it should.

'Would you not leave your hair down, love?' Jen suggested, sorry that both she and Dale had made such a thing of it. 'It really suits you.'

Alex subtly rolled her eyes. Jen caught it but decided not to pull her on it. Instead, she shoved a bowl of porridge into Alex's hands. 'Well then, can you at least eat your breakfast, please?' It had raspberry jam mixed through it, which is how Alex had eaten her porridge since she was a baby. She leant against the work surface, took three mouthfuls and put the bowl down.

'You need to eat more than that, love.' Jen picked the bowl up and held it towards Alex again.

'I don't have time and I'm not hungry.' Alex filled a sports bottle with water from the tap and put it in her backpack. 'Will you be at the match?'

'Shit,' Jen muttered, remembering. 'You're playing St Albans today. What time is tip-off again?' Her stomach tightened – she was going to be slammed at work today. Alex's basketball matches were usually at six p.m. and Jen knew she'd be lucky to get home by seven.

'Forget it.'

Jen exhaled loudly and squeezed the bridge of her nose. 'Oh, Alex, love. I'll do my best to be there, okay?'

Alex zipped up her bag and pulled her jacket off the back of a chair.

'I might be able to get there,' Dale said, without taking his eyes off his phone, as he sipped on Jen's coffee.

'I said, forget it.'

Jen glanced out the bay window to see Alex's friend and neighbour, Willow Higgins, and her awkward twin brother, Simon, outside waiting for Alex.

They lived in Honeywell Crescent, a small cluster of semi-detached houses, built in the shape of a horseshoe around a central green area. The Blakes, the Higgins and three of the other families who lived there all bought their houses back when the estate was first built.

Jen and Dale had easily afforded their nice suburban house back then. Now, they were so far behind on their re-mortgage repayments that Jen sometimes had nightmares about a literal wolf at the door. And selling wasn't an option either. By the time they paid back the money they owed, they wouldn't be able to afford a dog kennel.

'Okay, bye!' Alex shouldered her bag and headed for the door.

'Hey!' Jen held out her arms for a hug, which Alex gave her begrudgingly.

'Now can I go?' she asked, with a half smile and yet another roll of the eyes.

'Go. And have a great day.'

Alex hurried out of the kitchen and seconds later, the front door opened.

'She's always in such a good mood,' Dale said sarcastically.

Jen looked at him, scrolling on his phone, oblivious to the eye rolling as usual. 'That's because she has no idea how close she is to becoming homeless,' she said, sounding bitchier than she meant to.

He lowered his phone and leaned back in his chair, blowing a long breath up towards the ceiling. 'I know, I know, it's all my fault. I singlehandedly drove my American bosses back to the States and rendered us broke. Now, would you like me to lie down on the floor so you can kick me as well?' He pointed to the tinfoil-wrapped sandwich sitting on the counter, beside where Jen was standing.

'Alex, your lunch!' Jen called towards the still-open front door. She picked it up and hurried outside.

Alex groaned dramatically, trudged back towards Jen, took the sandwich and shoved it in the side pocket of her backpack. She did it in such a way that it would resemble something very different by lunchtime. 'Thanks, Mum.'

'Have a good day, love.'

Jen leaned against the door frame and waved. She could hear the excited babble of the two girls, as all three of them made their way across the green and out of the estate, on the short walk to school. Simon lagged behind them as always. He was a strange kid. His mother, Lia, called him *shy*, but Jen wasn't so sure. Her feelings towards his father, however, were much more straightforward. Jay Higgins was the reason why Jen had such mixed feelings about her time at St Brendan's. Jen and Lia were the athletic stars of that place back then. And Jay was the prick who wrecked it all. He was probably the real reason why she was more wary of Simon than she might other-wise have been. Because how far could an apple fall from a tree? Lia Higgins was also in her doorway on the opposite side of the green. She smiled and waved at Jen.

'What is she like?' Jen muttered sarcastically to herself as she returned a small wave and went back inside. 'Lia's over there looking like she's on her way to a Hilfiger photo shoot.'

'What's new?' Dale replied, punching various keys on his laptop.

'Why does she get so dressed up just to sit at home and wait for her husband and kids to come back for dinner?'

'Why do you care?'

She shook her head. 'I don't. I just don't get it. That's all.'

'Jen, Lia Higgins could pick up where Mother Theresa left off, and you'd still have a problem with her.' He turned to look at her at last. 'I tell you, no one can hold a grudge like a woman can,' he said with a shake of the head.

'I don't have a grudge…'

He laughed and turned back to his screen. 'Okay, if you say so. You just went from being best friends to…'

'Don't be ridiculous. That was high school, Dale.'

He held his hands up in surrender. 'So, on another note, are you going to make that match or what?' He got up and rattled the toaster to life. 'Only I have a load to do, so I doubt I'll get there.'

'Then why did you say you might?'

'Well, I just realised how many calls I have today.'

'I'll be there,' Jen said, determinedly.

'Really?' Dale was busy suddenly, making breakfast for one and getting ready to start his day.

'Toast for one, is it?' she mumbled, having resigned herself to the fact that her husband had reverted back to being a child when Alex was born.

He didn't respond. Instead, he made a show of looking stressed out by the very sight of his laptop. He'd already drained the cup of coffee that Jen had made for herself, knowing that she wouldn't have time to make, let alone drink, another one.

'Why aren't you going in today?' she asked.

'I told you, Gavin is away.'

'But won't he know?'

Dale sighed loudly and put his cup down on the table. 'Jen, I'm not skiving off or anything. I am actually working, you know. I'd be doing the same thing whether I was at the plant, or at my kitchen table.'

Now it was Jen who didn't respond, as she assembled

another less than fresh cheese sandwich for her own working lunch.

'Do you think I'd risk my job just to sit around in my baggy pants?'

'I think you're bored, and you hate your job,' she replied, trying not to sound as judgemental as she felt towards him.

'Of course I'm bored and I hate my job!' he barked back at her. 'My boss is literally half my age and has no idea what he's doing. Meanwhile, I could do his job with my eyes closed, but instead I spend my days talking about processed cheese slices, for a fraction of what the kids around me are earning. So, forgive me if I'm not beating a path to the cheese factory when I don't have to, Jen.'

She shook her head and roughly stuck more bread in the toaster. 'I have to do two vacation inspections today. An apartment in town and a house in Mayfield. Both have tenants waiting to move in, so they need to get done ASAP. Plus, I have three blocks of viewings.'

'Three blocks of viewings? They'll take all day.'

'Probably.'

He turned back to his laptop, where various windows were opening up. 'You should have just told Alex that you wouldn't be there. Again.'

This was just another version of the same argument they always had. Dale felt that Jen should be a stay-at-home mother, like the only other mothers Dale seemed to know. He'd never admit to the fact that they needed every penny that Jen earned to keep the roof over their heads.

'Have you forgotten our current situation?'

'How could I?'

'It's fine for you. You're not the one who has to come up with ways to make our equally shit salaries stretch from one end of the month to the next, are you?'

'Oh, I'm sorry. Does my money not go into that joint account as well?'

'When was the last time you thought about filling the cupboard with food, or buying Alex the new stuff she needs, or—'

'Alex doesn't need new stuff...'

'Really? Her basketball kit was too small for her. She got a whole new set last week. Did you know that? Her toes are about to burst out of her boots, but they'll have to wait until the end of the month. Did you know that her club membership had to be paid last week as well? And her school fees? And the car insurance two weeks before that? Did you know that the cost of a weekly shop at Aldi has gone up by about a hundred euro? Of course you didn't. You just rock up and either eat, or complain about, whatever is put on the plate in front of you and forget about the rest.'

He was concentrating on his laptop again, as if she hadn't said a thing. Her rising temper was ramped up by his refusal to engage further, but rather than letting it all out, she fumed quietly as she manually popped the toaster and scraped butter onto her barely warm bread.

'No doubt Lia will let us know if they win or lose today,' he mumbled finally.

Jen closed her eyes and cursed under her breath. He wasn't wrong. Lia Higgins would be the first one to launch the dreaded parents' WhatsApp group to life. But she wouldn't wait until the game was over. She'd send a blow-by-blow, basket-by-basket account from her prime spot on the supporters' mezzanine. 'The St Brendan's Bulldogs number one fan.'

Jen and Lia had absolutely nothing in common, aside from their children. Lia married a wealthy solicitor and aspiring politician, and she passed her days shopping, going to the gym, getting her nails done and cooking. *Everyone* knew about Lia's cooking. She also baked for every school event and was on *all* the committees. Most annoyingly, she knew about every new childish trend and craze before the kids did. She was the cool mom who took her kids to concerts on a school night, all while looking like she stepped off the cover of a magazine. She was infuriating.

'Yip,' Dale mumbled, then he smiled and said, 'Hello!' with a friendly wave to his computer screen.

Jen hurried over and rotated his laptop so that his colleagues wouldn't have a full view of their messy kitchen. Or of her, still wearing the shorts and vest that she'd slept in. Instead, she made them look towards their family photos on the opposite wall and wished that he'd find somewhere more appropriate to have these meetings if he was going to insist on working from home.

Jen took her sad excuse for breakfast upstairs. She'd been working at Murphy's Property Management for more than six years. She was part-time for the first three and she'd enjoyed it then. But having to ask for full-time hours after Dale lost his job, when she'd always insisted she could only work around her child, reeked of desperation. And James Murphy was the kind of boss who fed off that. Now he stamped his authority on her every chance he got.

She put her mobile breakfast down on her cluttered bedside locker. If she got dressed and left the house in the next ten minutes, she could get both properties inspected and at least one of the viewings completed before lunchtime. If she rushed the other two and perhaps cancelled a few of the viewing appointments, then maybe she could get home before Alex's match tipped off. She felt a twinge of guilt towards the people who were desperate to find a rental property in today's impossibly tough market, but they were not her priority. Her priority was to find relatively suitable tenants, tick the boxes and get to Alex's match.

She grabbed her bag and hurried down the stairs. Without saying goodbye to Dale, she left the house with a renewed determination that today would be the day when she would be there for her daughter. She'd be front and centre, alongside Lia Bloody Higgins, cheering on the St Brendan's Bulldogs. Come hell or high water.

# TWO

## JEN

'No, Jen! You can't just ring up a bunch of people and tell them, *Oh, I'm sorry, you can't find a place to live today because my child is playing a game.* And what would we tell our landlords when they ask why they're down a month's rent?' James waved another set of keys in her face, after she'd put the keys of both vacated properties and two of the viewings back in the lock box.

'I've missed her last three matches, James. Please? Can't someone else take this last one?' Jen pleaded, hating how pathetic she sounded.

'And by someone else, you mean me?' he said, raising an eyebrow.

Jen didn't respond, but she could have kicked herself for asking. James was handed this business when his father retired. He'd never had to work for anything in his life and she hated giving him the satisfaction of saying no to her. Which he nearly always did, just because he could.

'The girl is sixteen years of age. Isn't it time you loosened the apron strings a bit?'

'She's fifteen.'

'Well, I'm afraid the business world doesn't revolve around

a mummy's schedule. I made that very clear when *you* asked *me* for more hours. Remember that? Now there are only four couples booked in to view the apartment, so they shouldn't take too long. Unless, of course, you want to waste more time standing here arguing about it? But I can't do that all day.'

Jen silently reminded herself of just how much she needed this job, as a wave of depression washed in. She took the keys and left the office without another word.

It was four-thirty by the time Jen got back to her car and the last place she wanted to be headed now was to a slumlord's flat, where she'd have to explain to a string of hopeful tenants why they'd be lucky to be granted the keys to such a shithole. She hissed and slapped the steering wheel repeatedly, then pulled recklessly out into traffic.

It was seven twenty-five when she pulled up outside St Brendan's and as she jogged towards the indoor courts, a cheer rang out from inside. She pulled open the door and walked brusquely into the building that still felt so familiar to her. The enormous trophy case, which had always been there, still dominated the space. She glanced briefly at the many shiny awards, hard-won by St Brendan's athletes over the years, and at the framed photographs of Bulldog's stars, past and present, that were displayed behind them. One of those photos was of seventeen-year-old Jen and her best friend and teammate, Lia. Both beaming at the camera with their arms draped over one another's shoulders. That game lived on in St Brendan's folklore when they beat the All-Ireland champions by seventy-eight points to seventy-six with Jen and Lia scoring fifty-six points between them. Lia was stunning even then, and that snapshot in time showed two girls ready to take on the world together.

The supporters' mezzanine was packed, but she muscled her way through to the front. She wanted Alex to see her. To know that she was there, but just as she reached the rail, the final whistle blew and the crowd erupted all around her.

'Jen!' Lia shouted, while bouncing up and down in full Bulldog colours, including the jacket. Anyone would think *she'd* just scored the winning basket. 'You made it!'

Jen ignored her and leaned over the rail to look for Alex, but her back was turned to the crowd as the two teams congratulated each other.

'Alex played a blinder!' Lia hooted, finally stopping her incessant bouncing. 'She scored twelve points.'

Jen glanced at the scoreboard. Bulldogs, twenty-eight, St Alban's twenty. 'Alex!' she called hopefully, clapping and waving as if she could fool anyone into thinking she'd been there all along. Her eyes filled with tears. She'd missed it again.

'Hey.' Lia placed her hand on Jen's shoulder.

Jen looked at her finally and turned so that Lia's hand slipped away.

Lia's smile faltered, but not for long. 'So the twins want a garden party for their birthday in a couple of weeks' time. It'll just be pizza and what have you. You know they're too cool for anything else these days,' she said, still smiling.

Jen nodded.

'Sixteen already, eh?' Lia said wistfully. 'Where did the years go?' She nudged Jen then. 'Remember when that was us, tearing up the court?'

Jen's eyes were still on Alex, willing her to look up. But she was talking excitedly to Willow until another tall, blonde girl came and pulled Willow away into a huddle with one other girl. Alex's smile slipped and she looked around self-consciously, before falling in with some other teammates on the walk back to the changing room.

'Oh, well,' Lia tried again. 'At least match nights mean McDonald's for the kids. Less dinner prep and some peace and quiet for us at home, eh?'

Jen looked at her finally and forced herself to be civil. 'Yeah. Gotta love match nights. Have a good evening, Lia.'

Jen desperately wanted to stand by her car, waiting for Alex to come out. But being picked up by a parent after a home game was utterly mortifying for a fifteen-year-old, and post-match McDonald's was tradition. Interfering with that would help nothing, so Jen went home, knowing that Alex would be there with her by nine.

As she dropped her keys on the hall table, she could hear Dale's voice in the kitchen, so she opened the door just a crack and looked in.

He held his hand up, indicating that he needed another five minutes, while he continued a conversation with his screen. He sounded stressed and annoyed as he said, 'I should have been called at mid-day when you first realised this, Reggie! I would have come onsite and sorted it, and we wouldn't both be sitting here at eight o' clock at fucking night, would we!'

Jen's mood fell further as she pulled the door closed again and went to the bottom of the stairs. A part of her wanted to go up there and crawl into bed. But the kitchen was a mess, and she desperately wanted to see Alex before anyone went to sleep. She turned and went into the front room instead. She collapsed onto the couch, pulling her feet up under her and felt herself drifting off. The next thing she knew, she was being jolted awake by the front door slamming loudly.

The face of her watch blurred as her eyes adjusted.

'What's she doing home?' Dale came to the double doors and thumbed towards the hall.

'What time is it?'

'Quarter past eight.'

Jen rubbed her eyes and got up. 'Alex?' she called, going into the hall.

There was no response. Jen looked questioningly at Dale and started up the stairs. 'Alex?'

'Yeah?' came a reply at last.

Jen jogged up, knocked once on Alex's bedroom door and went in. She was sitting on the floor with her back to the bed and her tablet on her lap. She didn't look up.

'What a game!' Jen injected as much enthusiasm as she could into her voice.

'Yeah.'

It wasn't that Jen expected an elaborate response or anything, but she did expect a smidge of excitement. Or more than just one word at least, and she was disappointed not to get either. 'You're home early.'

'Saves you having to give out to me for being late.' Alex looked up at her finally and smiled.

'I'm making meatballs and spaghetti.'

'I just had McDonald's.'

Jen looked at her watch again. 'I'm surprised you had time.'

Alex shrugged and returned her attention to her tablet.

Jen wondered about the way those girls had pulled Willow away, excluding Alex from their little huddle. 'Is everything alright, love?'

'Why wouldn't it be?'

Jen shrugged. 'No reason. It's just that...'

'What?' Alex looked up again.

'Well, is everything alright with you and Willow?'

'What makes you ask that?'

'Nothing. I just saw those girls with her earlier and I...'

'What are you talking about?' Alex jumped to her feet and went to hold her open door. 'I'm tired, Mum. I'm going to bed.'

'At quarter past eight?'

'What?! One minute you're giving out that I'm home too late, now I'm too early. Same with going to bed! I'm tired, alright?'

'Alex? What is it?'

'You don't have to do this, Mum!'

'Do what?'

'Just because you're never here, doesn't mean you have to sit me down for a *talk* every time you are! Nothing is wrong. Everything is fine. I just want to go to sleep. Is that okay with you?'

Jen's eyes filled with tears, and she walked out before Alex had a chance to notice. As the bedroom door closed behind her, Jen stood on the landing suddenly overwhelmed with the pace of her life and the weight of her responsibilities. The kitchen was a mess. At least two loads of laundry required her attention and today was the use-by date on the meatballs in the fridge. If she didn't cook them, no one else would. Her bed called out to her, but once again, she ignored it and reluctantly went back downstairs.

Dale was leaning against the kitchen counter bringing a messy, thrown together sandwich to his mouth.

'Oh, for Jesus' sake.' She stalked over, snatched the sandwich out of his hand and threw it on the counter. 'I said I was making dinner, so I'm making dinner!'

Dale looked like he'd just gotten a slap of the wooden spoon from his mummy. 'What did *I* do? And when did you say you were making dinner?'

Jen leaned heavily on the counter taking deep breaths. 'I just wanted to celebrate her win,' she half whispered.

'With meatballs and spaghetti?' He made it sound so ridiculous.

'Yes! Because it's Alex's favourite. Only she somehow managed to get to McDonald's, order and eat something in the space of about twenty minutes.' She leaned on the counter and squeezed her eyes shut. She needed to calm down. 'They won. I got there at the end.'

'So what are you so mad about? I just finished work and I'm hungry.'

'I'm not mad! But if you were hungry, why wouldn't you think to put dinner on? For all of us!'

Dale huffed. 'Uh, hello!' he gestured towards his sleeping laptop. 'I was working! Plus, Alex went to McDonald's, and I didn't know what you wanted.'

Jen rolled her eyes, pulled the frying pan out of the pot drawer and slammed it down on the hob. 'Tomorrow is another day,' she muttered to herself.

Only the nagging voice in her head responded. *As if that'll be any better.*

# THREE

## JEN



The parents' WhatsApp group showed forty-seven unread messages when Jen opened it later that night. It had been set up back when their kids all started at St Brendan's, and it comprised of a group of women with not much else in common other than that their kids were at the same school. Jen usually steered clear of it, knowing that the simplest question could set off hours of notifications about nothing.



Of course Lia was first to reply to that with a rolling eye emoji. Jen made a face at her phone and waited for the advice to start pouring from Perfect Mamma. Alex spent a lot of time hanging out with Willow at the Higgins house. It galled Jen that Alex might tell Lia more about her day than she would tell Jen about her whole year. She just had that way about her with the kids.

LIA HIGGINS

I've started taking Willow out for coffee once a week. I think the one-on-one girl time, and the whole coffee culture in town, makes her feel more grown-up. Helps take the edge off and get her talking instead of hissing LMAO.

Jen groaned.

HELEN MARIA'S MUM

Good idea! That sounds like something I could do with!

Helen was relatively friendly but was an enormous gossip, and as such, no one else trusted her.

HELEN MARIA'S MUM

Can't believe they'll all be turning sixteen soon! It'll be college before we know it! Lia, are the twins planning a party?

LIA HIGGINS

I can imagine the girls sharing an apartment in the city, living their best college lives! Simon too, whether they like it or not!

Lia added not one, but two hysterical laughing emojis. But she dodged the question of the twin's birthday party, meaning that the guest list would be selective and Maria would not be invited.

Jen understood the avoidance. She never got the need to invite half the school to every party. But she didn't find Lia's comment about Simon funny. Surely, Lia would want Simon to get some friends of his own eventually and live his life with some level of independence. He relied on his sister for every-thing, including friendship.

The very idea of Alex moving out and going to college made Jen anxious. Not just that her child might want to leave the nest at some stage. But the fact that she and Dale could never afford for her to live anywhere but at home. They'd need all sorts of grants and assistance to make university happen at all, but somehow, they would. That was about the only thing that she and Dale agreed on nowadays.

'Hey.' Alex came into the sitting room and flung herself at the armchair. She'd changed clothes, and clearly she'd changed her mind about going to sleep at quarter past eight. Jen kept her mouth shut about that. Instead she left the chat and put her phone face down on the arm of the chair. 'Hey, you.' She smiled, surprised to see her. 'Nice T-shirt.'

Alex looked more like herself now. Her hair was wild, like it always was when she let it dry naturally, and she had her baggy jeans on, with a relatively new black T-shirt. It had Albert Einstein on the front and his tongue was painted in rainbow colours.

'Thanks,' she said, nestling into the chair and pulling a cushion into a tight hug before turning on the TV.

'I thought you were going to bed?' Jen ventured.

Alex looked away and shrugged. 'Sorry for the attitude earlier.'

Jen felt her shoulders sag. 'That's okay. Is everything alright, though?'

'Yes!' she stressed, settling on a re-run of *Friends*.

Jen held her hands up in surrender and the pair of them pretended to watch TV for a while. From time to time, she glanced at Alex, desperate to start a conversation that would lead to something meaningful, but not quite knowing how to start it without sending Alex storming up the stairs again.

'I hear the twins are having a pizza party for their birthday?' she tried.

'Mm,' Alex mumbled noncommittally, opening an app on her phone.

'That'll be nice. I'd imagine Lia Higgins makes the perfect pizza.'

Alex raised her eyebrows and inhaled with a slow nod. 'Yeah, no doubt. Seriously, though, what normal person bakes as much as Willow's mum? She had fresh apple and pear scones in her lunch this morning. I mean, like, they were still warm. Who's even *heard* of apple and pear scones?'

Jen grinned. 'You're just jealous that you don't get freshly baked goods in your lunch box,' she half teased, trying not to be a bitch in front of her child. Not when Alex had always adored the Higgins family.

'I'm quite alright with my cheese sandwich, Mum,' she replied with a wink.

'So... how's school going?' Jen asked, immediately wishing that she hadn't.

Alex shrugged and replaced the cushion against the arm of the chair. 'Grand.'

*Shit.*

'Anything interesting going on?'

'Nope. Same old, same old.' Alex got to her feet.

Jen stood up, too, and caught her gently by the arm. 'Alex? I'm sorry I missed the game.'

Alex shrugged. 'It's fine. You had to work.'

'I did. But you know you can still talk to me anytime you need to?'

Alex made a *duh* face. 'Yeah, I know.' She pulled her arm back gently, her cheeks flushing red. 'I'm alright, Mum. You don't need to keep asking.'

Before she had a chance to leave the room, Jen pulled her

into a tight hug. To her relief, Alex returned it, and Jen suddenly felt the stresses of the day begin to melt away. Not for the first time, she vowed to do better. To fight less with Dale. To find a job with a better work-life balance. And to somehow erase their ever-increasing debt so that she could give Alex everything she ever needed, including the stress-free, happy home that she deserved. From where she stood, Jen watched Alex slowly leave the room and trudge back upstairs, and only when she heard the bedroom door shut, did she move to close the blinds. As she reached for the cord, she saw Willow walking across the green towards home, at bang on nine o clock. Simon was ten feet behind her. Willow let herself into their house, allowing the door to close gently before Simon got there. But Simon didn't follow her in. Instead, he turned and sat on their low garden wall, facing the Blake's house. Jen moved out of sight but continued to watch, and for far too long, Simon just sat there, very, very still, staring straight ahead. Staring right at them.

# FOUR

## LIA

'What are you doing, love?'

Simon didn't respond. He just sat there on the wall with his back to her. She followed his line of sight straight to the Blakes' house.

'Come inside now, Simon,' she said, a little more forcefully. Lia used to think it was charming when Jay turned up unexpectedly outside her house back in the day. She thought a lot of things were charming back then.

He slid slowly off the wall and walked inside, passing her as if she wasn't there. Lia exhaled a shaky breath as her eyes were drawn to the descending blind in the Blakes' front room. Had Jen seen him watching their house? *Was* he watching?

'Can you get me some dinner?' Simon's voice snapped her out of it.

'Didn't you just have McDonald's?' she asked, closing the front door. 'Dad will be on TV in a few minutes. Grab some strawberries from the fridge and let's watch together.'

Willow was already sitting reluctantly on the couch. She was tired and desperate to go to bed, but Jay would want to know that they'd tuned in when he got home.

*'...and tonight, we join election candidate, Jay Higgins, who has been volunteering at the* Soup's Up *soup kitchen since eight am this morning...'*

Lia, Willow and Simon watched in silence as the camera panned through the messy dining hall, to a long counter where men and women worked to clear away the mess and leftovers from whatever meal they'd just served to God knows how many people. In the middle of them, with a grey apron on over his navy Hilfiger polo shirt, was Jay, looking more handsome than ever.

*'Jay, how did your day go?'* the reporter asked, jovially.

Jay blew upwards into his hair and smiled. 'You know what, Adam, these people are incredible. This was the most rewarding day I've had in a very long time.' He put down a stack of dirty plates and leaned heavily on the counter. He looked around for a moment, and if Lia didn't know him better, she'd think he was getting emotional. 'You know, we get up every morning, we have breakfast, we kiss our families goodbye and we go to work. We take for granted that food will be readily available to us at lunchtime, and again at the end of the day. And even though I make every effort not to, we can even take the love of our families for granted. That they'll be there, waiting for us when we return to our warm homes in the evening.' He rubbed both of his eyes roughly with the heels of his hands and shook his head sadly.

Willow tutted loudly, got up and left the room. Lia kept her eyes on the screen. On his tanned, muscular arms as he leaned on the counter again. His slightly dishevelled hair, his tired face and the five o'clock shadow that made him look ruggedly beautiful. That image of him on screen tonight would secure a huge female vote for him. 'The people who give their time here every single day are amazing,' he continued, his voice catching. 'The people who avail of these services are extraordinarily brave and they deserve more from us. They deserve to be the priority of our government. They deserve to be put first when it comes to the allocation of housing. They deserve to be able to put food on their tables, clothes on their backs and to have a warm bed at the end of the day, in a home they can call their own. Isn't that what we all deserve?' He looked around again, frowning, as if thinking of all the ways he could help. 'If I can earn your trust, then I promise you, I will not rest until the Irish people are prioritised. Until the cost-of-living crisis is addressed, and until the people of Cork can enjoy a basic quality of life that we all deserve.' He stood up straight then and ran his hands through his hair. He exhaled loudly and smiled his devilish smile. 'Now, if you'll excuse me, Adam, I have a mountain of washing up to do. Unless you want to join me?'

He always finished with a smile, and by making whoever interviewed him smile as well.

'Now can I have some food?' Simon's voice was whiny in contrast to his father's dulcet tones. 'I heard Dad telling you to make stroganoff when he was leaving today, and the smell tells me you did what you were told. So can you get me some?' He picked up his phone and started scrolling.

'What were you doing out there?' she asked, turning off the TV and getting to her feet, his words piercing her skin in a way that they shouldn't. He was her son. She needed to turn the tables before it was too late.

'Out where?'

She took a moment to respond, unsure whether or not to say anything. If Jay were home, she certainly wouldn't. But he was still at Soup's Up. She had some time. 'Do you like Alex, Simon? Is that it?'

He didn't look up from his phone and his expression made her wonder if he'd even heard her.

'Simon...'

'What are you on about, Mum?'

'What I'm on about, Simon, is that...'

He dropped his phone into his lap and deadpanned her. He tilted his head and then a small smile played on his lips. Ordinarily, Simon looked nothing like Jay. He was tall, big-boned, had thick curly hair and a chubby face, which would be severely acne scarred if Lia didn't see to it that it wasn't. But some of his expressions, like this one, made him look every inch his father's son and that unnerved her sometimes.

'All I'm saying is that if you like her, just talk to her.'

'As opposed to what?'

She squeezed her stomach to ease the discomfort there, as annoyance started to creep through. 'As opposed to sitting on a wall in the dark, watching her house.' She turned and walked into the kitchen before he could respond. She looked at the pot of perfect beef stroganoff. There was plenty of food there, but something in her refused to dish up a plate for Simon. Not because he'd just had a McDonald's. But because of how he'd been speaking to her lately. Simon was pushing boundaries now and if she didn't push back... She pulled a punnet of strawberries from the fridge, washed them, chopped them into a bowl and then went and placed it in his lap. His full attention was on his phone, and he didn't acknowledge the snack, or the effort to make it.

The front door opened and closed, and Simon stuffed his phone in his pocket and turned the TV back on. Lia started straightening cushions on the couch.

'Hiya, love.' Lia smiled as Jay came into the front room. 'I didn't expect you for a while yet.' She indicated the television. 'You looked great! How did it go?'

'That place is a hellhole.' He walked back out and headed for the stairs. 'I'm having a shower and then I'm burning these clothes. I'll have the stroganoff and a glass of red when I come down,' he called back. 'I want to erase all memory of that congealed shit I've been doling out to those cretins all day. Christ, they fucking stink.'

'A man of the people,' Simon muttered with a smile, as the bathroom door closed and locked.

Lia glanced down at him, then returned to the kitchen.

## FIVE

## LIA

'Christ, you look like you're asking for it,' Jay hissed, when Willow came into the kitchen wearing a short denim skirt with a pink cropped T-shirt. It was two weeks since his stint at Soup's Up and his popularity had soared. Which meant his family needed to work extra hard to keep it that way. 'Go back to your room, Willow, and try again.'

'But these are new! Mum just—'

'Well, Mum shouldn't have *just*, should she? Go.'

Willow's eyes brimmed with tears, but she refused to let them fall. Lia knew she wouldn't give him the satisfaction. Instead, she turned with her chin up and left the kitchen, headed for the stairs.

Lia's heart sank as she watched her go. Willow looked exactly like Lia had at that age, only twice as beautiful. She had Jay's olive skin and piercing blue eyes, and she was tall, with the kind of legs that looked amazing in anything. *She* looked amazing in anything. Perhaps he remembered how he'd acted with Lia when they weren't much older than Willow was now. Maybe that's why he came down so hard on her, always.

'Jay, it's her sixteenth birthday,' she softly pleaded for her daughter. 'She's spent weeks thinking about her outfit, and all the girls her age are wearing...' She stopped when he stepped into her personal space, bringing his face just inches from hers.

'Will you listen to yourself?' He pointed towards the stairs. 'If that's the best she can come up with after *weeks* of thinking, then God help her.' He lowered his arm and inched closer still, his breath warm in Lia's face. 'Remember, Lia, she is not *all the girls her age*. My family is not *all the other families*. How many times do I have to explain this to you? Are you so fucking stupid that you...' The doorbell chimed and he turned to look at it. 'Who's that?'

'The twins' friends, I'd expect.'

'Willow's friends, you mean.'

'They're Simon's friends, too.'

'If you didn't mother him like an imbecile...'

The bell chimed again.

He exhaled loudly and brought his hands to his temples. Lia moved around him with her head down and went to answer the door. She didn't particularly want to host a pizza party tonight. No more than Jay wanted any of them to be ordinary. But it was their children's sixteenth birthday. If Lia didn't give them a party that other parents would talk about, then he'd be down her throat about that, too.

His open disappointment in Simon was what made Lia put her own uncertainties aside as much as she could. The boy needed to feel like one of his parents believed in him. Simon wasn't sporty, like Jay had been. He didn't fit into many social circles, so it was up to Lia to bring those circles to him. To make sure he was included. But for a boy who was so unlike his father in many ways, he was beginning to remind her more and more of Jay every day. And that's where her uncertainties thrived.

'Alex!' Lia held her arms out wide when she opened the front door. 'My favourite neighbour. Come on in.'

'Hey, Alex,' Jay called from where he was now leaning casually against the kitchen counter. He popped a grape in his mouth and waved.

'Hi, Mr Higgins.'

'The other two are upstairs. Go on up, love.' Lia smiled. 'The pizza oven is warming up out the back. It'll be ready before the others get here.'

'Okay, thank you. I saw you on TV a few weeks ago, Mr Higgins. It was really good.' Alex called to him, then turned towards the stairs.

'Thanks, Alex.'

Jay's election posters had gone up all over the city and he was looking more and more likely to win his seat. No matter where they went now or what mode of transport they used, his gorgeous blue eyes were there to watch them. In his early fifties, Jay was a stunning man. Olive skin, thick, wavy black hair and those eyes. Also, he had the most handsome smile, filled with straight, white teeth. It was the smile that attracted Lia to him all those years ago, while they were still in school themselves. But she knew now that he could turn that smile on and off like a tap. It vanished before Alex was halfway up the stairs.

'Great. Just the type of supporter I need,' he whispered sarcastically.

'You'd be surprised. A few years from now, she'll be exactly...'

'Did you see the T-shirt? Has she gone woke or something?' He froze then and looked at Lia. 'Or is she... she better not have her eye on Willow.'

'It's just a T-shirt, Jay,' Lia replied wearily.

He turned to face her, his eyes darkening. She knew what was coming. 'What's with the tone, Lia?'

'Sorry. I'm just tired.'

'*You're* tired? From what? What's made you so tired?'

Lia bristled.

He ran his fingers through her hair. It was naturally blonde, just like Willow's. Then his knuckles brushed her cheek and down to her full, pink lips. Lia was in her mid-forties, but thanks to the laser treatments, Botox injections, Profilo injections, expensive facials and extortionate skincare routine, she looked ten years younger. She also had the body of a twenty-year-old. Lia felt her chest tighten.

'Sorry.' Alex came tentatively into the kitchen.

'Hey! What's up?' Jay inhaled and smiled brightly at her as he dropped his hands and moved away from Lia.

'Nothing. Willow's just getting dressed, so I'll wait here for her.'

'Good thinking.' Jay glanced at Lia. He popped another grape in his mouth and went out through the open double doors to the beautifully landscaped and furnished garden. The fire pit was lit out there and string lights gave the space a cosy glow, even on a chilly night. Willow had forbidden Lia to put up any form of bunting or birthday paraphernalia, so she didn't. It was simple and elegant. Very un-sixteenth-like.

'Here, give me a hand with this lot.' Lia smiled at Alex as she went and opened the fridge. She pulled out a large ball of fresh pizza dough. Lia saw the way the girl had looked at her and Jay. She saw an adoring man, gazing lovingly at his wife. Same as what everyone else saw. She was probably wishing her own parents could be more like that, too. Lia could see it written all over the child's face.

'Hey, Alex.' Simon arrived in the kitchen.

'Hey.'

Lia smiled at her boy as she began kneading the dough. 'Here's the birthday boy. Did he tell you he's started driving lessons this week? With me, I mean. I've been teaching him the basics up at the old industrial estate. He'll be an expert by the time his official lessons start next year, won't you, love?'

Alex shook her head. 'That's cool.'

Lia refused to admit that she was on a fool's errand. Simon

had no interest in learning how to drive and even less interest in taking instruction from her. Still, she told herself that her lessons would be good for his self-confidence. She glanced at Alex, who had yet to take her eyes off the dough ball and look at Simon. But Lia saw the way Simon had been looking at Alex lately. There was something about the intensity of his gaze that made her wish he'd set his sights a little further afield.

'Okay, I'm ready!' Willow swung off the bottom step of the stairs and breezed into the kitchen.

Alex laughed. 'Whoa! Now I feel seriously underdressed.'

Willow had cut her new skirt so that it didn't quite cover her underwear and ripped her T-shirt in such a way that her cleavage was exposed now, as well as her midriff. She beamed defiantly at Jen and threw her arm around Alex's shoulders. The pair headed out to the garden, with Simon close behind.

Lia glanced out the kitchen window just as Jay turned to see Willow coming. She moved out of his line of sight, dread pooling in her stomach. She exhaled a shaky breath and returned to kneading the dough.

# SIX

## ALEX

Alex trotted up the stairs in Willow's house, with the same comfort as she would at home. She knocked once and went into Willow's room. Usually neither of them knocked on each other's door, but Alex was feeling nervous suddenly. When she opened the door and saw Willow standing there, in her skirt and bra, with scissors in her hand, butchering the new top her mother got her for her birthday, her breath caught in her chest.

'Wh...?'

'Come in and close the door.' Willow smiled, but carried on cutting.

'What are you doing? That top is brand-new!'

'Pissing my dad off.' She grinned.

'Oh, Christ. I'll wait downstairs. I want no part of this.' Alex forced herself to laugh back and then she left the room. It was the perfect time to tell Willow everything that she'd practiced telling her for weeks. Months, even, but she was chickening out. As she pulled Willow's door closed, she looked at the crappy gift that she was holding. A scrapbook filled with photos from when they were toddlers, right up to a selfie taken last week. It was a broke person's gift, but Alex spent three weeks making sure it was the nicest broke person's gift Willow had ever gotten from her. She'd also spent three weeks deciding what to wear. Even going so far as to try on some of her mother's old "going out" dresses, which naturally she looked ridiculous in. She'd settled on black skinny jeans and her Albert Einstein rainbow tongued T-shirt, gathered into a knot so that her stomach was exposed. She'd fiddled with the knot when she felt her mother's eyes roaming over her and continued to fiddle with it on the walk over. She dropped her head and then opened the door again. 'Before I forget?' She smiled and threw the book like a frisbee, onto Willow's bed. Then she left the room again to avoid seeing her reaction and went back downstairs.

Jay and Lia looked like they were ready to rip each other's clothes off when Alex got back to the kitchen, and when Lia offered Alex some busy work, she could tell that Jay would have preferred it if she'd stayed upstairs and left them to it. But Alex needed the distraction. The others would be here soon, and she was running out of time to tell Willow how she felt. But then, of course, Simon came in.

'Here's the birthday boy!' Lia said, oozing pride as always. 'Did he tell you he's started driving lessons this week?'

Alex busied herself with Lia's dough, doing her best to avoid being pulled into a conversation with Simon. Of course he was learning to drive a year before anyone else was allowed to, but Alex couldn't have cared less. 'That's cool.' She forced a smile into her voice, but didn't turn to look at him.

Tonight was destined to be a series of awkward moments, beginning with her mother's – *you* are *comfortable over at that house, aren't you, love?* – chat before she left, which of course led to, *and there's no reason for you to ever be alone with Willow's dad, you know that, right?* A variation of the weird *chats* she always tried to have whenever she got a bee in her bonnet about the Higginses. But Alex had enough to be thinking about tonight. Willow's new friends, the bitches of Eastwick, would be arriving any minute, and in every way imaginable – looks, fashion, gift, the lot – they'd blow Alex out of the water. Since the bitches came along, Alex had been getting less time with Willow, but more time than ever with Simon. Everywhere she went, he was there. She hadn't said anything to Willow about it, because she didn't want to make her feel worse than usual about her annoying brother. But two days ago, Simon had followed Alex to the courts, while the rest of her class went swimming. When she asked him what he was doing, he got really upset. Then angry. He said he didn't follow her, but she knew that he did. Alex's fear of water was so ingrained that she was excused from all pool-based activities. But Simon *should* have been there with everyone else. He'd shoved her against the wall and accused her of leading him on. As if! Now Alex wanted to be as far away from Simon Higgins as possible. But she wanted to be as close as she could get to Willow. And she couldn't have one without the other. But that didn't mean she had to let Lia stick her with him for the night either.

But then Willow came swishing around the bottom of the stairs, her blonde hair fanning out to the side and landing perfectly over her left shoulder, and Alex forgot all about Simon and his poxy driving lessons. She was glued to the spot and it took everything not to let her jaw drop open. Everything Willow did seemed to end perfectly, and she made it all look so effortless. She was the most beautiful thing Alex had ever seen, and she felt like such a lump beside her.

'Okay, I'm ready!' Willow beamed and wrapped an arm around Alex's shoulders, pulling her towards the patio doors. Alex forgot about everything else then. They'd been best friends all their lives and Alex hated herself for falling in love with her. She felt her resolve melting away. If she were to tell

Willow how she felt, it would ruin everything, surely. Willow liked boys. Alex knew that. But saying nothing was torture. Especially now, when her bare arm was wrapped around Alex's neck and she both looked and smelled like heaven.

The doorbell rang before they made it as far as the rattan garden furniture. Mr Higgins was already out in the garden on the phone. He spotted Willow immediately and his features turned as dark as night. He pressed his phone to his chest and looked from Willow to the kitchen window, probably to see what Lia was thinking. Willow's outfit had had the desired effect. He ended his call and slipped his phone into his pocket, then he caught Willow gently by the hand and led her a few feet away from Alex. He spoke softly in her ear then pulled back and looked her dead in the eye. He held her gaze and her hand for a few seconds more, creating one more awkward moment for Alex, who stood like a spare part nearby. Finally, he returned his attention to his phone and walked away towards the other side of the garden. Willow's smile didn't falter, but Alex could tell when it stopped being genuine. She imagined that Willow had just been threatened with a grounding, or the loss of her phone. Or something equally devastating to a sixteen-year-old girl. Willow went out of her way to piss her dad off and never seemed to care about the consequences.

'Why do you do that?' Alex asked as quietly as she could.

Willow shrugged and Alex shook her head.

'I'll get the door,' Willow said, still smiling a strange fake smile. Alex watched her trotting inside and wondered why she couldn't see how good she had it. When Alex's parents weren't fighting about money, they fought about how shit their lives were. Alex would give anything to see her dad looking at her mother the way Jay had been looking at Lia earlier. The way he always looked at her with such adoration. No wonder she was always so happy. No wonder her mum hated them. Willow took it all for granted, but Alex still adored her.

'Ahh! It's Darina and Lucy!' Willow screamed her way out into the hall.

Alex dropped down on the rattan couch. *Great. Darina and Lucy.*

'Darina and Lucy?' Mr Higgins asked Alex, one eyebrow raised quizzically.

'Darina Hayes and Lucy Nagle,' Alex supplied half-heartedly. A.K.A the bitches of Eastwick, she wanted to add, but didn't.

'Don Hayes's daughter?' he asked, sounding pleasantly surprised.

Don Hayes was one of the best-known cardiac surgeons in the country, and his daughter was an asshole. But Alex didn't say as much. Instead, she forced a smile and a nod. He nodded, too, and she could tell what he was thinking. He was into politics in a big way and was probably pondering how much better Darina Hayes would be as Willow's best friend, than Alex, whose dad worked in a cheese factory. Without saying any more, he went back inside.

Alex watched him through the kitchen window as he spoke to Lia. His lips brushed her cheek as they talked quietly, and he placed his hand protectively on her lower back. Alex tried again to imagine her parents being like that with each other, but even her imagination couldn't quite conjure the image. Lia glanced up and saw Alex watching them. She smiled and gave Jay's hand a gentle squeeze. Alex looked away as Willow and her new crew came bouncing through the doors, all three screaming like idiots. Willow acted differently when they were around. Like she felt the need to dumb herself down for them. She put *like* at the beginning, middle and end of every sentence she spoke to those idiots, and *never* argued her point. Not like she always did with Alex. With everyone, in fact. Willow was badass, which was one of the things that Alex loved about her. But not with them. With them she became Barbie on steroids.

Darina let her smile slip dramatically at the sight of Alex sitting there on the couch. Her jeans and Einstein T-shirt, with the *tiniest* hint of Pride, seemed like a hideous choice of outfit suddenly. All three of them were dressed in mini dresses and new Converse high-tops, all fake tan, sleek hair and make-up. Darina, with her Sephora gift bag, pulled Willow over to the other side of the garden and was speaking in dramatic hushed tones, right into her ear. But her eyes were on Alex, and they made her want to crawl under the plump, weather-resistant cushions that surrounded her. Or maybe burn the house down, just to destroy the shitty scrapbook on Willow's bed.

'Oh, Christ.' Simon dropped down beside her, making her jump.

'What?'

'The bitches of Eastwick are here. Didn't anyone tell them that it's just pizza in the back garden?'

'It's not just pizza in the garden. It's your sixteenth birthday,' she said, shuffling further along the couch, putting a little distance between her and Simon, who annoyingly had taken to calling them by the nickname that Alex had mistakenly spoken aloud just once.

He looked pointedly down at the space between them, but he didn't move. 'You know Darina has been going out with a sixth year since the start of summer. Her parents have a home in the South of France, and she's been known to take "the chosen few" on holiday with her. The parties in *her* house are legendary. This "pizza party" is going to suck ass as far as she's concerned.'

'Your mum's pizza doesn't suck ass. Nothing about this house does.' *Except maybe you.*

'Yeah, well, nothing is as perfect as it seems. That lot included.' He nodded towards the long-limbed creatures across the garden. 'Darina lost her virginity at the back of the rugby clubhouse. Did you know that? At least two of the players had a go.'

Alex looked sharply at him, deeply uncomfortable all of a sudden. She could feel the redness spreading across her chest and up along her neck, and she brought her hand to her throat. It wasn't that the mention of sex embarrassed her. She and Willow talked about sex plenty. Or more about who was having it. But coming from Simon, it sounded... ugh.

'Listen, I'm sorry about the other day over by the courts.' He turned in his seat so that his broad body blocked her from the others suddenly. 'Obviously, I didn't mean to be a prick.'

Alex nodded, shuffling towards the edge of her seat, to both see and be seen. She looked to Willow, wishing for her to look over. Or better still, *come* over. But she didn't.

'Don't worry about them.' Simon leaned forward, forcing her to look at him again. He nudged her playfully on the inch of bare skin between her T-shirt and her jeans, making Alex spring up from the chair. She pulled open the knot, making her midriff disappear.

'I'm not worried about anything.' Her throat tightened.

'Here, drink this.' Simon stood with her and held a can of Coke towards her. He threw an arm lazily around her shoulders and her whole body tensed. Simon smiled and looked at the can, which she refused to acknowledge, and eventually he placed it on the glass-topped table in front of them.

'Stop touching me, Simon,' she whispered, moving another couple of inches to the right, her eyes still on Willow's back as his arm slipped away. She knew she should shout at him. Slap him even, but she couldn't make a scene. Not in this house. He wasn't worth losing Willow over. Or making herself look like an even bigger idiot in the eyes of the bitches. But even before the thing outside the courts, she'd caught Simon looking at her from time to time. And whenever she did, it took him ages to look away. It was like he was in a world of his own and hadn't noticed that he'd been caught. But he seemed bolder now. More determined, and Alex didn't like it.

She glanced from Simon to Willow, who was laughing with her new friends at something that Alex wasn't privy to. She was glad suddenly that she hadn't told Willow how she felt. It would have made this infinitely more awkward. Her insides slackened with the realisation that she might never be able to tell Willow just how much she loved her. Or that she was slipping further and further out of her league.

Simon's fingers brushed Alex's lower back, startling her again. 'I'm going to see if your mum needs any help.' She knocked her shin against the table in her haste to get away and go back inside the house.

'Can I help with anything, Lia?' she asked, as brightly as she could.

Lia smiled at her. 'You're a star, Alex. Can you get the sauce out of the fridge?'

Alex nodded and went to the fridge with its double doors. It was jam-packed, as always, with fresh food. Lia made everything from scratch, including the bowl of pizza sauce that sat on the middle shelf.

'Thanks, love.' Lia took the bowl from her with a smile. 'Now, I'm not going to have you standing in here making pizzas with me, when all your friends are out there.' She nodded towards the window. 'There should be a few more arriving shortly.'

'They're not really my friends,' Alex mumbled.

Lia's shoulders sagged and she looked at Alex with sympathy. It made Alex's cheeks flush red.

'I didn't mean it like that. I just meant...'

'I know what you meant, pet.' She rubbed Alex's back. 'It's a big year for you guys and there's bound to be some changes. But you're a part of this family, Alex Blake. And you always will be, so don't you forget that, alright? Now, if you really want to help, then you can pop upstairs and grab some throws out of the linen press. It'll be getting cold out there soon.' She glanced out the window. 'And Lord knows, my little Willow could use the coverage.' There was both humour and sarcasm in her tone as she looked out the window.

Alex followed Lia's gaze to where Willow was smiling in delight at her new and expensive gifts. It was that smile that made Alex always want to be the funny one. These days it made her want to kiss her. And when she reached behind and pulled her hair over one shoulder, it made Alex want to run her hand slowly through it. She brought her hand to her chest, feeling her breathing quickening.

'Alex?' Lia squeezed her shoulder gently.

Alex blinked. 'Yeah, sorry. Throws.' She returned Lia's smile and headed for the stairs. 'Leave it with me.'

'Are you alright, pet?' Lia asked after her.

Alex waved over her shoulder. 'I'm grand.'

Upstairs, Alex opened the linen press on the landing, breathing in that familiar Higgins house scent – something between fresh laundry and expensive aromatherapy oils. Though their houses were identical from the street, stepping into the Higginses' felt like entering a boutique hotel. Every surface gleamed, every item seemed brand-new, a stark contrast to Alex's own home.

'Hey.' Simon tapped her on the shoulder as she bundled the gorgeous grey-and-white throws on top of each other. A whole matching set of them. Each one must have cost a fortune.

'Jesus!' She startled. Her chest tightened and began reddening again as she glanced over his shoulder towards the stairs.

'Have you ever heard of Wally Funk?'

'Who?'

'Wally Funk. Come on!' Simon beckoned her into his room with a smile. 'She's right up your street.'

Alex glanced towards the stairs and then back to Simon. He did share her love for random facts, and he always came up with great ones. A part of her wanted to know who, or what, Wally Funk was. 'I need to get these down to your mum.' She placed her hand on the bundle of throws and glanced again towards the stairs. She heard Lia moving around down in the kitchen. Alex had never felt uncomfortable in this house before and Lia was right there. Alex could hear her, which meant that Lia could probably hear them, too, right? He'd hardly try anything with his parents so close. Besides, anything was better than watching a live version of *Mean Girls* playing out in the garden. She hesitated a moment longer, then followed him to his room.

'Wally Funk was the oldest woman in space,' Simon said excitedly, bringing his laptop to life on his desk and beckoning her over. It was as if she'd imagined him being a creep earlier. 'But not just that!' he continued.

Alex glanced around the room she'd been in many times. It didn't really look like a teenage boy's room. It was too neat, and like the rest of upstairs, it always smelled nice. It had Lia written all over it. Definitely not Simon. She sat on the end of his bed, like she often did, and watched the screen. An elderly woman with short white hair and a huge smile came up. Alex could tell immediately that she was no ordinary pensioner and there was *nothing* Alex loved more than a trailblazing woman. She shuffled in closer to see what it said about her.

'Look at this!' Simon said. 'By the age of twenty, she was a flight instructor, training male air force candidates, even though they wouldn't allow her to join the air force herself on account of being a girl. Can you imagine being that bad ass at twenty?'

'I'd be happy to be that badass at any age.'

Simon turned towards her. He had the same expression of pity in his eyes when he looked at her now. If Simon Higgins felt sorry for her, then she really was pathetic.

'Christ, I'm getting all the pity tonight.' She half laughed at herself.

'I don't pity you.' Simon sat down beside her. 'Why would I pity you?'

'Well, when you put me standing next to that lot...' She thumbed towards Simon's bedroom window and the garden outside it. 'I do look a bit... *ah, bless.*'

'How can you say that?' Simon leaned back and looked at her. 'Alex, you're gorgeous.'

Those words coming out of Simon's mouth... She laughed uncomfortably because she had no idea what to say. Why had she said *any* of that to him?

'Why are you laughing? What's so funny?'

'I'm not laughing. Not really, I mean. That's not what...'

He shook his head vehemently. 'What if I told you that I've thought you were gorgeous since we were seven years old?'

She gave another involuntary chuckle, but her skin prickled, and she felt hot all of a sudden. She shuffled towards the edge of the bed and that's when she noticed that the door was closed. When had he closed the door?

'Don't laugh, Alex. I'm being serious now. I know you think of me as' – he shook his head and shrugged his broad shoulders – 'baby Simon, or whatever. But I'm not baby Simon. And I'm not *your* brother either.' He caught her by the arm as she went to stand up.

Alex's quivery smile faded and then died completely. She had no idea what to do. This was Simon. She couldn't slap him or scream at him or *hurt* him in any way, because this was just... this couldn't be what it felt like it was. His mum and dad were right downstairs. Still, she wanted to get away from him.

'Simon, I...'

'Just hear me out, okay?' He turned to face her, catching hold of her other arm now. His grip was tight, making the skin on her arms burn.

She pulled, gently at first, but when he didn't release her, she pulled a little harder. 'Let me go, Simon,' she said quietly, a ridiculous quivery smile back on her face. It wasn't like she could scream Willow's house down.

'Alex... I love you. I've loved you for years.'

She shook her head. 'Simon, I don't think... I mean, we're like...' She pulled again, harder this time, but he still wouldn't let go. Alex looked towards the door. He must have shoved it closed when they came in. Could Lia hear them? Wasn't she wondering what was taking Alex so long with the blankets?

'Don't say we're like brother and sister.' He began shaking her. 'Please don't say that, Alex. We're not. I'm not a kid. I'm a man and I'm telling you that I love you. And I know you love me, too.'

'But I don't...' She stopped. She didn't know what else to say. Then finally, she said the only thing she could think of. 'Look at my T-shirt. Do you see this?' She pulled on Einstein's tongue. When she opened her eyes, Simon's head was tilted to see what she was talking about.

He frowned. 'What? No way.'

Alex nodded, looking him in the eye. She'd never actually come out as being gay because, well, why should she?

Simon laughed briefly.

'Why are you laughing?' Alex's stomach dropped.

'I'm laughing because it's bullshit.'

'What?'

'You've been sucking face with boys all summer, Alex.'

Alex frowned and shook her head. She had let a boy kiss her at the end-of-year disco, because she couldn't be the only one not to. But he tasted like vodka and Red Bull and she'd hated every second of it.

'More than sucking face, from what I hear.'

He released his grip and Alex immediately stood up. 'What are you talking about?'

Simon stood up, too. 'Kyle Fuller has told everyone what colour knickers you were wearing at the end of year, Alex.'

Alex shook her head and stepped back.

Simon closed his eyes and tilted his head to one side. Then he reached out and took her hand, clutching it tightly. 'I knew it was bullshit. I'm sorry, Alex. I shouldn't even have told you that. He wishes, right? Come here, sit down.'

She did. She felt like crying. Kyle Fuller was an asshole, and she could easily see him bragging about something that never happened. Truth be told, that's partly why she picked him. She *wanted* people to hear she'd kissed him because she desperately wanted not to be in love with her best friend.

'I'm sorry, Alex,' Simon said again, more quietly this time.

Alex blinked and a tear rolled out of each eye. 'I'm gay, Simon,' she said, the words sounding strange coming out of her mouth. She had imagined herself saying it for so long. She wished he didn't have to be the one she told first. But if it put a stop to this, then it was worth it.

But Simon smiled, brows furrowed as if confused. 'No, you're not.' His voice was low, too, and he put his hands on her shoulders again. This time he pushed her down onto the bed.

Alex pushed up against him, but he was strong. Suddenly he wasn't Willow's pity-party brother anymore. He was a giant man, with meaty hands that had somehow found their way up inside her T-shirt. He moved so that his thigh was between her legs, and he used his knee to push hers apart.

'Simon...' Alex cried quietly, turning her face away as he tried to kiss her. 'Please, let me up.'

'You let Kyle do it...'

'No, I...'

He pulled her T-shirt up and shoved his hand under her bra. He squeezed hard.

'Ouch, Simon...' She started crying now, as she pushed uselessly against him, while he wrestled his way on top of her. Crushed under the weight of him, she couldn't breathe suddenly. 'Stop, please...'

'Simon!' Lia came through the door and Simon jumped to his feet. His face now was that of baby Simon again. A deer caught in the headlights.

Alex jumped up and ran from the room, pulling her clothes back into place, her face hot with tears and shame as she took the stairs down two at a time and ran from the house.

# SEVEN
## LIA

Lia hurried to the top step of the stairs and stopped. She looked from the front door to Simon in disbelief. Simon looked terrified now. 'I... I didn't...' he stammered.

'Get back in your room and do not leave it,' Lia hissed at him. In that instant, the sight of her beautiful boy revolted her. She knew what it felt like to be pinned down by someone more powerful than her. To have her autonomy taken away, and when she walked through that door, it wasn't Alex and Simon she saw. It was her seventeen-year-old self, and Jay.

She turned her back on him and hurried downstairs and out the front door. She stood there looking across the green, towards the Blakes' house. But she couldn't see Alex. She looked all around and over towards the woods. There she was, hurrying towards the treeline. Lia glanced at the Blakes' house again. She should call Jen. She knew she should. But Jen would fly off the handle and make this so much worse for everyone, including Alex. The woman was so caught up in the mundane, that she had no idea how to handle anything with delicacy. Lia pulled the door closed and jogged after Alex. She *would* bring her home to Jen. Once she knew the girl was alright.

'The woods' was actually just a copse of trees between one estate and the next. But the kids had been building forts in there since forever. Even now, they still hung out on the tyre swing beside the remains of a timber cabin that was erected by some of the dads back when the kids in both estates were small enough to make it their whole world.

'There you are,' Lia said softly when she reached the tree from which the old tractor tyre dangled on a rope.

Alex was sitting on the swing, crying. She wiped her face with the palms of her hands.

'Are you alright, love?'

Lia walked slowly towards her, reached out and gave her knee a gentle squeeze. Then she lowered herself onto the grass beneath her.

Alex nodded brusquely. 'I'm grand,' she said, her voice full of teenage bravado.

'I saw what Simon did, Alex.'

'It's fine.' She sniffed.

'It's not fine. He had no right to touch you like that.'

Alex looked at her with a slight frown.

'Alex, just because you two are friends and I'm his mum... you don't have to cover for him. I saw what he did.'

They both stared at the grass for a few seconds.

'He's been falling for you for some time.' Lia spoke softly, but her insides churned as she made the same excuse for her son that Jay had made for himself back then. She'd been silly enough to believe it, but she wasn't sure that Alex was. 'I see how his face changes whenever you walk through the door,' she continued. 'How much more effort he puts into his appearance when he knows he'll be seeing you. I also know that my son is an idiot, Alex.' She smiled. 'Teenage boys tend to be.'

Alex looked at her and gave her a half smile. They were both quiet for another while, before Alex said, 'I didn't know that he liked me.'

Lia smiled sadly and nodded. 'He does. Clearly, though, he has no idea how to show it.'

'But I'm not... I mean, I don't...'

Lia reached up and put her hand on Alex's knee again. 'Alex, it doesn't matter. You don't have to explain yourself. Whether the feeling is mutual or not, it still doesn't give him the right to touch you without your permission. And that goes for crushes, boyfriends, husbands... wives' – she shook her head – 'and complete bloody strangers. None of that matters. No means no.'

Alex wiped her tears away again and nodded.

'You did nothing wrong here, love. Do you hear me?'

Alex nodded again.

'And as for Simon... he's a boy trapped in the body of a man, Alex. He has no idea what to do with it or how to act. But I know I raised him better than that.' Lia might have tried to raise him better than that, but she wasn't raising him alone.

Alex got down from the swing and sat alongside Lia on the grass, under the giant oak tree. Lia reached an arm around the girl's shoulders and pulled her close.

'I promise you, Alex – Simon will never do anything like that to you, or to anyone else, ever again. Do you hear me? No one in my family will ever hurt you. We love you.'

Alex leaned her head on Lia's shoulder. She could feel her nodding and when she said, 'I know that,' there was more false confidence in her voice. They sat quietly for another few minutes, Lia trying to gauge where to take the conversation next.

'Alex, can I ask you something?' she asked gently, after a minute had passed.

Alex sat up.

'You can tell me to mind my own business if you like, but... I'm wondering if you need someone to talk to. About...' Lia brushed her fingers against the little rainbow flag coming out of

Einstein's mouth. 'Are you gay, sweetheart? Is that what you've been keeping inside you all this time?'

'What makes you think I'm keeping anything inside? It's just a T-shirt,' Alex said defensively, scrabbling to her feet. She was crying again. Big fat tears.

'I've known you since the day you were born, love. For the past while you've seemed...' Lia shook her head, thinking of the right word. 'Apprehensive. Like you have something important to say, but the words won't come out.'

Alex lowered her head, and Lia saw the girl's shoulders sag. Relief, maybe?

'But why are you crying? It's 2025, Alex! People are free to be themselves! Here, sit down.' Lia patted the grass beside her.

Slowly, Alex came back over and sat down. Lia put her arm around her again.

'Yeah, well, straight people don't have to *come out* about their sexuality, do they?'

Lia half smiled and shook her head.

'No! So why is it any different for me?'

'You're absolutely right. You love who you love, and you don't have to explain *why* to anybody.'

'I just wanted to tell people in my own time.'

'And that's absolutely fair. This is your news to tell, not mine. It's not really something you should have to think about at all, is it? Falling in love is the most natural thing in the world. Unfortunately for my dumb son, he's feeling misguided. *I'll* be putting him straight, don't worry. So...' She raised her eyebrows and looked at Alex. 'What's really been eating you up? It can't just be the fact that you're gay. Not in this day and age, surely?'

Alex laughed. 'You sound like my mum: *not in this day and age.* I forget sometimes that you and her are the same age. You're so much more...'

'Your mum is a good woman, Alex. Me and her were like you and Willow, once upon a time. As you know.'

'What actually happened?' Alex said, looking at Lia intensely.

Lia shrugged, her gaze falling on the treeline. 'Nothing happened. Not really. I suppose life just sort of took over and got in the way.' Again, memories filled her head as the lie spilled out.

Alex's smile faded. 'She wouldn't get any of this.'

'Does she know?'

Alex shook her head.

'Why don't you talk to her about it?'

Alex laughed. 'I can't talk to her like I talk to you. She just... she geeks out about stuff when she doesn't know what else to do.'

Lia laughed. 'What do you mean?'

'I mean... when I tell her I'm gay, first, she'll pretend like she already knew. Then she'll go on and on about it, smothering me with her *support*. Then she and my dad will probably start fighting over which one of them isn't being supportive enough, or some crap like that.'

'So you know she'll support you.'

Alex shrugged and shook her head. 'Yeah, well, she's never around long enough for me to tell her anything anyway. And when she is home, she's so stressed out.'

Lia looked down at the grass, her smile gone now. As she spoke, she sounded sad again. 'It's not as easy for your mum and dad, Alex. They work really hard, and they have a lot on their plates. The cost of living has gotten to the point where ordinary, hard-working people are struggling to keep a roof over their heads. Especially after your dad... Well, it's hard to prioritise other things when you're fighting to survive and provide for your family. You'll understand that more when you're older.'

'But you still have time to sit under a tree with the weird kid from across the green,' Alex said, her face creasing into an awkward smile.

'You mean the amazing girl from across the green? Well, I guess that makes me the lucky one.' She got to her feet and wiped the seat of her cropped white pants. Then she held a hand towards Alex and helped her up, too.

Alex looked at her for a second, then hugged Lia tightly. Lia hugged her back. When she let go, she held her at arm's length. 'Now you listen to me. If what happened tonight with Simon is bothering you...'

Alex shook her head. 'It's fine. I told you... I just...'

'I know, love.' She smiled and tucked Alex's hair behind her ear. 'You're so strong. There is *nothing* you can't handle, is there?'

Alex smiled a teary smile.

'But while it might not bother you now, it might at another time. Promise me that you'll come to me, pet? I'm here for you, any time. You hear me? Any time.'

# EIGHT

## JEN

'What in the name of God is wrong with you, Alex?' Jen stormed around Alex's room the following weekend picking dirty clothes up off the floor and dumping them in a laundry basket that she was carrying around under her arm. 'I specifically asked you last night if you had a clean kit for today, and you said yes! So what the hell is this?' She held up Alex's basketball kit. It smelled like deodorant and sweat. The room was dark except for a sliver of morning light that managed to find its way through a crack in the curtains. It came to land on the giant Lego space shuttle in the corner of the room. That thing had taken Alex nearly three months to build. Jen would never have had the patience for it, but Alex was at her most serene when she was surrounded by those annoying, spiky little bricks. Lego was a phase she never quite grew out of.

Alex, who was lying on her bed staring up at the ceiling, turned on her side, ignoring Jen further.

Jen felt her head start to throb. Even though it was Saturday, she had to show two properties before Alex's match in the afternoon and *now* it seemed she had more laundry to do, despite being up late last night to get through the mountain that was waiting for her when she got home from work. It seemed washing machine instructions were too complicated a thing for anyone but her.

'Alex!'

'What?' she spat.

'What's wrong?' Jen had never seen her daughter like this before. Despite her annoyance, she wanted desperately to pull her into a hug but fought against her impulse.

Alex jumped up off the bed and went to her wardrobe. 'There's nothing wrong. I just wish you'd get off my case for five minutes. Or is that too much to ask?'

'Alex.' Jen sighed. 'I'm not trying to be on your case. But you have a basketball match this afternoon and your kit is dirty. I have to work this morning, so how am I supposed to get this washed and dried on time?' Her work phone rang and vibrated loudly against the kitchen table downstairs, but she ignored it, knowing that it would be James.

'You don't have to. That match was yesterday. You missed it. Today is just training.'

Jen was silent, as she ran through the entire week in her head. She didn't forget the match completely, surely? 'Wh... what do you mean, the match was yesterday? Why would the match be on a Friday?' She wrestled the laundry basket to one side and pulled her phone out of her back pocket. She quickly opened WhatsApp and the muted parents group chat. Thirty-seven unread messages. Lia's running commentary rendered silent. *Shit.*

'It was on at three. The whole school attended. Like, part of the school day, pretty much. Parents were notified on the school app.'

'The school app...!'

'Plus, I did tell you. Last week.'

Jen's heart sank. How had she missed that? 'So, today...?'

'Training, but they're going to the pool instead.'

'The whole team?'

'Reward session.'

'And you're not going?' She sounded like an idiot trying to catch up.

'To the pool?' Alex looked at her, like she *was* an idiot.

Jen shook her head and blew out a long breath. Of course Alex wasn't going to the pool. She had a mortal fear of water, ever since she slipped into a pool on holidays when she was five years old. She went straight to the bottom. It took about six seconds for Dale to reach her, but those six seconds were the last that Alex spent in any body of water. All of her teachers and her coach were aware of this, and Alex was excused from all water-based activities.

'Well... how did yesterday go then? Did you win?' Jen asked brightly.

Alex shrugged. 'I think so. But I didn't go.'

'What? What do you mean, you didn't go?' Alex had been playing basketball since she was seven years old. She loved it. 'Alex, you're an integral part of that team. Isn't that important to you anymore? You can't just decide not to turn up for a match. They won't tolerate that.'

'Look, just because you were the shining star of St Brendan's, doesn't mean I have to be!' She made a face and changed her voice when she said *shining star*, with more uncharacteristic sarcasm. 'It was just a stupid friendly.' She got up and grabbed a heavy coat out of the wardrobe and put it on. Then she left the room and went downstairs. Jen followed, feeling utterly confused.

'Where are you going? You'll roast in that coat.'

Alex didn't answer. She disappeared out of the house just as Jen's work phone rang again. She hurried to the kitchen, grabbed it off the table and hit accept. 'James, I'm on the way.' She picked up her handbag and left the house. And the pile of laundry.

'I've been ringing you for half an hour,' James snapped. 'I need you to do Douglas Road as well today.'

'What? James, it's Saturday!'

'You're getting paid, aren't you?'

James hung up. Jen squeezed her eyes shut and let out a silent scream. Even though she was outdoors now, standing by her car on a sunny autumn day, she felt claustrophobic. Like her life was suffocating her. She wanted to release the pain and frustration she'd been holding in for months. She wanted to cry loud, heaving sobs, but even more desperately, she needed some space to breathe.

When she opened her eyes again, she saw Willow walking towards the entrance to the estate. She was with Darina Hayes and Lucy Nagle. They all had their kitbags on their shoulders, but they didn't look like a basketball team. They looked like something from an American high school movie. Short shorts and bra tops, with perfect hair and make-up. She frowned and looked around the estate, towards the woods. She saw the back of Alex, in her baggy jeans and winter coat. She was heading into the woods, alone. Jen looked at Willow again and the girl waved when she saw her. But it wasn't the usual, enthusiastic wave that Jen was used to. Jen pointed towards the woods to let Willow know where Alex was, but she just lowered her head and continued on her way. She looked again towards Alex, who suddenly looked like the loneliest child in the world. Jen let her arms hang down, while she watched her beautiful daughter walking away from her lifelong friend and the sport that she'd always loved. Something was wrong and Jen was hit with a wave of guilt over the way she'd barked at her about her stupid laundry.

Her phone rang. It was James. Again.

'I'm coming.' She rolled her eyes, opened the car door and got in. By the time she turned the car around, Alex was gone from sight. Jen sat there for a minute with her eyes on the woods and her mind on her daughter. But while they were three months behind on their mortgage repayments and had a crippling gas bill to pay, Jen had no choice but to leave her, for now.

Dale picked up on the fifth ring.

'Where are you?'

'What do you mean, where am I? I'm in the same place I was when you called five minutes ago – working overtime, remember?'

Jen rolled her eyes and made a face at the phone. 'Yes, well, you didn't answer five minutes ago.' She was driving through the city on her way to the first of three viewings now. 'I mean, what time will you be home? Something's up with Alex.'

'This again? What exactly do you think is up with her?'

'I'd have led with that if I knew what it was, Dale.'

'She's fifteen years old, Jen. We've been warned about this often enough, haven't we? And to be fair, we've been getting off fairly lightly up until now, hormone wise.'

'Exactly! So why the sudden change? And please don't tell me her age again because I know how old my child is. I'm telling you, I don't think it's...'

'It's one of two things: teenage drama, or teenage hormones. But she's not just a teenager, is she? She's a teenage *girl*, which means it's probably a strong combination of the two. Either way, I'm sure having her mother sticking her oar into every little thing is *really* helping her.'

His sarcastic dig made her want to scream. He might be right, but he was always so self-righteous that she refused to agree with him. '*Something* is wrong, Dale!'

'And where are you?'

'Where do you think I am?'

'I thought you were supposed to be off today. It's Saturday.'

'It is Saturday. But the gas bill is up to eight hundred euro because we haven't cleared it in two months, so I have viewings today. I'm on my way to one of them now.'

'Ah. So you're not *that* worried about Alex then, obviously.' There was a loud noise in the background. Dale was on the factory floor. 'Look, I have to go. You're not the only one who has to work on the weekend.'

The line went dead, and Jen let out an exasperated growl. Tears of frustration rolled off her chin and she wiped them angrily away as she came bumper to bumper with the car in front. The quays were at a standstill, and she was going to be late. She dialled Alex's number. It rang once and then she cut the call. Jen let out another groan as she inched her way further into the heart of the city, and away from her daughter.

# NINE

## LIA

Lia watched from her doorstep as Jen stood by her car looking like she wanted to kill someone. Instinct told her that it was more to do with the phone call she'd just ended, than anything else. But she had noticed Alex walking in the opposite direction to Willow and the girls and Lia thought briefly about following her to check in. But as important as it was to keep Alex close now, Lia just didn't have it in her today. She stood there for another minute and watched Jen's car revving its way out of the estate, then she closed the door and went upstairs.

Lia used to hate the silence in the house when everyone left. The days seemed to stretch out endlessly before her, with nothing but domesticity to occupy her time. That, and the weighing scales.

She closed her bedroom door and went to her wardrobe. From the top shelf, she pulled down a Christian Louboutin boot box and brought it with her back to the bed. She ran her hand over the glossy surface and then removed the lid. She did this from time to time, when she needed reminding of how far she'd come. The first photo she picked up was a family photo, taken when Lia was about ten. She was wearing a summer dress that had belonged to both of her sisters before her. They stood either side of her, looking equally tatty. She put that picture aside. The next one was of her and Jen holding a gold trophy between them, smiling like they were fit to burst. Jen was the only person who knew that Lia's kit was from the charity shop. Or that Lia sometimes went to school hungry because her father drank whatever money her family had. Jen knew every embarrassing thing about her back then and she never thought anything of it. The next photo brought a smile to her face. The pair of them singing karaoke in a bar that, at seventeen, they were still too young to be in. Jen, Lia and a few of their other friends always looked older than they were when they wore make-up, and they weren't above flirting playfully with the bouncers. Whenever she looked at that picture, she could almost feel the ache in her face that she'd felt from laughing that night.

'Mum?'

Lia jumped and shoved the photos back in the box, along with all the other memories of her old life. She hurried to put the box back on the shelf and cover it over again with knitwear.

'Mum?' Simon called again from downstairs.

'What are you doing home?' she asked, coming to the top of the stairs and heading down. Simon had left not long after Willow had. He usually went wherever she was going, so in today's case, he should have been at the pool. But Lia suspected that Willow's new friends weren't as welcoming as Alex had been, and that wasn't good.

'Can you make me some scrambled eggs?' he asked, rather than explaining his sudden return home. Lia bit her lip and looked to the ceiling. 'Simon, you do know that scrambled egg is literally the easiest thing in the world to make. You're fifteen. You need to start learning to take care of yourself.'

'Can you put white pepper in it?' he said, still looking at his phone, ignoring her comments.

She blinked slowly and went about preparing his second

breakfast, hating herself for doing it. But now was not the time for volatility. She needed to tread very carefully where her family was concerned. 'Have you spoken to Alex yet?' she asked, keeping her tone light.

Simon looked up as if waiting for her to start making sense. Lia hated that look. She got it from Jay all the time. 'About what?'

'You know what, Simon. What were you thinking?' She couldn't keep the edge out of her voice.

He sighed and dropped his phone. 'What are you talking about, Mum?'

Lia squeezed the bridge of her nose and turned to the fridge. 'You want me to say it, eh? You *need* to hear the words coming out of my mouth? Fine.' She pulled out the box of eggs and slapped them down in front of him. 'Have you spoken to Alex about the fact that you tried to force yourself on her, right here in our house?'

Simon exploded up out of his seat, knocking it to the floor, and he walked away. He made it halfway to the front door before turning back. 'How can you say that to me? You make me sound like some kind of... like, a rapist or something.'

Hearing that word coming from her son felt worse than any blow she'd taken over the years, physical or emotional. Her arm wrapped instinctively around her belly, which started to ache. 'I'm not saying...'

'I tried to kiss her, Mum. That's all. I was never going to... I'm hardly going to hurt Alex, am I? How could you think that about me? What kind of mother *are* you?'

His face was masked with pain. Not the pain of having hurt his friend. But the pain of his mother questioning him like this. Lia's heart broke. He was her son. Her baby. And looking at him now, she felt nothing but shame for having spoken to him like that. Of course he wasn't trying to hurt Alex. He wasn't a vindictive boy. He was inherently good. Innocent, if not a little misguided. And that's what he needed from her now: guidance. Not judgement.

'I'm sorry, love.' She reached out and touched his arm. 'I didn't mean for it to sound like that. It's just that, when I walked into your room...'

'You saw the tail end of something. But, Mum, Alex kissed me first.'

Now it was Lia's turn to frown in confusion.

'A couple of weeks ago.'

'Really?'

'Why'd you say it like that?'

'Like what?'

'Like you think I'm lying? Or that she couldn't possibly be attracted to me?'

Lia shook her head.

'She said she was confused. That she wanted to try it... to see if she liked it.'

'Confused about...?'

He looked at her now like she was thick. 'Being gay.'

'Oh.' This made sense. Teenagers needed to experiment with... 'But not that night? The night of the pizza party?'

Simon's expression returned to neutral, and he walked past her, back to the kitchen. He straightened his chair, sat up at the island and picked up his phone again. 'Yes, that night, too.' He was studying his screen instead of looking at her. 'But then she changed her mind.'

'She changed her mind?'

He nodded. 'About a second before you came into the room.' He looked up again, his face softened once more. 'So, you see, Mum, I wasn't doing anything to hurt Alex. We were kissing, like she wanted to. Then she changed her mind just as you walked in.'

Lia stood looking at him for a few seconds, while he returned his attention to his phone. She nodded slowly. 'Okay.

Just... make sure she knows that you're sorry for any misunderstanding, okay?'

'Why aren't you having this conversation with Willow, by the way?'

'Willow? Why would I be having this conversation with Willow?'

'She's been the one icing Alex out, not me.'

'What? Why?'

Simon laughed. 'Jeez, Mum. I thought being on top of these things was, like, your *thing*? Willow has new friends now. Alex doesn't fit in with them so... Alex is out, full stop.'

Lia shook her head. Alex had been a part of their family forever. She was the last link that Lia had to her old life. Her one-time best friend and the girl she used to be. Before Jay. She looked at Simon and frowned when she saw the grin on his face. Now was not the time to push Alex away. Now was the time to keep her close.

'Willow wouldn't ice her out.'

'Darina mortified her when she saw the shit present Alex gave her for her birthday. So Alex has officially been cancelled.' He looked up at her again. 'Shouldn't you be at Pilates or something?'

Lia glanced at the clock. *Fucking Bikram yoga.* Lia hated Bikram yoga, but the class was run by the wife of one of Jay's colleagues. She not only had to attend, but she had to be a poster girl for its benefits. She went and picked up her bag from the hall.

'What about my eggs?' Simon called after her.

Lia left the house, closing the door quietly behind her. Her chest felt tight as she walked to her car and her breathing was shallower than it should be. She climbed in and closed and locked the door. Then she sat behind her tinted windows, her knuckles whitening as she gripped the wheel. She stayed there, employing every method she'd ever learned to slow her breathing and stave off the panic attack that threatened. Lia was the proverbial swan. Calm and graceful on the surface, but no one ever saw what went on underneath.

The sight of Jen on the other side of the green distracted her momentarily. She must have forgotten something at home and was now running to her car for a second time that morning. She was haggard looking as always, but a part of Lia envied the woman. No one talked about her hair or her clothes or her handsome high-flying husband or her perfect kids. There was absolutely no pressure on Jen Blake to do anything other than go to work, fight with her husband, and slouch on the couch with a glass of wine and a bag of Doritos every night. It didn't matter that her once stunning looks and athletic figure had slipped away. She had the freedom to just let it all go.

Jen glanced up as she was about to get into her car and caught Lia looking. Lia forced a smile and waved through the windscreen at the woman, who waved her phone half-heartedly in return. Jen slid into her car and continued to talk on the phone as she pulled away from the house. Lia sat with her keys in her lap, watching her go.

# TEN

## JEN

The crowd was relatively large and boisterous. Most parents were there, along with other students, but then it was the first match that mattered in the championship season. Lia was down on the sidelines placing tubs of homemade protein balls on either end of the bench. She moved out of the way when the doors leading from the court to the locker rooms burst open, and the home team came bounding out, looking like they were about to take over the world. The crowd cheered and in the school gym, the sound echoed, making it seem like there were hundreds in attendance. Jen craned her neck to see Alex among them. To see if she was one of the girls high-fiving Lia as she made her way past them and back to where she was supposed to be, on the supporters' mezzanine.

'Where is she?' Dale asked.

Jen shrugged, leaning further over the railing to see.

They all bounded across the court to their coach and their bench. Seconds later the away team entered the same way. They were singing a cheerleader type chant in an attempt to intimidate their rivals. But the home crowd just cheered louder, chanting *bulldogs, bulldogs, bulldogs* over and over, drawing out the word and stamping their feet for the St Brendan's Bull-dogs, the home team. Jen and Dale joined in the chant and the cheering, but they still couldn't spot Alex in the throng of gangly players. Then Dale elbowed Jen in the ribs and nodded towards the doors. Alex eventually came through from the locker rooms alone. Her shoulders were slumped and her arms hung loose by her sides. She didn't look up towards the supporters, or even check out the competing team. She just strolled towards where her own team were in a huddle without her.

'Christ, she looks like she's headed for the gallows,' Dale drawled.

Lia elbowed her way to the railing, too close to Jen. 'Is Alex alright?' she asked, brow furrowed.

Jen bristled. She wanted to tell Lia to fuck off and mind her own business. But for Alex's sake, she didn't.

'Mm,' she answered instead, but honestly, she had no idea. Her mood slid off its low peak. Every minute she spent at home now was spent trying to coax Alex out of her room. While also having to cook, clean and ruminate over their bills. But she was still no wiser and with perfect Lia and her heavenly scent pressing her for information, Jen said the only thing she could think of. 'I think she might be coming down with something.' She wouldn't give Lia the satisfaction of admitting that she was clueless.

'Poor thing,' Lia said, still clapping and stamping her feet, though too gently to make any sound at all. She was too much of a lady for that. 'They're all a bit funny these days, if you ask me. Teens, right?'

Jen looked at her with her sleek ponytail and perfectly applied make-up. But the harsh gym lighting also showed up the puffy skin beneath her eyes that her expensive concealer failed to erase. Jen saw her bony sternum above the V-neck of her Bulldogs T-shirt, too, and she wondered if anyone else could see the cracks in the woman's perfect exterior. Or did Jen only notice because she knew for sure that they were there.

'There you are.' Jay smiled, squeezing himself between Jen and Lia, wrapping his arms around Lia's waist, while simultaneously smiling at Jen.

Jen rolled her eyes and looked down at the court, bitter memories rising. God, where was the Lia who used to dance on tables and down shots with them at the bar? The wild child of their group, Lia Carey, always up for anything. Right up until Jay swooped in and moulded her into the perfect Lia Higgins. It was like she couldn't erase her old self fast enough. Now she floated around like she'd been born with that silver spoon in her mouth and Jay permanently glued to her hip like she was some kind of trophy he'd won.

Alex glanced their way, and Jen gave her a subtle thumbs-up, but she ignored them and walked around her huddled team.

Alex hardly played at all. She wasn't cheering or chanting or getting involved full stop. Even when they won by fifteen points, it was like she didn't even notice.

'Hormones have entered the building,' Dale announced for the parents around him to hear, and they all giggled and rolled their eyes in agreement. The men jibed that they had their work cut out for them. Jay smirked, making Jen feel slightly protective of her husband, while simultaneously wanting to slap him.

'Oh, shut up, Dale,' Jen growled in his ear and walked away towards the gallery exit, feeling Lia's eyes on her back as she went.

Dale jogged after her and caught her by the elbow. 'What are you doing?'

'I'm going to see if she's alright,' Jen said as Alex left the court while her team continued their celebrations.

'Jen, the last thing a fifteen-year-old needs is their mummy walking into the team locker room and checking their temperature. Especially in front of her friends.'

Dale was right and she knew it. 'Fine. I'm going to wait in the car then.'

Dale glanced back apologetically at the other parents, shrugged his shoulders dramatically, and followed Jen out of the gym.

'That wasn't embarrassing at all,' Dale said, as he finally caught up with her near the car.

Jen didn't respond, which took all the restraint she had.

'Will you calm down about all this, please, Jen?'

She stopped walking and turned to face him. 'Are your eyes working, Dale? Have you not noticed *anything* over the past few weeks? Not the attitude? Not the fact that she's spending every evening in her room? Not the fact that she hasn't been seeing Willow, or anybody else, for that matter?'

Dale looked incredulous now. 'Jen, you give out when she spends too much time over at the Higginses' house. Now you're complaining that she's not going there enough! Which is it? Do you want her there, or at home?'

Jen rolled her eyes and walked on ahead of him.

'Look, why don't we stop at the Wholly Ground on the way home? I'll get us a couple of nice, strong coffees. Maybe Alex could start drinking it, too. Lia was saying that she and Willow went out for coffee this morning. A mummy-daughter thing. Maybe you two could do that. It might perk the pair of you up a bit.'

She looked suspiciously at him. Coffee from anywhere other than home was one of the luxuries they'd had to cut. Jen would kill for a decent coffee from the Wholly Ground, but... 'I think that money would be better spent on the gas bill, don't you?'

'What?'

'The gas bill, Dale. There's still eight hundred euro outstanding on it.'

He stopped walking and stepped closer, lowering his voice. 'Jen, what do you want me to do? I'm working my bollocks off while little snowflakes sail past me into management positions.' He inhaled through his nose, his face reddening. He lowered his voice further and Jen heard it crack when he said, 'I reek of cheese all the time, and I feel like crying when I see my monthly payslip. Is that what you want to hear from me? You're not the only one who's bloody miserable, but we can't harp on about it all the time!'

Tears pricked her eyes again. He was right. But that changed nothing.

'The team are heading to McDonald's after to celebrate,' Lia called as she headed for her brand-new Tesla, which was parked four spaces down, making every car around it look like Jen felt.

Dale cleared his throat and turned to look at Lia. 'Lovely stuff.' He gave her a thumbs-up and she waved and got in. 'Does she have money?' he quietly asked Jen then.

'I gave her a tenner this morning.' They reached their car and Jen got in the passenger side.

'So, look, you're getting that coffee, alright?'

She tried to smile, for his sake, and nodded.

'And would you mind dropping me off in town then?'

She closed her eyes and shook her head. 'I knew something was coming.'

'What? I told you about the Liverpool match last week, didn't I? The lads are all going out to watch it, so I said I'd go. Don't worry, I have my allowance. I know how much I can spend,' he said sarcastically.

She hated when he spoke to her like she was *his* mother. Like she was the one who decided that they would live as frugally as possible. Jen *never* went out. She never got to go anywhere. But now he'd made sure she couldn't argue about it, by telling her how crappy he felt about his job.

He pulled over opposite the Old Goose bar and they both got out. Jen walked around to the driver's side.

'Jen,' he said, before walking away. 'Go home and take a break. Throw up your feet and take it easy, yeah? Stop worrying for one afternoon.'

*Oh, fuck off.* She returned a fake smile instead of saying exactly that, and of course Dale chose not to notice as he headed off on *his* worry-free afternoon. Jen felt a pang of jealousy and a surge of resentment. She desperately wanted to round up her friends, get dressed up and hit the town. Not only that, but she wanted to check into a hotel where no one would wake her up in the morning, and when she *did* wake, someone would place a cooked breakfast under her nose.

Instead, she went home to a quite house and a pile of laundry that was big enough to eat two hours out of her afternoon. When she finally did sit down for the coffee that she so desperately needed, except in instant form, she picked up her phone, scrolled through her WhatsApp until she came to one of her group chats. One that had been dormant for weeks. Not that it would matter when she started it up again. Dee and Ellen had been Jen's friends in school and in all the years that followed. Dee and her wife, Chrissie, had two kids under the age of three. They were in that stage of parenthood that left you wondering if the person you once were would ever return. Or if she even existed in the first place. Ellen, on the other hand, would probably be spending her Sunday afternoon recovering from the weekend and swiping through Tinder, setting up the weekend yet to come. They used to be a foursome which included Lia, but she wasn't in this chat.

JEN BLAKE

I've been abandoned by my family & have morphed into Cinderella. Send help.

She didn't have long to wait for a reply from Ellen.

ELLEN DRUMMOND

You're alive!!! And just in time too! Myself & 4
women from my yoga class are going to Bere
Island next weekend. You HAVE to come!!! It's
technically a yoga retreat, but it'll be pure
DEBAUCHERY! BYO Fizz

The message was followed by twelve clinking champagne
flutes and six aubergines which made it clear that it was not a
women's-only retreat. Not that she needed to be told that
because Ellen wouldn't be going if it was.

A yoga retreat?

Dee had joined the chat.

I haven't showered in 3 days and today I ate an
entire share bag of Monster Munch for
breakfast.

JEN BLAKE

How about dinner when you get back, all 3 of
us? Dee, 1 night when you'll get to eat dinner
while it's still hot and have a glass of wine. Then
we'll send you back home when everyone's
asleep!

DEE KEATING

Oh God yes!!

ELLEN DRUMMOND

I can definitely do dinner! Friday week?

DEE KEATING

Chrissie is working on Friday week. Saturday
week?

ELLEN DRUMMOND

I have a thing on that Saturday.

**JEN BLAKE**

Sunday week?

**DEE KEATING**

Can do.

**ELLEN DRUMMOND**

Me too!

**JEN BLAKE**

Sunday week it is!

Jen felt excited momentarily, but she was also calculating the cost in her head. Dinner and some wine would probably run close to a hundred euro, due to the fact that Dee would drink gin and tonics like they were water, and they would split the bill three ways. Still. She needed this night out with her friends, so to hell with it. Why should *she* be the only one to sacrifice?

**DEE KEATING**

Eh, should we ask Lia?

Jen groaned. But a small part of her already knew that she'd be cancelling on them with a few days to go. She wasn't ready to admit that yet, but still, she wouldn't argue. There was no point.

**ELLEN DRUMMOND**

Well, it's been a long time, hasn't it? Maybe she's bored of suburban life & is craving a return to the wild side!!! BTW did ye see Jay on TV at that soup kitchen? Christ he's still lush, isn't he? She landed on her feet there.

**DEE KEATING**

Eh, we ALL live the suburban life now. Or had you forgotten? And no, I didn't see him. I always thought he was a bit of a dick.

**ELLEN DRUMMOND**

Is that a NO to Lia?

Jen closed her eyes and lowered her head. Then she exhaled loudly before typing another message.





She inserted two hysterical crying emojis and one eye roll and her whole body sagged with disappointment when she hit send. Not because Lia might have been there – but realistically, Jen was never going to be. She simply couldn't afford it. But it was nice to let herself believe for a moment that she might.

'Hey.' Alex came through the kitchen door in her rainbow shorts and Einstein T-shirt.

Jen looked up in surprise. 'Where'd you come from? I didn't hear you come in.'

'I was upstairs.'

'Upstairs? I thought you all went to McDonald's?'

She shook her head and went to the cupboard. She pulled out a box of cornflakes and poured herself a bowl.

'Have you been upstairs all this time? Why didn't you go?' Jen placed her phone face down. Group chat over. She'd respond to the incoming notifications later.

'Because I didn't want to.' Her reply was snarkier than normal. It seemed it was the *new* normal.

'Are you feeling okay?' Jen got up and went over to feel her forehead, but Alex pulled her head away.

'I'm grand, Mum. I just didn't want to go. Can I not decide for myself where I want to spend my time?'

Jen exhaled and rubbed her forehead. 'Of course you can. It's just that you don't usually choose to miss out on these things. And you didn't look very enthusiastic coming onto the court today either. Are you sure you're alright?'

'Will everyone just get off my bloody back for five minutes?' Alex snapped. Then she took her bowl back out to the hall and upstairs, leaving Jen staring after her.

Jen's phone blinged again. She glanced at it: another Whats-App, this time from Lia.

**LIA HIGGINS**

Willow & the girls are heading to the cinema by the looks of it. I told Willow I'll collect them afterwards. Will I pick Alex up too?

Jen slid the phone onto the table and went upstairs. She knocked on Alex's door, but she didn't let herself in this time. 'Alex?'

'What?'

She opened the door. 'What's wrong?'

'I told you, nothing is wrong.' She tutted then and swung her legs off the bed. 'I wouldn't have bothered with the cornflakes if I knew they'd come with an interrogation.' She shoved the bowl onto her bedside locker.

Jen didn't respond to the strop. 'The girls are going to the cinema,' she said softly. 'Why aren't you going with them?'

'And if the girls jumped off a cliff, would you want me to jump after them?'

'Okay, that's enough, Alex. You can be in a mood all you want, but don't speak to me like that, do you hear me?' The words came out sharper than Jen intended, her own frustrations boiling over. For God's sake, the girl had zero responsibilities, nothing to actually worry about, nothing to... Jen's stomach twisted with guilt. How could she think that about her own child? Something was clearly wrong, and here she was, dismissing it like every other parent she'd sworn she'd never be.

'Well, just leave me alone and I won't bother you at all, will I?'

Jen bit her tongue before a sharp retort came. She forced

herself to step out of the room and pull the door closed, then she went back downstairs. She needed to give them both some space to calm down. She picked up her phone and opened Lia's annoyingly perky WhatsApp.

JEN BLAKE

Still not feeling great but raging to miss it! I hope the girls have a great night.

She inserted a smiley face in direct contrast to her own scowling one. Then she returned her phone face down to the kitchen table.

# ELEVEN

## LIA

'Why isn't Alex going to the cinema with you and the girls?' Lia stood in Willow's bedroom door, watching her daughter drag a mascara wand through her lashes for the third time. The vanity mirror cast a harsh glow across Willow's face as she leaned in close, inspecting her work with practiced precision. A faint cloud of hairspray still hung in the air from her earlier efforts, and discarded outfit options lay crumpled on her bed.

'I can only assume it's because she doesn't want to.'

'Why not?'

Willow shrugged and went about examining her choices of lip gloss. Willow had gotten the best of both gene pools. She was long and lean like Lia, with the same naturally blonde hair. But she had Jay's olive skin and piercing eyes. She didn't need the amount of product that she'd recently started using on herself. She already stood out in every crowd. But Lia was seeing the changes in her since she started hanging out with Darina Hayes. Up until then, she only paid this much attention to her appearance when it was about getting under her father's skin. Now it had become routine. Her day started two hours before school did, because her hair, skin and uniform all needed to be groomed to perfection before she considered leaving the house. But the smile that used to melt Lia's heart seemed to have vanished overnight and that's what saddened her the most. Everything she did was for the good of her children. To give them security. A happy life. But seeing her daughter become more insecure and more miserable by the day made her want to cry out, what's it all for?

'Why don't you leave the girl alone?' Jay's voice came from behind her, causing Lia's stomach to tighten on instinct. Willow's lip gloss wand paused momentarily, but she didn't look away from her mirror.

'I'm only asking...'

'Willow is clever enough to know which friends are good for her and which ones are deadweight. Aren't you, sweetheart?' he said, smiling at Willow, but his voice had an edge and Lia watched as he silently critiqued her outfit. Ridiculously expensive sports leggings and a cropped top, which, crucially, covered her midriff. He nodded in approval and walked away towards the stairs. He didn't know about the bra top she was probably wearing underneath. *That* would her real outfit. Lia knew because it was how Darina, Lucy and all the other girl's their age dressed. And because she did Willow's laundry. She also saw her old self in her daughter – the defiant streak to do whatever the hell she liked, to spite him.

'So, your best friend since you were five has become a deadweight, has she?' Lia asked quietly, when Jay was gone.

Willow huffed sarcastically. 'It's just the cinema, Mum. If she doesn't want to come, then I can't very well force her, can I?'

'Did you ask her?'

She threw the gloss back in her make-up bag. 'What is it with you and *Alex, Alex, Alex*?! It's like you love her more than me sometimes.'

Lia rolled her eyes. 'Don't be ridiculous, Willow. I just hope you're not allowing these new friends to dictate who you—'

'Nope. That's your thing, Mum, not mine.'

'Excuse me?'

Willow laughed meanly and it hit Lia in the gut. 'Come on, Mum. I love you, but *you're* the one who lets people tell you what to do. Not me.'

Willow walked past Lia and down the stairs. She paused on the last step and turned. She walked more slowly back up again. 'Look, I'm not freezing Alex out if that's what you're thinking. It's *her*. She's acting weird lately and it's getting a bit annoying.'

'Weird, how?' Lia's stomach tightened again.

Willow shook her head. 'She just has no interest in anything anymore. Like, if Darina or Lucy are talking, she'll roll her eyes right in front of them. Or if we say we want to do something' – she held her arms out wide – 'like, go to the cinema, it's like she's too good for us or whatever. Like we're not cool enough for Alex Blake.'

'That doesn't sound like Alex. Maybe she's just insecure about Darina and Lucy, love. They're not the most...'

'Don't you start, Mum. I get enough of that from Alex, too. She thinks everyone's out to get her all of a sudden, when really, *she's* the one being odd.'

'I just don't think it's the right time to push Alex away, love.' She lowered her voice gently, not wanting Jay to hear her. He couldn't find out about Simon and Alex.

'I'm not pushing Alex anywhere! But we're not five years old anymore, Mum. I'm allowed to have more friends than just the ones I grew up with.'

Willow was right, of course. But she couldn't help but feel like they needed to keep an eye on Alex. Now more than ever.

'Take Simon with you,' Lia said, more as an afterthought, as she turned to go back upstairs.

'Ugh.' Willow groaned dramatically and lowered her voice again. She was clever enough not to let her father hear everything she had to say. 'When does he stop being my responsibility?'

'He's your twin brother,' Lia hissed.

'That doesn't make me his keeper. He freaks Darina out! She's not Alex. She's not willing to put up with a tagalong in order to be my friend.'

Lia could feel her voice becoming breathless as anxiety gripped her. 'What does that tell you?' she asked eventually.

'That you need to take him off my hands. I can't fucking breathe with him.' She walked back down the stairs and left without giving Lia any more time to come up with a response.

Lia stood on the landing, looking through all the open doors to the perfect rooms in their perfect house. Willow's with her designer clothes and high-end cosmetics neatly arranged everywhere. Lia and Jay's room, with its enormous bed and a ridiculous number of decorative pillows, and Simon's room. All she saw when she looked into Simon's room was Alex Blake's tear-streaked face. And the look on Simon's face when he realised he'd been caught. That moment between taking what he wanted from the girl beneath him, as his father had done the first time he'd had sex with Lia, and the shocked innocence that he presented to her. His mother. She blinked slowly and turned towards the stairs.

'It's coq au vin tonight, right? Did you get the Chianti?'

'Hmm?'

Jay looked at her as she walked into the kitchen, his face completely blank. Lia pulled herself back into the moment.

'I'm sorry, love. What?'

'Graham and Maeve.'

*Oh fuck.* Graham Dunleavy, senior partner at the solicitor's firm where Jay worked and major financial backer of his political campaign. She'd completely forgotten that he and his obnoxious wife, Maeve, were coming for dinner.

'Did you forget?' His face was still impassive, but Lia could see the torrent rising behind his eyes.

'No, I...' She rubbed her forehead. 'There's been a lot going on with the...'

Jay stepped closer. 'You *know* how important this dinner is, right?' He tapped the side of Lia's head roughly. 'Can your little brain comprehend the weight behind Graham Dunleavy? His support will drive me into office and all I'm asking from you, is to present a few pieces of fucking chicken on a plate.' He brought his hands down by his side and lowered his voice with them. 'You have one job in this family. One. And a blind monkey could do it, Lia. They'll be here at eight and everything about this night had better reflect the family that we are.'

Lia nodded, not daring to speak. Her hands gripped the countertop behind her. When Jay got like this, things would go one way or the other. More often than not, the other.

'And wear something nice.' He was about to leave, when he turned and looked her up and down. 'If anything still fits.'

Lia exhaled when the front door closed behind him. She smoothed down her top, letting the palms of her hands linger around her stomach. It was flat and hard and yet he somehow saw the two pounds she'd gained over the past few weeks. She glanced through to the sitting room window and saw him standing near his car, a friendly smile on his face, as he waved at the neighbour three doors over, who was also getting into her car. They were passing banter back and forth when she pulled her eyes away and looked at the clock. She had four hours. Despite her mounting dread about the night ahead, she took her phone from her bag and scrolled until she found Alex Blake.

LIA HIGGINS

Hey! I hear you're not feeling great. Come over if you're free. I think I know what's going on.

She inserted a winky face emoji and a heart. Two blue ticks told her that Alex was online, and that she'd seen her message. But a few seconds later, she went offline.

'Shit.'

## TWELVE

### LIA

'Eh, hi.' Alex looked uncertainly at the strangers milling around Lia's kitchen. Muriel, her cleaner who normally came on Friday, but was happy to return today for a price. She worked diligently around an off-duty maître d' from La Provence – Jay's favourite restaurant. Muriel was erasing all traces of the fact that a family of four lived in their house, while Gregory, the maître d', was creating a fine dining atmosphere in their own dining room. The perfect coq au vin would arrive just ahead of their guests. And ahead of Jay with a bit of luck.

'Oh, don't mind them.' Lia rolled her eyes and waved away the silliness of it all. She was relieved that Alex had decided to come over and was suddenly sorry to have an audience. 'Come. Let's have coffee in the garden.'

'I don't really drink coffee,' Alex replied uncertainly.

'Well, maybe it's time you start.' Lia smiled. She set the machine going and poured two cups, making Alex's a foamy latte. She handed her a tall cup and led her outside to the garden, away from the staff. Lia let out a long sigh as they sat down on the rattan couch with the late September sun on their faces. There was so much that she needed to explain to Alex, but she had no idea where to start. Or how to phrase it all in a way that she'd understand. Jay was still oblivious to Simon's behaviour, and she wasn't sure how long she could keep it that way. Or how he'd react. He'd blame her for sure. The children were *her* job after all. The job a blind monkey could do apparently.

'Are you okay, Lia?' Alex craned her neck to look at Lia, who smiled in return.

She reached out and squeezed Alex's knee. Then she shook her head. 'Do you ever feel like everyone just... expects too much from you?'

Alex raised her eyebrows in surprise.

Lia laughed quietly. 'I'm sorry, love. I'm grand. Besides, aren't *I* supposed to be the one cheering *you* up?'

'That's okay,' Alex replied, her voice soft and full of concern. She turned to face Lia.

Lia looked at her with a soft smile on her face. 'Let me tell you something, Alex. That feeling you have right now – that everything is impossible. It's true. Everything is. But only for women.' Lia gestured between the two of them. 'We're expected to be perfect in every way. But not *too* perfect. Good-looking. But not *too* good-looking. Thin. But not *too* thin. Clever, but not *too* clever. We're expected to meet everyone else's expectations of us, aren't we?'

Alex inhaled deeply and blew out with a slow nod.

'It's bloody hard.'

'But not for you. You, like, always have your shit together.' Alex glanced at her then. 'Sorry for the language.'

Lia laughed. 'What does that even mean?'

'My mum would *never* sit in the garden, drinking coffee with me and talking to me like this. She still treats me like I'm five years old.'

Lia reached out and gently lifted the girl's chin to look at her. 'Alex, you have a fantastic mother. She doesn't sit in the garden like this, because she doesn't have the time. I consider myself very lucky that we don't have the kind of financial pressure that a lot of families feel, so please don't think less of your mum for working her backside off. She does that for you.'

Alex nodded slowly and took a sip of her coffee. Lia could tell by her face that she liked it.

'I know your mum and I aren't as close as we once were, but I still consider her to be my friend. So, let me be here for you when she can't, okay? And, Alex?'

Alex looked at her nervously over the rim of her coffee mug and then cast her eyes to the ground.

'Anything you say to me, stays with me. So... what's going on up here?' She gently tapped her temple.

Alex half smiled but there was no joy in it. 'Just like you said. That it's all impossible.' Her voice was no more than a mumble.

Lia sighed. 'Is this about Willow and those new girls?'

Alex shrugged. 'It's not just them.'

Lia nodded, but this worried her. 'Love, your circle of friends will grow and change throughout your life. But by the time you're my age, that circle will have narrowed back down again. And those left behind will be your true friends.' In Lia's case, that circle had shrivelled away to nothing. She had no friends, true or otherwise. Jay saw to that, but she continued to issue consolations on the matter.

Alex was nodding and staring absentmindedly into her coffee.

'Or are you still thinking about what happened here, with Simon?'

Her head shot up and she shook it adamantly.

'Are you sure? Because, love, you don't have to put on a brave face for me. Honestly, I'm so mad at him I could...' She shook her head angrily. 'I could bloody well throttle him.'

Alex's eyes welled up and she nodded unconvincingly. 'So am I.'

'And so you should be,' Lia assured her. 'Because that's the other thing about being a woman, Alex.' She lowered her voice now. 'Men will think they have certain rights to you.' She leaned in closer. 'And you can allow yourself to become a victim of that by letting them take over your thoughts and your happiness. Or you can show them that you're stronger than them. That they can't break you down or make you doubt yourself.'

Lia could have laughed at her own hypocrisy. She'd become such an expert at talking shite, but really, she wanted to cry. Movement in her peripheral vision made her glance towards the house. She thought she saw someone at the upstairs window, but there was no one there. Muriel was moving around in the kitchen, just inside the patio door, which was probably what drew her attention. Lia felt sweat pooling at the back of her neck. What if Alex told someone about Simon? She couldn't let that happen. But really, what could she do to stop her?


It was after midnight when Graham and Maeve left, and as expected, it was a torturous evening of business talk and politics. The men became louder and more self-righteous as the Chianti flowed, while Lia plastered on her practiced smile and counted the minutes until she could escape. From Maeve's vacant stare and tight grip on her wine glass, she wasn't enjoying herself either.

'That went well.' She smiled at Jay, as they stood, arms around each other, at the front door, waving their guests off in a taxi.

'The food was very nice,' he replied into her hair, as he kissed the top of her head.

'Thank you, I'm glad.'

Once they'd gone and the front door was closed, Lia returned to the dining room to start cleaning up.

'Why are you saying thank you? It's not like you cooked any of it.'

Lia froze momentarily as dread began to swirl in her stomach along with the red wine she'd been knocking back to get through the evening. She suddenly felt light-headed but tried to keep her voice light. 'True... by the time you reminded me, it was...'

'You don't think Graham and Maeve are frequent visitors to La Provence?' he said, in a low, menacing tone. 'You made us look like we couldn't be fucking arsed.'

'No, Jay, I...'

'Give me your purse.' He held his hand out.

'Jay...'

He grabbed her by the arm and shoved her towards the kitchen, where her handbag hung on the back of a chair. Simon was standing in there, eating a bowl of cereal. The kids spent the night in their rooms, while their parents entertained. That's how it always was. But now Simon stood watching her with a bowl in his hand and what looked, in the dim light, like a small smile. The only trace of emotion on his face. She lowered her eyes as shame crawled through her and with trembling hands she picked up her bag. She returned to the dining room and handed it to Jay, who tipped the contents out all over the table.

While he rummaged through everything, Lia's mind was on the next few days. Her period was due, and she'd let herself run completely out of sanitary products. Perhaps she could borrow some from Willow, assuming... Jay picked up a half-eaten packet of mints. He waved them accusingly in her face and then threw them towards the kitchen, where they skipped across the floor. Then he picked up her purse and removed all of her bank cards. He threw the purse, still open and empty, back on the table. 'Phone.' He held his hand out again.

Panic gripped her when she couldn't immediately remember where she'd left it. Her eyes flitted around the room until she saw it, resting on the arm of the chair. She quickly retrieved it and handed it to him.

He opened it easily. Of course he did – Jay had everyone's password. Lia's stomach clenched as she watched him delete her Google Pay app, that small act of control he loved so much. How many times had he done this now? Again, she thought of her need for sanitary products, which she would not ask him for, and her cheeks burned with the familiar shame of being treated like a child.

'If you need to buy groceries, you do it online. Place everything in the basket and then you *ask me* to pay for it. *If* I'm happy with your purchase, then I'll do exactly that when I have time.' He threw the phone at the couch and went upstairs.

Lia's hands trembled as she swept the scattered contents of her handbag back in, her throat tight with unshed tears. The wine glasses and coffee cups clinked too loudly as she gathered them, desperate to busy herself with anything but her thoughts.

'It's okay, love,' she managed, forcing a smile she didn't feel for Simon. He stood in the kitchen, methodically chewing, those cold eyes taking in every detail of her humiliation.

'Did you have a nice chat with Alex today?' he asked quietly.

Lia couldn't respond, but his words added an icy chill to the angst she was feeling. She lifted her eyes to look at him. 'What?'

'Does Dad know how chummy you two have become?'

Lia just stared at him. Her stomach, already a ball of tension, tightened even more.

He left the dirty bowl on the counter and cocked his head to one side before fixing her with a smile that didn't reach his eyes. Then he left the kitchen.

# THIRTEEN
## ALEX

The halls of St Brendan's were busy and noisy as always. It was ten minutes before the first class of the morning and the day stretched out intolerably long before Alex. She walked in with her head down and a beanie hat covering the fact that she'd shaved all her hair off the night before. She'd given up on the ridiculous hair straighteners and all the other crap she'd been attempting in an effort to keep up with Willow's new friends. Willow knew the real Alex just as well as Alex knew the real Willow. Every inch of her was beautiful, from her smile, to the dimple that appeared in her left cheek when she chewed. But as much as Alex needed to stop thinking of her like that, she found herself struggling to think at all, or even to *breathe* properly whenever she was near. It was torture and it had to end. Hence, the shaving of the head. She was done being Alex Blake, the quiet lovesick idiot that people like Simon Higgins and Darina Hayes thought nothing of. She reached up and pulled off the hat, still moving forward through the wide corridor. She ignored a sharp intake of breath and a snigger that came from somewhere nearby. They wouldn't bother her. She wasn't *that* Alex Blake anymore. She was Alex fucking Blake now and anyone who didn't like it, could go fuck themselves.

Alex felt Simon's eyes on her before she looked up and saw him. He was standing close to, but not quite with, a group of boys who were loudly taking the piss out of each other near the bank of lockers. He looked shocked at first, but then he grinned broadly. Normally, she would have at least made herself smile at him, or wave, or something. But now everything about him made her feel sick. For the past fifteen years, the three of them had walked to school together. Now she walked alone because Willow wasn't ready on time. She was too busy perfecting her already perfect hair. And Alex had been avoiding Simon as much as she possibly could. A small part of her still wondered if she was overreacting. It was Simon after all, and Lia was probably right. He just liked her and didn't know how to show it. She, of all people, knew how that felt. He'd always been so awkward. But twice now he'd been forceful with her, first accusing her of leading him on when he followed her to the gym, and then that thing in his room, the memory of which was invading her sleep now. So while she didn't have to spend time with him for Willow's sake, she was choosing not to. Plus, Simon would be repulsed by a bald girl. She knew him well enough to know that.

Even now he looked so out of place. He never really gelled with other boys, but the way he was hovering around that group made him look desperate to change that. *Actually* desperate. If Willow were here, she'd be mortified by him. And perhaps by her now, too. But she wasn't here, and Alex wondered how long it would take those boys to smell the desperation on him. Then, like sharks getting the scent of blood, they'd tear him apart and Willow would get the blame at home.

But Alex ignored her natural instinct to protect Willow, and she carried on. When she glanced back, Simon was staring at her as she walked towards her own locker further along the hall.

His face was kind of blank, the way it went sometimes. She turned and walked a little faster now. Every time she closed her eyes, she felt the weight of him pressing her down onto his bed. She felt his hands, groping her body and she smelled the cheese and onion crisps on his breath. *Was* she overreacting? Or had he told everyone how gross her body felt or how small her breasts were? How the flab on her stomach squished in the palm of his hand? Alex felt her face burning up and her newfound confidence slipping. She didn't need anything from her locker, but she opened it anyway and used the door to shield herself from everyone. It was better than facing the hordes of boisterous people all around her, who seemed to fit so naturally into their surroundings. Unlike her. Not now that she was pretty much alone. And bald.

When she glanced back again, she saw that Simon had inserted himself into the group of boys. They were all nudging each other and looking at her, while Simon spoke animatedly. She slammed her locker door shut and hurried off with her head down and her face on fire but not before she caught a glimpse of Simon cupping imaginary breasts. His new friends, who would have had nothing to do with him an hour ago, couldn't get enough of him now.

The end of the school day couldn't come soon enough for Alex but with it, came the end of her life as she knew it. She wouldn't have taken much notice of the small crowd that had gathered in the hall, if it weren't for Willow. Alex had finished her day with woodwork, while Willow was coming towards her locker from the biology lab, in the opposite direction. She was walking with Darina Hayes and both of them had been smiling about something, until they got a little closer to the group. Then a sudden look of horror came over Willow's face, and after a brief moment where she seemed to be glued to the spot, she ran towards the crowd. Darina hung back, but she was very clearly entertained by whatever she saw.

Alex frowned and brought her hand self-consciously to her head, her heart starting to pound as she moved toward the exit. What was everyone looking at? Willow's voice cut through the whispers – 'Take it down!' – high and desperate in a way Alex had never heard before. Then she saw where everyone was looking. Her locker. Oh God, her locker. When Willow's eyes met hers, they were filled with tears, and Alex's whole body went cold. The tiny hairs on her arms stood up and her stomach plummeted as if she'd missed a step in the dark. Whatever was up there, whatever had made Willow look at her like that – this was going to be bad. Really, really bad.

'There she is.' Someone sniggered and everyone turned to look in Alex's direction. The group parted, as more and more curious students arrived. But all eyes were on Alex.

'Al, I...' Willow mouthed, slowly shaking her head. Her eyes were filled with tears as they flitted from her shaven head to her face.

Alex's locker, along with the ones on either side of it, were completely covered with a montage of sorts. A blown-up image of a naked, heavily overweight woman, cupping her breasts in her hands. But she didn't have a head. At least, not one of her own. A photo of Alex, her face flushed red and sweating with her mouth open, had also been blown up and roughly attached to the body. That photo in its original form, had been taken when Alex scored the winning basket in the school's cup final the year before. She looked grotesque. But to make the whole thing even more horrifying, the red, sweaty, fat, naked Alex had a string of pink love hearts floating away from her, towards an equally magnified, but stunningly beautiful image of Willow. A text bubble was drawn beside Alex's head and in it was written, *PLEEEEEASE DO ME, WILLOW. PLEEEEEEASE!!!*

The words burned into Alex's brain as her insides turned to

ice. Her heartbeat exploded in her ears, drowning everything else into a distant roar. The hallway tilted and spun, faces blurring into a wall of pointing fingers and cruel laughter. Someone was making a sound like a wounded animal – was that coming from her? A teacher's voice cracked through the fog, but Alex could barely hear it over the rushing in her head. Everyone scattered except Willow, whose stricken face reflected back all the horror and shame coursing through Alex's body. *Move. Please move*, she begged her legs, but they'd turned to concrete, her knees threatening to buckle. When she finally forced them forward, they betrayed her – wobbling, knocking together, each step a fresh humiliation. Her ankles rolled inward like they couldn't bear her weight anymore. She stumbled toward the exit, her body as broken as the rest of her, every eye burning into her back as she fled.

'Alex!' Mr Henderson, the principal, called after her, but she kept going.

As she hurried down the steps outside, Simon appeared in front of her, faux concern etched across his face. He'd been hiding from Mr Henderson behind a low wall. 'Hey, you okay?' Alex flinched at the sight of him and staggered past, her head thumping and her body trembling. *I'm going to be sick.*

# FOURTEEN

## JEN

Jen had been standing on her front doorstep for the past five minutes watching out for Alex. It was after six. She should have been home from school hours ago. But Jen had only just gotten in herself, and Dale was still at work. She saw Simon approaching the Higginses' home and waved him over.

'Hey, Mrs Blake.'

'Any idea where the girls are?' She half smiled, keeping her tone light. A hint of worry had started to niggle in her gut, but it hadn't gone full-blown yet. It wasn't that late after all, and she didn't want to come across as hysterical.

'I think Willow should be at home.' He nodded in the direction of their house. 'Or at least, that's where she told me she was going.'

'Oh.' Jen pulled her shoulder away from the door frame. 'And have you seen Alex?'

Simon shook his head.

By now, Jen could easily tell when Alex or Willow were hiding something. But for as long as she'd known those kids, she could never get a read on Simon. Not even when they were younger. He could be totally expressionless sometimes. 'Is everything okay with you guys?' she asked, her smile melting away.

Simon shrugged, his eyes still hidden behind his curls.

'What is it, Simon?' she probed.

'Erm, well...' He stepped a little closer. 'It's just... is everything okay with Alex, Mrs Blake?'

This caught Jen off guard. *She* was the one hoping to get that information from *him*. 'What do you mean?' The knot of worry in her stomach began to grow.

'It's just that... well, she's been acting a bit strange lately.'

'I know,' Jen replied, instinctively biting her thumbnail, an anxious habit she'd not been able to break. 'She hasn't been herself. Is there something going on at school?'

Simon made a face and shook his head. 'No more than usual. But she's been... look, never mind. It's nothing.'

Jen reached out and caught him by the arm before he could leave. 'Tell me, Simon. Please.'

She knew she was probably freaking him out, but she needed to know what was going on.

'She's been picking arguments with everyone for no reason,' he said quietly, like he was sharing state secrets. 'And she... I don't know...' He ran his hand through his hair, finally pushing it back off his face. 'She's been acting a little bit paranoid or something.'

'Paranoid? About what?'

He shrugged. 'It's like she thinks everyone is out to get her. Ever since Willow started hanging out with those dickheads... sorry.'

Jen's brow furrowed and she nodded. 'So, she and Willow...?'

'Willow will always do her own thing. She loves Alex, but... she also loves being popular.'

Jen's heart hurt for her daughter suddenly. Was Alex losing her best friend?

'She's kind of stopped talking to me, too.'

Jen nodded absentmindedly. That made more sense. If Willow wasn't Alex's friend anymore, then Alex had no reason to spend time with Simon.

Simon shrugged, a look of self-pity on his face. 'I guess my sister was her best friend. I always thought I was, too, but I guess I was more of a hanger-on than I thought.'

She probably should have consoled him in some way about being a hanger-on. Maybe even pretended that he was wrong. But instead, she asked, 'Have you tried talking to her about it?'

'I tried.' He turned to walk away. 'Alex doesn't seem to like any of us anymore. Anyway, bye, Mrs Blake.'

Jen's arms fell loose by her sides, as she watched him walk away. Before he was halfway across the green, Lia came to the door. She was illuminated by the hall light behind her and even now, at the end of the day, she looked stunning. Jen wrapped her ancient cardigan around herself self-consciously, waved and shut the door.

She tried Alex's phone five more times. It was ringing, but she wasn't answering. As she finished leaving another voice message for her, each one sounding slightly angrier than the last, Dale arrived home.

'Alex hasn't come home yet,' she said, before he'd even closed the front door. She could hear the frantic breathless tone in her own voice as she paced the hallway, her eyes refusing to land on the photograph of Alex on her first day of school with a beaming smile and pigtails, which hung on the wall.

Dale looked at his watch. 'Quarter to seven.'

'I know what time it is, Dale. She should have been home hours ago.'

Dale dropped his bag in the hall and took off his coat. 'She's probably over at the Higginses'.'

'She's not. Simon said that Willow was at home, but he hasn't seen Alex since school. He said she's been acting weird.'

Jen saw the flicker of worry in Dale's eyes before he responded, 'Well, *that's* a case of the pot calling the kettle black, if ever I heard one. What kind of a young fella spends all his time with his sister and her friends? *He's* fucking weird, not Alex. Anyway, she's probably on the court, shooting some hoops.'

'That closes at six.'

'What time did you get home?'

'I was home before six.'

'So, for all you know, she came home, made *herself* something to eat and went back out again. But you weren't here so she couldn't tell you.'

He walked past her into the kitchen where he stood looking around, as if wondering where his dinner might be hiding.

'Do you even care?'

'She's a teenager, Jen...'

She squeezed her eyes shut. 'Say that one more time, Dale. She's fifteen years old. She's a fucking child. She's *our* child and it's getting dark outside. She should be home.'

'Call her.'

Jen waved her phone at him and raised her eyebrows.

'Check her location.'

Jen frowned and looked at her phone. 'What? How do I do that?'

Dale shrugged. 'I think on their Snapchat or something like that.'

Alex had only been given a phone when she started at St Brendan's, for this exact reason. As far as Jen knew she wasn't overly active on social media. In fact, she often complained about how much time Willow spent on there. She closed her eyes again and squeezed the bridge of her nose. Was she really stupid enough to believe that she didn't spend time there?

'Will you check it, please?' She held the phone towards him.

'Me?' Dale asked, rooting in the fridge for something edible and making a right show of it. 'What do I know about Snapchat and all that?' He shut the fridge door. 'I thought all the mothers were on top of this kind of thing, Jen? It's probably not rocket science, like.'

Jen brought the phone to her ear again and walked out of the room.

'Jen?' Lia sounded surprised to be hearing from her. And so she should.

'Hey, Lia. Is Alex there?'

'Um, no. She isn't. Has she not come home yet?'

Jen rolled her eyes thinking, *I wouldn't be bloody ringing you if she had.*

'Sorry. You wouldn't be calling me if she had. Hang on. Let me check with my two. I'll call you back in a few minutes.'

'Okay, and um, Lia?' Jen lowered her head, feeling more stupid than ever. 'Do you know if Alex is on Snapchat? Or one of those platforms that have location tracking?'

There was silence for a second and Jen thought she might choke on her pride.

'I think she might be, yes,' Lia answered finally. 'Willow is and so is Simon. I have their passwords, and I've told them they get to keep their phones only as long as their location stays on. And of course, I get to look through their content any time I like. Obviously.'

Tears welled in Jen's eyes. When had she become so stupid?

'So, if you just go into Alex's phone,' Lia explained gently, 'there should be a family link for parents app.'

'I don't have her phone.' The words barely came out and Jen never felt like more of a failure. The fact that Lia Higgins was there to witness it was unbearable.

'Okay... Look, I'm sure there's no need to worry. I mean, she probably just...'

Jen lowered the phone to her chest and squeezed her eyes shut. Then brought it back to her ear.

'Can you please ask Willow if she knows where Alex is?' She tried to keep her fear and embarrassment out of her voice.

'Of course. Of course I will. I'll...'

Jen hung up, unable to endure anymore. She glanced again at the smiling junior infant on the wall. 'Where are you, Alex?' she muttered, as a single tear rolled down her cheek.

# FIFTEEN

## LIA

'Willow?' Lia called.

'Yeah?' came the reply from upstairs.

Lia went up to her, rather than calling her down. Jay was away on business and wasn't due home until later that evening, so she wasn't worried about him coming in and hearing their conversation. But Willow was in a mood lately, too, and she didn't want to start this conversation off on an argument. 'Hey.' She popped her head around Willow's door.

'Hey.' She was sitting at her desk doing her homework. That was one good thing instilled in them by their father. Homework being completed before dinner was non-negotiable. It was habit now, even if Jay wasn't here to see to it.

Lia went into her room and sat on Willow's bed. Then, keeping her tone as light as she could she said, 'I need to ask you something, love.' She gave Willow a few seconds to turn around, but she didn't. Lia counted to ten in her head. *Keep calm. Don't lose it.* 'Is everything alright at school?'

'Yeah, why?'

'Alex hasn't come home yet, and her mum is a bit worried about her. Do you know where she might be?'

'She shaved all her fucking hair off.' Willow looked over her shoulder, sounding more angry than surprised by her friend's actions. Like Alex's choice of hairstyle somehow reflected poorly on her.

'She wh... Why would she do that?'

'Why are you asking me?' Her voice rose with a hint of hysteria.

'What's going on? Have you two had some kind of falling out?' Lia could feel her own dread rising. Was Alex breaking down? Giving a cry for help that would eventually bring do-gooders flocking to their door?

Willow threw her pencil at her desk and swivelled her chair finally, to face Jen. 'No! But she *hates* Darina and Lucy and she's being a right bitch about it. It's like she doesn't want me to have any other friends or something. Christ, when did everyone become *my* responsibility?! First Simon and now Alex! Why can't everyone just leave me alone?' she all but screeched.

Lia nodded, forcing herself to be calm. Getting angry would get her nowhere with Willow. The girl craved attention and a softly, softly approach worked best. Lia needed to make this all about Willow if she were going to get anywhere. 'Pretty much the same thing happened with me and her mum, you know. Except it was your dad that Jen didn't like. Or rather, they didn't like each other. She asked me one day to choose. Her, or your father.'

'And what did you do?'

Lia forced a smile. 'What do you think? I chose your dad.'

Willow frowned, but she readjusted her expression almost immediately. 'Yeah, well, that's not all.'

'Oh?' Lia's stomach tightened. Had Alex told Willow about Simon? Who else had she told?

'Yeah... I think she likes me.' Her cheeks flushed red, and she began fidgeting with the hem of her T-shirt.

'Oh? Has she told you that?'

'Did you know?' The question was accusatory.

Lia shrugged, not wanting to let on that Alex had confided in her, rather than in Willow.

'She told Simon.'

Lia frowned. 'So, Simon told you that Alex has a crush on you?'

'Simon's told the whole school!'

Lia brought her hands to her temples and squeezed her eyes shut. 'So the whole school knows that Alex has a crush on you, before she's even had a chance to come out on her own terms?'

Willow nodded. She looked like she might cry. What the hell was Simon trying to do?

'Are they giving her a hard time about it?'

'*Her?*' Willow jumped up from her chair, incredulous all of a sudden. 'What about me, Mum?'

Lia frowned again. 'What about you, Willow? How many boys fancy you at this moment in time?'

'I don't know,' she spat. 'A few.' She started pacing. Then, not knowing what else to do, she started tidying her vanity table.

'And are you worried what people might think about that? About boys having a crush on you?'

'No, but...' She swept up her make-up brushes and threw them at the bed in frustration. Two landed in Lia's lap, but she ignored them.

'Exactly. What's one more admirer? But Alex isn't quite comfortable in her own skin yet, is she? Put yourself in her shoes for a minute.'

'I know, alright!' Willow shouted. 'I don't care who fancies me. But how am I supposed to know if she's being my friend because she wants to be my friend? Or if she's only my friend because she thinks that maybe something will happen some day?'

Lia mentally rolled her eyes. 'She knows you're not gay, doesn't she?'

'Yeah, but...'

Lia held her hand up. 'Look, I'm not going to tell you who to be friends with and who not to. That's up to you. I just don't want to give Alex Blake any reason to turn her parents any further against our family, okay?'

'If Dad is the reason why Jen turned against you, then shouldn't you be having this conversation with him?' She smiled then, knowing full well that Lia could never initiate such a conversation with Jay. Willow seemed desperate to reclaim some control, the feeling of having the upper hand, and Lia couldn't blame her for that.

'You don't...'

'What did he do, anyway?' she asked, turning her back and rummaging through her make-up again. 'Aside from what he always does.' She turned again, looking like she suddenly had it all figured out. She was so bloody naive. 'That's it, isn't it? He tried to treat Jen Blake the same way he treats you, and you took his side over hers. That's why she hates you, isn't it?'

Lia breathed deeply, pushing down the memory of Jen confronting Lia's rapist. The way she'd sought him out so fearlessly the morning after it happened, when she noticed the bruising on Lia's thighs while they changed for training. She remembered how fiercely she'd thumped him and threatened what would happen when they reported him. Lia could still feel Jen's fist punching into *her* chest instead of Jay's, when she threw herself in front of him. And the look on Jen's face when Lia called her a jealous little liar, despite the blood that still trickled out of her. Confusion at first, then shock. Eventually her disgust was all that was left, and Lia did her best to forget it. She fought the urge to scream at Willow. To tell her how little she actually knew and how much Lia had protected her from over the years. Instead, she got to her feet and forced an authority that she did not feel she had into her voice. 'If you hear from Alex, you're to tell me. And if your new friends decide to make her a target, then you're to nip it in the bud, you hear me? You don't have to be friends with her, but I didn't raise my kids to be bullies either. Plus, your father will not be happy with any negative attention on us right now. This is a very important time in his career.'

Willow just looked at her, those piercing blue eyes so like Jay's, and Lia saw what she'd become reflected in them – a woman who preached against bullies while cowering before one in her own home. Her daughter returned to her desk without another word, dismissing her. The familiar shame crept up Lia's throat as she turned to leave. The worst part wasn't that Willow pitied her – it was that she deserved every ounce of that pity.

# SIXTEEN

## LIA

When she returned to the kitchen, Simon was there. He sat on a high stool with his legs crossed and his hands joined together on his knee.

'So, my sister wants to be rid of me,' he said, not sounding too bothered. But Lia knew that he was.

'Of course she doesn't. She's just upset about Alex.'

'What about Alex?'

'They've had a bit of a falling out, that's all. Normal teenage stuff.' She tried to sound like that's all it was. 'I'm sure it'll all blow over soon.'

Simon chuckled. 'Is that what she told you?'

She turned to look at him but hated what she saw. That tilt to his head, like he was studying her.

'So she didn't tell you about the circus at school today?' He laughed.

'What?' Her voice filled with dread as her throat tightened.

'I'll let Willow fill you in. But it was hilarious. Genius, even.'

'What did you do, Simon?' She spoke quietly, sure that he *did* do something.

He stood up, bringing his hand to his chest, feigning innocence. Why was he doing this? Why didn't he care what she thought anymore? Easy, she realised. Because he knew that she would protect him. Like she protected his father – at all costs.

'Shouldn't you be at hot yoga, or wherever it is that you pretend to go?'

Her skin prickled. 'Excuse me?'

'It's okay. I know you lie to him all the time. It's what you do, isn't it? Women.'

'Simon... where are you getting this from?' Tears filled her eyes. This was not her awkward little boy. 'I never lie to your father.'

He nodded, knowingly. 'I suppose time just got away from you then. I mean, it started ten minutes ago, didn't it?' He smiled again. 'Don't worry, I won't say anything. And he can't watch you all the time, right?'

Lia inhaled sharply as she searched his face for any trace of the stoic little boy, who was always old for his age. But all she saw was his father. 'Do you know where Alex is, Simon?'

He frowned. 'Why would I?'

'Did you do something?'

'You mean aside from letting others know what a teasing little bitch she is?'

A strangled sound escaped her lips, and she brought her hands to her face. She turned away from him, no longer able to control her emotions. There were too many. 'You stupid boy, Simon,' she hissed, her fear growing with every passing second. 'What were you thinking?'

'What was *I* thinking?' The pitch of his voice never changed but his bemused smile had disappeared. 'I was thinking about all the times she laughed at my jokes, touched my arm, talked to me about all her bullshit and then turned on me the second I responded. I was thinking what a teasing little whore she is. They all are...'

'Who?' The word barely came out, her eyes wide now as she watched him. He believed every word he was saying. He believed he was right.

'Girls! Women! Why do you do it?'

There it was. The lost little boy, pleading with her to teach him. 'Simon...' She reached out and touched his arm. He just looked at her hand, then stared at her. 'What exactly did you do?'

'He put fucked-up photos of Alex *and me* all over the school.' Willow's angry voice came from the doorway and Lia turned to see her tear-streaked face. The way she looked at Simon now, it was as if she hated him. *Really* hated him. 'He destroyed my life.'

Lia's phone buzzed in her back pocket. Jay was due home at any time and she pulled out her phone, sure that it would be him. And Simon was right. She *was* supposed to be at Bikram yoga. It *was* Jay. But there was also an unread message from Alex that she'd somehow missed earlier in the evening. She opened that one first and frowned at her screen. Bile rose up her throat. *Alex.* Then she ran from the house.

# SEVENTEEN

## JEN

When Jen pulled up outside the school, a huge sense of relief washed over her when she saw that the car park was full. There was a game on in the gym. That's where Alex was. Of course she was. Jen slammed her door shut and hurried inside, taking the stairs two at a time up to the supporters' mezzanine. Her emotions alternated wildly between elation and rage. She wanted to scream at Alex, never to do this to her again. She also wanted to hug her as tightly as she ever had. But as she reached the rail and looked down, she immediately knew that this wasn't Alex's team. Of course it wasn't. Willow, the star of the team, was at home and the kids on the court looked no more than twelve years of age – first years. She pushed back and scanned the crowd, which wasn't that big. She saw vaguely familiar faces, but Alex was not among them. Fear swept back in, rendering all other emotions void. She jogged down the stairs again and into the player's locker room.

'Alex?' she called, striding through the deserted changing area and into the toilet block, pushing open the door to each empty stall. 'Where are you?' she muttered through clenched teeth as she hurried back towards the exit door.

'Alex?' she shouted when she got outside, her eyes frantically scanning the area.

'Mrs Blake?' Simon came through some parked cars towards her. 'Is everything alright?'

Jen ignored him and continued to look wildly around for her child.

Simon tilted his head and looked at her. 'You know, she's probably just upset about today. In fact, I was just speaking to Mum about it.'

Jen looked at him then, her breath halting. 'Upset? Why would she be upset? What happened?'

'You know...' Simon mimicked running a shaver over his head and made a buzzing sound. He was smiling like an idiot.

Jen frowned and shook her head. 'What?'

'It was a bit drastic, to be fair, Mrs B. She should have known she'd get grief for it. This is St Brendan's. You can't just pull a Britney Spears and expect no one to notice.'

Jen wanted to shake him, but she held back, desperate to know all that she didn't. But she couldn't keep the ire out of her voice. 'Simon, what are you talking about?'

He tilted his head again, making Jen desperately want to swing for him. He looked like he was watching a hamster in maze. 'Didn't you see it? She shaved all her hair off. She was as bald as an egg when she rocked up at school today.'

'Wh... she what?' There was a loud whooshing in Jen's ears. This was not Alex. This was a cry for help, or... something.

Simon's smile disappeared. 'What, you really didn't know?'

Jen's eyes filled with tears.

'Mrs Blake? Is everything okay?' Simon asked again. 'I mean, why would she do something like that? And she kind of, like, used it to make a statement or something. Like, she arrived first thing wearing a hat, then kind of just whipped it off in front of everyone. Like, a big reveal or something.'

Jen was finding it hard to breathe. How could this have

happened? How could Alex have gotten to the point of something so drastic without Jen knowing? 'I need to find her.'

'Isn't she in there watching the match?'

Jen shook her head again. 'Help me, Simon. Please, help me find her,' she said, desperately.

Simon reached out and touched her on the arm. He looked so much like his father in that moment. Less the weird little boy and more the man who raised him 'I'll walk back towards home and see if she's somewhere along the way. I'll check the woods, too. She might have gone there if she felt like being on her own.'

Jen nodded, again looking frantically around, not knowing where to try next. She'd already checked the woods, but Alex could still go there, if she was wandering around looking to be alone for a while. That's what Jen would do if she'd had a day like Simon described Alex's to be. 'I'll check back here.' She indicated the grassy area at the back of the gym, near the player's entrance. 'Simon, you have my number. Call me if you find her. And ring your friends. See if anyone's seen her. Please.'

'Okay.'

Simon took his phone out of his pocket and Jen watched him as he looked blankly at the screen. She remembered then that, aside from Willow, Simon probably didn't have any other friends to call. But she didn't care about that now. She needed to find her daughter.

'Alex?' she called, walking away from Simon and around the back of the building. 'Alex, it's me. Please, love – answer me if you can hear me?'

There was no response. A loud cheer rang out from inside the gym, but there was no one outside the building. As she headed back across the front of the main school building, she sat down heavily on the steps to think. To try putting herself in her daughter's shoes. But how could she? Alex was nothing like Jen. Jen would never have had the courage to shave off her hair. Not at fifteen years of age. Not at any age. As she sat there, her legs started to bounce on the balls of her feet, and she felt her ribs shaking in time with them. A loud sob broke free and she felt more helpless than she ever had. She got to her feet again, wiping her eyes. She had no idea where to go, but sitting still was torture. As she moved away from the steps, something shimmered on the ground and caught her eye. When she looked down, ice-cold fingers of dread crawled through her insides. It was a silver unicorn keyring. Jen didn't need to pick it up to know that if you turned it a certain way, it became rainbow coloured. She knew that because she'd been with Alex when she bought it at Covent Garden the year before, when she and Jen got to tag along on a trip that Dale had won on a radio station phone-in. Jen bent to pick it up.

'Dale?' She brought her phone to her ear and held it there with a shaking hand.

'Did you find her?'

Jen squeezed her eyes shut and cried, loud sobbing tears. She'd needed to hear him say, *she's home!*

'Jen?'

'She shaved off all her hair today.' Her voice was so low, she hardly heard it herself.

'What?'

'Her hair... she shaved...'

'She shaved her hair off? What? Why would she do that?' She heard him inhaling loudly and his voice rose. 'Did some fucker shave off her hair?'

The thought hadn't occurred to Jen. *Would* someone have shaved her head by way of bullying? *Did* someone do this to her. But no. Simon said she arrived at school this morning, wearing a hat, and then pulled it off as if to make a statement. 'Check the bathroom. Check your shaver.'

She could hear Dale thumping up the stairs, huffing and puffing in her ear. 'Fuck.'

'What?'

'The bathroom bin is full of hair. She bloody shaved her head!' He sounded more impressed than worried.

Bile rose up Jen's throat and she vomited into the nearest bush.

'Jen?'

'Something's happened to her, Dale.' She coughed, wiping her mouth on the back of her hand.

There was a moment of tense silence before he said, 'Well, she shaved her head. She's probably off somewhere regretting her choice and worried about our reaction.' He sounded almost relieved and what he said might have made some sense. But she could still detect an undercurrent of fear in his voice, too.

She looked at the keyring in her hand and hoped against hope that Dale was right. But she couldn't settle on his theory. Not because it wasn't plausible, but because her gut was telling her that it was something more. Alex wouldn't shave her head for no reason. Something pushed her to do that. Something was wrong and Jen could feel it in her bones.

'I've been telling you that you needed to be there more!' Dale finally said, his own worries now manifesting themselves into blame. 'I'm just her dad! She *needs* her mother...'

'This is not about us! It's about Alex. We need to find her!' she all but screamed at him, and hung up the phone. If Dale was standing in front of her now, she'd punch him for his last comment, rather than wondering if he felt as shitty about his parenting abilities as she did.

Jen stood looking all around. She had no idea where to go. Simon was right. Alex always went to the woods when she wanted to be alone. They all did. How many times had Jen fantasised about being able to go for a long walk with no one but an audiobook narrator for company, rather than face her seemingly endless list of daily responsibilities? Even Dale sometimes sat in his car outside the house for twenty minutes, or more, after arriving home from work in the evening. Everyone needed to be alone sometimes. She almost believed that that's what this was, as she hurried towards her car. That Alex was sitting under a tree somewhere, contemplating her day. But when she got into her car and started the engine, she didn't drive directly back to their estate. After all, she'd checked their woods already. Instead, she drove around the surrounding area. She parked up and ran in and out of shops, and another wooded area that bordered a neighbouring estate. But there was no sign of Alex. She redialled her number over and over, but it just kept going to voicemail.

'Alex, love, please! Please call me. I just need to know you're okay. I won't ask any questions, and you don't have to talk to me until you're ready. But please. I need to hear your voice. Just, call me.' She left a fourth voice message, each one sounding more desperate than the last.

When she ran out of places to look, she convinced herself again that Alex would be sitting on the tyre swing, or under the big oak. With Simon. Who hadn't called her yet. Jen was sweating, but a chill ran through her then. Why had she let Simon go alone to look for her? Jen turned the car towards home and drove too fast to get there.

Her phone rang as she pulled into their estate. 'Where the hell is she, Jen?' Dale no longer sounded relieved. He sounded as frightened as she was now, which amplified her own fear even further. Dale was the king of denial. If he was entertaining the possibility that something had happened to Alex, then it really was time to panic.

'I can't find her. I'm going to check the woods again.' Her voice sounded like a stranger's, and she felt sick to the pit of her empty stomach.

She hung up before Dale had a chance to seek reassurances from her. She pulled up outside their house, slammed her car door and jogged towards the woods. By the time she got there, she was feeling less convinced that Alex would be there, and as she moved through the trees, the only sound she heard was her own shallow breathing. Was Simon still here, or had he gone home? Did he even bother to look?

Soon the giant oak was in sight and the tyre swing. Alex wasn't there. But Simon was. He was sitting on the ground with his back to the tree. His phone was on the ground with the screen lit up. Jen could see that he was looking at a photo of Alex. She knew the one. Lia had taken it when she brought the girls to Garryvoe Beach the summer before. Willow had been sitting beside Alex on the sand, the pair laughing hysterically at something that Jen wasn't privy to. Another moment she'd missed. But on Simon's phone, Willow had been cropped out. Simon's hand was in his pants and his eyes were on the screen. On Alex in her swimsuit.

Jen stumbled backwards away from him. Her stomach churned and whatever was left in there rose up into her throat. But she couldn't leave those woods. She doubled over, breathing noisily as she retched over a pile of dead leaves.

'Mrs Blake?' Simon's voice came through the encroaching darkness around her. 'Are you there?'

Jen straightened up and walked towards the oak tree, her legs feeling weak. Simon was standing now with his hands, and his phone, in his pockets. She could barely bring herself to look at him. 'Where is she?'

'I've checked everywhere here. I can't find her.'

He didn't seem to know that he'd been caught. Or at least, he didn't seem embarrassed about it. But his face was in shadow, as the woods became so much darker suddenly.

'If anyone will know where she went, it'll be Willow,' he said with confidence.

'Why do you say that?' Jen's voice was as steady as she could make it. 'From the looks of things, Willow's been busy with her new friends and you.' She glanced towards his pocket and the shape of his phone. 'What's going on, Simon?'

He frowned. 'I told you. Kids at school have been giving her a hard time, and…'

'Where did you get that photo?'

'Which one?'

'If I look on your phone right now, am I going to see my daughter's face?'

Simon shrugged. 'Oh, that. It's from my mum's Facebook page. You can probably get it there if you want a copy?'

He did that thing where he tilted his head to look at her again and Jen felt another chill.

'Do you know where Alex is?' She stepped towards him, her voice low and suddenly steady, filled with rage.

He laughed. 'You already asked me that, Mrs Blake.' He feigned innocence. 'That's why I came here, remember. To help you look for her?'

'Did you do something to her?'

His smile faded away and he looked scared suddenly. 'Wh… me? Mrs Blake, Alex is my friend.' His voice was small again. His bravado gone, if that's what it was.

'I saw you.' She glanced towards the phone in his pocket again.

He looked horrified and Jen could see a sliver of doubt creeping in. But she carried on. 'You had her photograph open on your phone just now. But only Alex. No Willow.'

His face flushed bright red. 'Please don't tell my mum, Mrs Blake. I'm sorry! I just… I really like her and… I've never done that before!' he cried, like he was the first person ever to masturbate, and to make matters worse, he'd been caught. But none of it was genuine. She knew that suddenly. His little boy lost act was exactly that. An act.

'Do you know where Alex is?' she asked, louder now, cutting him off.

'No! I swear, I…'

'If I find out you're lying to me, Simon, I swear I'll make

your life a living hell.' She looked him up and down, her chin quivering uncontrollably. She turned and walked away before she wasted any more valuable time on Simon Higgins. Her baby wasn't there. She wasn't anywhere.

'Where are you, Alex?' she whispered, crying as she exited the treeline.

# EIGHTEEN

## JEN

'Jen.'

Jay Higgins positioned himself in such a way that his whole body blocked the doorway. His pristine white shirt was untucked from his charcoal grey trousers, and his tie hung open around his neck. He was one of those men who, annoyingly, got better with age. Physically at least and he knew it, too. The more grey flecks that appeared in his black hair, the more handsome he became. In his tailored suit, with his charming smile, and confidence oozing quietly from his pores, he could literally stop women in their tracks. Jen hated him. She'd hated him for more than twenty years. Ever since he started dating her best friend and alienating her from everyone else. From Jen, her basketball teammates, and away from basketball altogether. Eventually he steered her away from the gap year she and Jen were supposed to take together, and the college degree she always planned on getting. He'd shrunk Lia's world so much, that she became her own little planet, orbiting around him. And Lia gave him the power to do it.

'I need to speak to Lia.' Jen craned her neck to see past him, into the kitchen.

Jay moved to block her view. 'Lia's not here.'

'Oh. You let her out without you? That's nice. But I need to speak with her, now.'

With the advantage of a six-inch doorstep, Jay was able to smile down upon her. He knew exactly how to wind Jen up. He'd been doing it since they first met.

'Do you?' He grinned. 'Well, your needs are very important to me, as you know. And you have so many. But I'm afraid I can't help you this time, because like I said, I just got home myself, and Lia isn't here.'

Jen squeezed her eyes shut and ground her teeth painfully. 'Alex is missing, Jay. So can you stop being an asshole for five minutes and tell me where Lia is?'

He raised his eyebrows. 'Why do you think Lia can help you with your runaway teen?'

Jen frowned. He couldn't have cared less. 'Because something's been going on between the kids, Jay! If you could take your blinkers off for two minutes, you'd know that.'

'They're hardly kids anymore, are they? They're adolescents and they're making new friends. You know how that goes. Alex has probably gone off somewhere sulking about it. You remember what that was like, too, I'm sure?'

He was patronising her and Jen wanted to slap him in the face. She'd done exactly that once, when she overheard him calling Lia a slut because she laughed at Paul Greene's joke in biology class. That was nearly six months after Jay had raped her in the back seat of his father's car. Lia sided with Jay then, too, which was when Jen stopped defending her. But a small part of her wondered again if he was right this time. If maybe Alex had run off because of her hair. Or whatever it was that pushed her to shave it off.

She frowned then and looked away to the side, thinking. What could make her do that? 'She's being bullied,' she said quietly, realisation dawning.

Jay's eyes narrowed, as they looked down upon her. He was debating with himself about whether to close the door in her face or pretend to help her. It was three months before the local elections and Jay Higgins was pushing his golden-boy image all over the city. The family solicitor. The family *man*. The all-round good guy. Jen knew exactly what he was thinking. He was looking for an angle. One that would benefit him.

'My daughter is missing, Jay. Your family can help, or you can close that door in my face, which is what I know you *want* to do. But I'll be screaming from the rooftops until I find her. And about anyone who stands in my way.'

He sighed heavily, let the door swing open and took his jacket down from a hook on the wall. He put it on and picked his car keys out of a bowl on the hall table. 'Lia is already looking for her, from what I gather. I'll give her a ring and I'll take a drive around. Okay?' He held out his arms and raised his eyebrows.

She turned and walked away from him, back towards her own house and car. She didn't trust Jay to speak to Lia, so Jen went searching on her phone for Lia's number. She didn't trust Jay, full stop. For all Jen knew, he was lying through his teeth. Lia could still be inside that house, so she refused to take his word for anything.

She found herself pressing dial on Alex's number again, before Lia's. 'Alex, love, please! Pick up the bloody phone or call me back. I need to know you're okay!'

As soon as she hung up, her phone rang. But it was Dale's name on the screen, not Alex's. 'Did you find her?' His voice was more high-pitched than usual and held an urgency that told her Dale was panicking.

'You drive to the park and look around there,' she said, trying to make herself sound calm.

'Okay. I'm near there now. Where are you going?'

Jen had no idea.

'What about Pennie Greene's house? Could she have gone there?'

'Pennie?' Jen sounded more confused than she should have about the suggestion. Pennie Greene had been in Lego club with Alex since they were about seven years old and it was the only activity that Alex did without the twins. Alex and Pennie did get along well, though they didn't really hang out with each other outside of that. 'Alex hasn't been to Lego club for months, Dale. Why would she go to Pennie's house?'

'Well, maybe she wanted to spend time with someone whose surname isn't Higgins, Jen – I don't know! Do you have any better suggestions?'

He was right. 'Okay, I'll try Pennie's house.' Jen started the car and took off, too fast again inside the estate.

She hung up from Dale and called Lia. It went straight to voicemail. The next number she tried was Willow. She answered on the first ring.

'Hello?' Her voice was low.

'Willow, it's—'

'I know. Your name came up on my phone.'

Jen exhaled loudly, turning onto the main road and narrowly avoiding a collision which would have been her fault entirely. 'Willow, I need you to tell me where Alex is.'

'I don't know where she is,' she shot back, a steely edge to her voice.

Jen knew Willow Higgins almost as well as she knew Alex. She knew that she needed to use honey, not vinegar, if she were going to get anywhere with the girl. 'Okay, well... I'm really worried about her, love. It's not like her to stay out like this and not answer my calls or messages.'

Willow stayed silent, but Jen could hear her breathing.

'Can you tell me what happened today, love?'

'How did *you* hear about that?'

Jen glanced at the phone, which was sitting on the

passenger seat. Willow wasn't talking about Alex's hair. She was talking about something Jen would have *heard* and not seen. 'I'd like to hear it from you,' she said, as softly as she could.

'It's just idiots who think they're funny.' Her voice sounded like it was gaining strength in bursts but losing it just as quickly.

'It always is. So, tell me.'

'They... It was just a stupid picture of Alex... *and* me,' she added defiantly. 'They plastered it all across the lockers.'

Jen felt as if the wind had been knocked out of her as her imagination ran wild. She tried to clear her throat but couldn't. 'What kind of picture?' she croaked.

'The stupid kind. Why did she do that to her hair?'

'I thought you might be able to tell me that?'

There was silence again and this time Jen realised that she'd need to be the one to break it.

'Willow, whatever is going on between you two, you know that Alex loves you. That Dale and I love you. You're part of our family, so please, whatever you two have fallen out over, I'm begging you to put it aside for now and help us to find her. Please.'

Willow exhaled loudly. 'Okay. I'll go check up by the pool.'

'By the *pool*?' Jen frowned.

'Not *in* the pool. *By* the pool. It's where we hang out sometimes.'

Jen blew out a long breath, and let her tears fall as she pulled into Pennie Greene's estate. 'Thank you, Willow. Call me if you hear from her.'

# NINETEEN

## JEN

Jen hurried up Anna Greene's driveway and rapped on the door.

'Jen? Hi,' Anna said as she opened the door. She glanced over Jen's shoulder, seeming a little confused as to what might have brought her here.

Jen sometimes regretted not making more of an effort to get to know Anna. She was what Jen's mother would have called a homely woman. Small and heavyset with curly hair and rosy cheeks. She mixed and matched pretty much the same small variety of clothing all the time. Mostly cardigans and stretchy pants. Pennie was always well turned out, though, and Jen knew that that was because Anna, a single mother, spent all her money on her child and none on herself. Not unlike the Blakes.

'Anna, hi. I'm so sorry to turn up like this.'

'Don't be silly! Come in.' She stepped back and opened the door wide. Jen was greeted by the smell of home cooking. Something warm and hearty.

'I'm sorry, I can't. Alex is missing, Anna. Can I speak to Pennie? I just need to know if she's seen her.'

'Pennie!' Anna called loudly towards the stairs. Her worry for Alex was already clear in her expression.

'Yeah?' Pennie came to the top step.

Pennie looked like a much younger version of her mother, right down to the curly brown hair and rosy cheeks.

'Come down, love. Mrs Blake needs to speak to you.'

Pennie came quickly down the stairs.

'Have you seen Alex, Pen?' Anna asked, before she reached the bottom step.

'Not really,' Pennie replied.

'When was the last time you saw her?' Jen asked, still standing outside on the doorstep.

Pennie shrugged, looking worried. 'I've seen her around school and that. But she hasn't been back to Lego club since we finished up before summer. And she doesn't really... I mean, we don't really hang around together at school anymore.' Anna put an arm around her daughter's shoulders and Pennie leaned into her.

Alex hadn't mentioned Lego club all summer, so Jen didn't ask if she wanted to sign back up. It was just a hundred and forty euro that she didn't need to spend every couple of months. 'Do you have any idea where she might have gone?'

Pennie shook her head. 'Up by the pool, maybe? That's where most of them hang out.'

'Willow is checking there now.' Jen looked away for a minute, despair clawing at her insides. Then she looked back to Pennie and asked, 'Did you know that she was being bullied at school?'

Anna frowned and looked to her child. Pennie nodded. 'They've been pretty awful to her. Darina Hayes and Lucy Nagle. And some of the boys as well.'

'Oh, Jen, I'm sorry, love. Poor Alex,' Anna said, and Jen appreciated the flicker of anger in the woman's expression.

Tears filled Jen's eyes and poured down her cheeks. 'How long has it been going on?'

'Um, I think since around the time of the twins' birthday party.'

Jen shook her head. 'I didn't know.'

'Of course you didn't know,' Anna said sternly. 'Sure, they tell us nothing, do they?' She reached out and squeezed Jen's arm. 'Grab your coat, Pennie. We'll get out and help you look.'

Anna Greene hardly knew Jen. Yet here she was offering more help and consolation to her than anyone else had. Her kindness was the last straw for Jen, and she let out the sob she'd been doing her best to silence.

'Oh, don't worry, pet. We'll find her.' Anna hurried back into the kitchen, while putting her coat on. Jen watched her turning off the cooker and unplugging something else, before hurrying out the door, with Pennie close behind her. She locked up the house and double-checked it before all three of them left.

Jen paced from window to window, her phone clutched in her hand, watching shadows move in the darkness. No Alex at the pool. No Alex at the courts. No Alex anywhere. Her calls went straight to voicemail now, each one more desperate than the last.

'She must be at Willow's,' everyone kept saying, their voices too bright, too hopeful. But Jen knew better. A mother knows. Her hands shook as she looked at the clock again. Almost midnight. The voice she'd been fighting all night clawed its way up: something is terribly wrong.

'I'm calling the guards.' The words came out raw. 'We should have called them hours ago.'

Dale nodded helplessly. He'd hardly spoken since he and Jen met up at home less than twenty minutes earlier. Jen felt chilled to the bone and light-headed. She hadn't eaten since breakfast and couldn't bear the thought of trying to force herself to. Her mind was a jumble of every sharp word she'd spoken to Alex, every time she hadn't been there for her. As she brought the screen to life and opened the phone app, a loud thumping on the front door made them both jump. Jen dropped the phone and ran to open the door.

Standing there, looking more haggard than anyone had ever seen her, was Lia Higgins. She was crying and breathless and she was holding her phone up to Jen.

'What? What is it?' Jen implored.

Lia all but fell into the hall. She handed the phone to Jen. 'I got this... it's from Alex.'

Jen's stomach roiled as she clutched Lia's phone in both hands, trying to hold it steadily enough that she could read the screen.

> **ABLAKE**
>
> I can't do this anymore. I just want it all to end. Tell my mum and dad not to blame themselves, or each other for this. It's not their fault. It's mine. Everything is my fault. Tell them I love them. And tell Willow I'm sorry.

'Wh... what is this?'

Dale took the phone from her and read the message. He staggered backwards against the stair banister.

'Where is she?' Jen sobbed, grabbing Lia by the shoulders. 'Why would she send this to you? Where is she, Lia?'

'I... I don't know.'

'You do! You know something. Why would she send this to you? Why wouldn't she send it to me?'

Lia's face changed, but it was such a subtle shift it could easily have been missed. Jen didn't miss it, however. She saw the hint of judgement that was thrown her way, even now.

'Did you find her?' Anna Greene came breathlessly through the front door behind Lia. She'd been walking the neighbourhood for hours. Pennie was with her, until Anna sent the girl home some time after ten.

'Jen.' Dale's voice cracked as he quietly called her from the kitchen doorway.

Everyone turned to look at him and Jen's knees buckled when she saw his pale and crumpled face. She shook her head, her lips trembling.

He held up his phone helplessly. 'The Gardaí just received a report of someone in the water down by the quays. They lost sight of them before help arrived.'

Jen shook her head more vehemently. 'No.' Whatever else was true, Alex would never willingly go into the water of the river Lee. Not in a million years. 'That's not her.'

'They said that a St Brendan's kitbag was pulled out of the river, right near the edge.'

'No!' Jen reached out to steady herself against the banister, but she missed. Both Lia and Anna grabbed her and held her upright as she cried. 'No! No, no, no!'

'Don't you fall down,' Anna muttered fiercely in her ear, as she wrapped her arms tightly around her. 'That girl of yours is as strong as an ox. Do you hear me? Now, let's go.'

The woman's words sank into Jen's soul, and there they released some of the strength with which she'd spoken them. Jen pulled herself upright, roughly wiping the tears from her face. She zipped her jacket up to her chin and picked up her car keys.

'I'll drive,' Dale said, his voice breaking. 'The report went into the Bridewell station. We'll head there.'

'I'm not going to the police station, Dale.' Jen was already out the door with Anna close behind her. Lia still hadn't moved. She looked like she might crumble at any moment. But not Jen. Not anymore. 'I'm going to bring my baby home.'

. . .

Whatever strength she'd borrowed from Anna Greene evaporated when she reached the quays. There were lights everywhere and voices. Lots of voices coming from out on the water. Small boats bobbed and swirled and danced on the calm surface, while beams of bright spotlights lit up the murky river before them.

'Excuse me!' Anna shouted at a man in bright orange waterproof gear. She went running over to him. When she had his attention, she lowered her voice as she spoke urgently to him, gesturing towards Jen as she did.

A numbness had come over Jen. It was as if she were on the set of a movie – one of the thrillers she liked to watch before they had to cancel their Netflix and Sky subscriptions. A scene where fictitious rescue personnel searched for a fictitious victim. But this was real. The victim was her daughter.

'Mrs Blake?' The man in orange came and touched her gently on the elbow, his expression grim. Anna stood behind him, wringing her hands.

Jen tried to focus on his hand. She managed a nod and tried to stop the shaking that had now taken over her entire body.

'At the moment, we don't know anything,' the man said, as reassuringly as he could. 'There might be no reason at all for us to be here. Someone found a bag and then your husband called to say your daughter has one just like it and she hasn't come home yet.'

Jen gave another semi-automated nod. 'But someone said they saw her in the water?'

'Someone did make a call to say they *think* they saw someone, but when they looked again, there was nothing there. It was the same person who found the bag when they went for a closer look. The bag might have been the only thing there, for all we know. Can I get you to take a look at it? Maybe you can tell us if it belongs to Alex or not. Do you think you can do that?'

Given the job he was currently doing and the conversation

he was being forced to have, his voice was one of the calmest she'd ever heard and filled with sincerity. Without knowing anything else about him, Jen trusted him more than she trusted anyone else in that moment, such was the man's presence. He held his arm out and led her towards a van with *Cork River Rescue* written on the side of it. He pulled open the side door and gestured to a black kitbag with the red St Brendan's logo on it. Hanging off the zip was a metal loop, missing its unicorn keyring. Jen's chest tightened and a loud sob escaped her. She moved towards the van and opened the zip on the bag. Inside was the St Brendan's basketball strip, with AB embroidered onto the right side of her vest. AB – Alex Blake.

'Alex.' Jen keened and doubled over as bile rose up her throat.

'Okay, Jen, I've got you.' Jen felt Anna's arms supporting her.

Jen crouched close to the damp ground and looked across to the other side of the river. There were two fire trucks over there and several people moving slowly along the quay wall. She listened as the man answered Anna's questions about their search strategy.

'We have four boats on the water and three divers already in. It's slack tide now and that's a good thing. It means there's not much movement so *if* she went in the water sometime in the last hour or so, she won't have been taken too far. But like I said, we don't *know* that she went in there. All we do know is that this *is* her bag and that she hasn't returned home. Is there someone at your house, in case she does go home?'

'My son is there.' Lia's voice came from behind Jen. She hadn't been there before. 'I asked him to stay at your house, Jen.'

'Is there anyone with him?' Anna asked, her tone icy.

'My husband is just across the green,' Lia responded, defensively.

Anna looked like she wanted to say more, but she stopped herself.

Jen saw a lone figure approaching a group of firemen on the other side of the river. It was Dale. She'd know his form anywhere, along with his lumbering gait.

'What's your name?' she asked the man, as Anna helped her up off the floor.

'Michael,' he said with a gentle expression that told her he understood everything.

'I'm Jen. Alex is my baby, Michael. She's five foot four inches tall. She has bright blue eyes and black hair, which she just shaved off because she's so damn brave.' Her voice cracked, but she kept going. Alex needed to be real to all of them, so they'd put everything into their search for her. 'And she's funny. She's funny and kind.' A hint of anger returned to her voice. 'She's kind to everyone. She's smart, too. But she has a mortal fear of water, Michael. If she's in there...' She looked at the hauntingly dark river and her mouth twisted in anguish. 'She can't be in there.' She shook her head adamantly. 'She wouldn't. If you knew how afraid she is of water...'

Anna's strong arm was around her shoulders again. 'Let's not get ahead of ourselves, now,' she said firmly. 'Michael here looks like he's been doing this since Alex and Pennie were in nappies. Isn't that right, Michael?'

'Maybe even longer,' he said. 'I know exactly how you're feeling right now, Jen. Believe me when I say that. I know the kind of hell you're in. But I need you to stay strong and trust that everyone out on that water tonight, knows exactly what they're doing. And we won't give up.' He reached out and squeezed her shoulder again, then started to move away. 'I'm going to get back to work now, and if we learn anymore, I'll find you.'

# TWENTY

## JEN

As the night wore on and the tide completed its turn, the search moved downriver, closer to the Blackrock Castle. One of the fire trucks had given Jen, Anna and Lia a lift down there. The River Rescue van pulled up alongside them and Dale climbed out, along with Michael, the search coordinator. Their eyes met and lingered helplessly on each other for a while. She saw only her own devastation reflected back at her and there was nothing they could do for each other in that moment. All Jen could think about was Alex. She couldn't be in there. Surely they were wasting their time here, when she was probably at home by now, wondering where everyone had gone.

But what if she *was* in there? How cold she would be. How frightened and terrified. Jen had been slumped against a boulder for a while, but as she looked out upon the slow-moving river, she thought she saw something breaking through the surface. She jumped to her feet and ran into the water. 'Jen!' someone called from the shore. It sounded like Anna, but Jen didn't stop.

The bottom dropped away before she got knee deep and she went under for a few seconds. But Jen was a strong swimmer.

She'd become one, after her daughter almost drowned on a family holiday. Perhaps the last happy one they'd had. Dale blamed her for not keeping a close enough eye on Alex that day. No doubt he blamed her tonight as well. And perhaps he was right.

She kept going until she caught sight of the head again. But it was a seal. She stopped swimming before she reached it, and as she treaded water, she could feel herself drifting slowly downriver, until a floatation device was slung around her chest, and she was pulled backwards towards the shore.

'You're alright, love,' a man's voice said in her ear.

'I thought it was her,' Jen cried, and allowed herself to be pulled to shore, as her strength drained into the murky depths.

Within seconds she felt the stony ground under her feet again and another pair of arms around her. Anna, almost up to her own knees in water, helped the man to remove the floatation device, and then she led Jen back to dry land.

'Lia, watch her,' Anna ordered Lia who was standing nearby with both hands covering her mouth. 'I'm going to check in with that lot and see what's happening.' Anna stumbled her way across the loose shale towards the rescue coordinator, leaving Jen to be held upright by Lia.

'Oh, Jen,' Lia whispered in her ear, her voice weak and shaky.

'Over here!' someone called.

The quay, the slippery strand, and the water, all came alive with movement suddenly as everyone converged on that one boat, and on the man who was hauling the lifeless body from the river. People slipped and stumbled and scrambled past. Medics moved in, and instructions were called out. But it all happened around Jen and Lia, who were rooted to the spot where they stood. Jen no longer felt the cold of the dirty water which had soaked through the layers of her clothing. She no longer felt anything. Her legs died and she slipped from Lia's grasp and landed on the ground. Lia lowered herself shakily alongside her. Anna was the first to scream the word, 'No!' Jen saw the shape of her falling to the ground, too. Like it was her own child being pulled from the water.

Her own, dead child.

She would have no memory of what happened after that. She wouldn't have to remember her baby girl being pulled out of the boat and onto a waiting stretcher. She wouldn't have to remember her bloated face and her blue-tinged skin. She wouldn't have to witness the hands of strangers pumping Alex's chest or the involuntary arching of her back as they tried to shock her back to life. Instead, Jen would be carried, oblivious, to a second ambulance, and transported behind the body of her child, all the way to Cork University Hospital, where she would spend two days wishing she never woke up.

# TWENTY-ONE
## LIA

The heater blasted hot air at them, but Anna Greene wouldn't stop trembling. Lia gripped the steering wheel, her own hands shaking now as the reality of what they'd just witnessed crashed over her. Alex's body being pulled from the water. Jen's screams, and Dale's. The way Anna had crumbled to the ground like she'd been shot, while Lia had just closed her eyes and prayed. *Thank God it wasn't one of mine.* The thought made bile rise in her throat – what kind of monster was she, to feel relief in that moment? She glanced at Anna, who sat rigid and silent beside her, refusing to acknowledge a single word Lia said. The silence felt like an accusation.

As they pulled up outside Anna's house, she had the passenger door open before they'd even come to a full stop. She got out and walked like someone twice her age towards her front door, while Lia stayed idling in the driveway. She couldn't go home yet. She couldn't face her own children. She wouldn't be able to look at Willow without seeing Alex's lifeless face. She couldn't look at Simon without wondering... She squeezed her eyes shut against the thoughts threatening to overwhelm her.

•   •   •

'Where've you been?' Jay asked, in an accusatory tone when she did arrive home a while later. He looked at her more closely then. 'Jesus. What happened to you?'

'I was down by the river, helping with the search.'

Jay rolled his eyes. 'Christ, they're being a bit dramatic, aren't they?'

Lia glanced at Simon and Willow, who were sat on the couch. Willow was pretending to read a book for Jay's benefit, while Simon was on his Nintendo Switch. She shook her head solemnly at Jay.

'What?' he asked, but she pretended not to hear him. She could only say this once, and Willow, in particular, needed to hear it from *her*. She felt sick to her stomach and her whole body trembled, but she had to get the words out before she choked on them. Jay wouldn't be happy, but Lia deserved whatever punishment came her way tonight.

'Willow, Simon,' she said softly, to get the attention of her kids. Jay frowned at her, but she kept going before she couldn't. 'I'm afraid I have some really bad news.'

Willow put down the book and sat up straight, her face already draining of colour.

'Alex has... She's...' Lia brought her hands to her mouth.

'No, Mum.' Willow stood up, her eyes brimming with tears. She knew what was coming.

'I'm sorry, love.' Lia held out her arms and Willow ran into them.

'Did she kill herself?' Simon asked, without looking up from his Nintendo. His thumbs were still working overtime on whatever dumb game he was playing.

Lia blanched.

'Christ,' Jay said. 'That family is a bloody car crash.' He walked away, back to the kitchen. 'Lia, can I have a word?' he added, over his shoulder.

Lia nodded and kissed Willow on the top of the head. But

her eyes were on Simon. He was never a sensitive boy by any means. But with every year that passed, he grew colder and colder. Seeing him now scared her. His lifelong friend, who he'd apparently grown feelings for, had been pulled from the river and he couldn't bring himself to look away from his game.

'Lia?' Jay called.

Willow ran up the stairs sobbing.

A wave of tiredness crashed over her as she went over to Jay, supporting herself on the kitchen island. The suddenness with which his hand wrapped around her throat caught her off guard and her knees buckled. He tightened his grip and pulled her upwards, until she was balancing on the tips of her toes.

'What was that?' he hissed in her face.

She tried to respond, but she couldn't. She couldn't breathe. He *would* let go before anything happened. She knew he would, but being choked still terrified her.

'Next time you decide to drop a bomb on my children, you run it by me first. You hear me?' He moved even closer, so his body was pressed against hers. 'You can't just *hurl* something like that at them. You need to be *told* how to word it. You do not make decisions about our family by yourself.' He squeezed a little tighter and she started to claw at his arm. 'You know that,' he said more gently. Then he let her go and stepped back.

Lia fell against the island, with her hand to her throat, gasping for air.

'Were any of the media there?' he asked then, taking a bite of an apple.

'I...' Her voice croaked, so she just shook her head and shrugged. She picked up a glass from the draining board and filled it with water from the tap. Her hand shook as she brought it to her lips.

Jay nodded. 'It'd be nice to have a pic for the front page. My wife assisting that poor family.'

Lia turned her back on him, pretending to check her phone

as she tried to gather herself. *How could he? Callous bastard.* All he could think about was the upcoming elections. She shuddered to think what might happen if he didn't win. Jay took his apple into the sitting room and sat down beside Simon. He picked up the remote and turned on the RTE news, no doubt hoping for a scene where election candidate Jay Higgins' stunning wife was front and centre, offering help at a local tragedy.

She looked at her husband and son – Simon still lost in his game, twisting and turning his console like his life depended on it, and Jay watching TV and eating an apple – feeling the twist of disgust and shame in her stomach. She climbed the stairs, pausing on the landing. She wanted to check on Willow, but first she headed to the bathroom for some arnica cream, of which she had a lifetime supply. She massaged some onto her throat, the image of Alex's lifeless body being hauled from the river replaying over and over in her mind.

# TWENTY-TWO

## JEN

Death by drowning. That was it. The only explanation Jen and Dale were given for the gaping hole that had been left in their lives. Jen had been sitting on Alex's bed for two days. In her hand was the broken rainbow unicorn keyring, and on her body, Alex's basketball jersey, still unwashed and would forever remain that way. She ran out of tears some hours ago, and now she was just numb. Dale was somewhere else in the house being silently tortured by his own self-loathing. She'd just about forgotten he was there. Whenever she heard him moving around, a part of her expected it to be Alex arriving home like the whirlwind she used to be, throwing random facts at them like confetti. She had one to suit just about any occasion, and any topic of conversation. But of course, it wasn't Alex arriving home. And it never would be again.

'Hey…' A shadow of Dale slowly opened the bedroom door, but he couldn't bring himself to step inside the room. He looked like maybe he'd died as well. 'Are you hungry?'

Jen shook her head. Hungry? How could anyone be hungry when Alex was gone?

He kind of staggered backwards, away from the door and

when he met the wall, he slid down it, to the floor. 'Why would she do this?' he whispered into his hands.

Jen frowned. 'Do what?'

He looked at her, confused and in pain. 'Wh... This!' His voice cracked. 'Why would she do *this*?!'

'She didn't do this, Dale,' Jen said with conviction.

Dale started to cry, his body hunched and shaking. Jen looked away. She had no comfort to offer now. Their tether had been cut and she felt more adrift from him than ever. But the fact that he actually thought Alex had *chosen* this was the rock their marriage would perish on.

Jen looked around her child's room, its walls patched with posters of female trailblazers. She could hear Alex's voice in her mind, telling Jen about each of them as she hung them in their place. Rashida Adeleke, Ireland's athletics phenomenon; Rosa Parks, whose refusal to give up her seat echoed around the world; Marie Curie, who wasn't just the first *woman* to win a Nobel prize, but the only *person* to have won it in two scientific fields. And of course, Alex's biggest hero, Malala Yousafzai. *I mean, I don't even have to tell you about her!* But she did anyway. For more than thirty minutes.

The mirror on her dresser was framed with photos. Alex was one of the few people Jen knew who went out of her way to print pictures. Most of them were of Alex and Willow. A couple of her with Dale and Jen, and one of her and Pennie, beaming behind their enormous, prize-winning Lego space shuttle. Alex was the kind of friend that everyone should be so lucky to have. She never turned her back on people. A dull pain spread across her chest. Thinking of her baby in the past tense was unbearable. She picked up Alex's pillow and hugged it tightly, breathing in the scent of her again. Then Jen found her gaze drawn to a picture of Alex and Willow. Both girls were sitting on the grass between their houses, laughing hysterically at something. Carefree and beautiful, both of them. Simon stood awkwardly in the background, watching the pair. The reality of that day was probably such that Simon was involved somehow – that he was a part of what they were laughing about. It was just a snapshot in time, but suddenly it was a haunting one. One where he appeared to be lurking in the background, watching. Jen thought about him that day in the woods. When he was supposed to be looking for Alex, but instead he was masturbating to an image of her. Was it the same image of her beautiful daughter, which had been warped and used to torture her?

She put down the pillow and got up off the bed. Her legs felt stiff and aching from lack of use, but her insides simmered as she looked at the image of *him* watching Alex. She hurried from the room, flew down the stairs and opened the front door, then she ran outside without closing it behind her. Rather than taking the footpath around, she crossed the road, stepped onto the green and made a beeline for the Higginses' house on the other side.

'Simon!' she called loudly, as she neared the house. 'Simon Higgins, get out here!'

Jen didn't notice the curtains twitching, or the shapes appearing in their neighbours' windows. Unlike Jay Higgins who stepped outside, pulling the door shut behind him as he looked around at their poorly hidden audience.

'Jen? Are you alright?' he asked, with a forced smile, his eyes still glancing around at his neighbours.

'Simon!' she called over his shoulder.

Jay reached out and caught her by the shoulders, to stop her from going any further. She pushed against him, but he pulled her into a tight and unwelcome hug. His lips touched the tip of her ear when he said, 'Go home, Jen,' through gritted teeth. As always, his cool exterior never faltered.

Jen struggled until he let go, then she took a step back from him. But she raised her voice. He might not have wanted their witnesses, but suddenly, she did. 'Where is he? Where's that perverted son of yours?'

Jay was incredulous. 'I beg your pardon?'

Even in her blind rage, Jen could tell that he was restraining himself. Holding in the torrent that he desperately wanted to unleash upon her. Their ill feelings towards each other had always been mutual.

'You heard me. It was him!' She pointed at the house. 'He's the reason my baby...'

'Jen!' Lia came hurrying out, pain and worry etched on her face. What did she know about either? She came to Jen and gently shoved Jay out of the way. She placed an arm around Jen's shoulders, but Jen shrugged her off.

'Don't touch me. You're not my friend.' Jen tried to step around her. 'Simon!' she called again.

Jay came and said something in Lia's ear, then went inside and closed the front door. Lia, for her part, looked like she hadn't heard him, and she kept her eyes firmly on Jen. Finally, Jen broke down crying.

'Has everyone seen enough?' Lia called to her neighbours, shaming them into looking away, momentarily at least. 'Please... this isn't for anyone's entertainment.'

Some had the good grace to look sheepish, as they closed their doors and let their curtains fall. Others just moved to a different window and continued to intrude upon their neighbour's pain.

'Jen,' Lia said softly. 'I'm so sorry.'

'It was him,' Jen said, her own voice sounding dull and detached from herself. 'It was your Simon.'

Lia shook her head. That's when Jen realised that that look on her face *was* fear. But fear for her own child. Lia *knew*. Jen made for the house again and this time it was Lia who stood in her way.

'Jen! You're not thinking clearly. No one *would* be in your place, but...'

'In my pl—'

'But my son had nothing to do with this. Simon is broken-hearted, Jen, and so is Willow. My children are grieving and it's my job to protect them now.'

'Are they?' Jen laughed suddenly. 'Have you seen *him* crying then? Is he all broken up, really?'

'Jen, please!' Lia looked disbelieving. Like she couldn't imagine someone implying that her son was some kind of psychopath. 'You're not—'

'He was masturbating to her picture when he was *supposed* to be looking for her!' Jen snapped. 'I saw him!'

Lia stepped back, looking like she'd been slapped.

'Yeah. He's brokenhearted, alright.'

'Jen.' Dale's arms wrapped around her from behind, gently pulling her away. He was out of breath. She struggled against him at first before her strength drained and she collapsed into him.

'I'm sorry, Lia,' he mumbled to the other woman.

Jen shoved him away from her, but she continued towards home. Before she went inside, she looked back towards the Higginses'. Lia was still standing on the green where they'd left her. She was hugging herself, watching them go. Through the open sitting room curtains, she saw Jay sitting on the couch, watching them through the window. But in the upstairs master bedroom window was the full silhouette of Simon Higgins. He was standing with his hands in his pockets looking right at her. Before Jen stepped inside her own house, Simon raised one hand and waved.

# TWENTY-THREE

## JEN

'What are you doing, Jen?' Dale asked, like he genuinely couldn't understand her behaviour.

'It was him,' she hissed, pointing towards the front door.

'It wasn't him. It wasn't anybody. It was...' He dug the heels of his hands into his eyes and doubled over.

'No!' Jen said, more forcefully, shaking her head adamantly. 'I know my child, Dale. She—'

'And I didn't know her?' he cried, straightening up again, his eyes painfully red.

'She didn't do this. She would *not* do this.'

'But she did, though.'

Jen cried, too, and looked away from him, hopeless. He didn't believe her. He'd rather accept this and cry quietly into his cornflakes, than make a scene. Rather than demanding to know the truth, however awful it might be. But what was the truth? And when it came to the perfect Higgins family, who would believe it, if not her own husband – Alex's father?

'Where are you going?' He caught her by the elbow as she reached for her jacket, which hung on a hook in the hall.

She pulled out of his loose grip. 'Anywhere but here.'

'Jen, leave it.'

Jen looked him up and down, suddenly loathing him. 'You leave it.' She picked up her car keys and walked out.


The whole time she was driving, Jen was thinking about Alex. Her smile, her laugh, the way her voice sounded when she was upset. The way she'd sneak up behind Jen sometimes and wrap her arms around her, bear-hugging her mother when she needed it most. Usually while she was cooking, and then she'd sneak a taste of whatever was almost ready. How could she just be gone? What were they supposed to do now?

She was pulling up near Blackrock Castle before she knew where she was going. Right by where Alex was found. She parked the car and got out, pulling the zip of her jacket all the way up to her chin. It was a mild evening, but she immediately felt the cold of the night when she stood drenched to the skin on the shore, while her baby was dragged onto a boat. That cold stayed with her even now. It had seeped into her bones. The tide was high, and the river moved much faster towards the sea. A little further along the water's edge sat a lonely figure on a bench. It was a woman – small and round with an unruly mop of hair. She was only a silhouette, but even still, there was something familiar about her. Jen kept going and as she neared the woman, she didn't so much as glance in Jen's direction. Her hands were in her lap and her eyes were on them. Jen stopped and looked at her. It was Anna Greene.

'Anna?' she asked, stopping near her bench. She stuffed her hands deep into her jacket pockets.

Anna inhaled sharply and stood up. 'Jen!' She glanced around then, seeming embarrassed. 'I'm sorry, I...' She looked at Jen, her eyes brimming with tears. 'I shouldn't be here. I'm sorry.'

There was something about Anna that made Jen wish she'd

made more time for the woman over the years. They had, after all, known each other since they were girls. But Anna always kind of faded into the background. Jen went and sat on the bench.

Anna shook her head. She looked like she hadn't slept in days. 'I don't know. I just keep thinking about...' She glanced at Jen. 'I'm sorry, I shouldn't... I'm so sorry, Jen. I'm so sorry for your darling Alex. She was such a special girl.'

Jen looked at Anna's tear-stained face, wringing her hands in her lap. 'How's Pennie?' she found herself asking. Even though it hurt to ask about another fifteen-year-old girl who was tucked up safely in her home, while Alex was not. But suddenly she wanted this woman's company. She wanted to talk to someone who knew Alex, and knew how special she was.

Anna shrugged. 'She's at her dad's. But I don't expect she'll stay the night as planned. She rarely does.'

Jen vaguely remembered that Anna had had an affair with her married boss back in the day, and Pennie was the result. She wasn't the only result. Anna was given some ridiculous reason why her services were no longer required at the company, which of course wouldn't be tolerated now. But back then the news was met with, *well, what did she expect?* She became a single parent, fodder for gossip, and had spent the past fifteen years alone. Or at least, that was Jen's understanding.

'That could have been me,' she half whispered.

'What?'

Anna looked at Jen. 'It could have been me, watching Pennie being taken from that river.'

Jen frowned.

'I'm sorry. You don't need to hear this and I shouldn't be putting myself in your shoes. What you're going through...'

'What do you mean, it could have been you?' Jen asked. She desperately wanted to talk. Could this woman have *some* idea of what she was feeling? Could anyone?

'Pennie's been asking about her father since she was old enough to speak.' Anna's soft voice had a hint of resignation to it. 'Back when the girls were small, she was probably the only child in the class who didn't have a daddy at home. It's not so unusual now, but... ah, sure what child doesn't want the same as what every other child has? Anyway, Declan had his own family. A wife, and he had one child before Pennie came along. And he had two more after her.' She shrugged. 'He didn't want to know her, which of course was *his* loss,' she said, without a hint of bitterness.

Jen lowered her eyes. 'Idiot,' she muttered.

Anna issued a small smile. 'Yeah, well, unlike her father, Pennie *isn't* an idiot. I sat her down and told her the truth about him when she was about nine. We only have each other so, you know, we can't be telling lies. Not about the big stuff. Anyway, despite it all, she found him, and without telling me anything about it, she just turned up at his house one day.' She inhaled deeply and blew out a long breath.

'What happened?'

'She came home in floods of tears. He'd hissed her off his doorstep, like he didn't want anyone to see her standing there. He told her never to come back.' She looked at Jen again, her face suddenly more defiant. 'I never wanted a thing from that bastard. But when he took it upon himself to hurt that child' – her mouth turned down – 'he wasn't going to get away with it anymore. That's when I went after him for child support and everything else I'd allowed him to dodge. It got very nasty there for a while, as you can imagine. Then a couple of years ago...' She took another deep, shaky breath.

'What?'

Anna raised her eyebrows and shook her head. 'I'll spare you the details, but Pennie spent a bit of time inside in St Michael's.'

'St Michael's? You mean—'

Anna nodded. 'The psychiatric ward. Yes. Bulimia, depression... overall crying out for help. Screaming for it. My beautiful little girl who never hurt a fly.'

'Oh, Anna.'

She shrugged. 'I was afraid to leave her out of my sight for a long time. She was just so sad. So low in herself, you know?'

Jen turned her gaze to the deep black river. Why hadn't she felt any such fear for Alex? She *knew* that she was struggling. She knew something was wrong. But it never occurred to her that...

'Don't you do that,' Anna said sharply.

Jen lowered her head and sobbed.

'Don't you be thinking, *I should have known*. You couldn't know.'

'You did.'

'I don't know what the hell I know. What *do* I know? Nothing. None of us knows a fucking thing when it comes to raising teenagers. Especially at a time when there's more pressure on them than there is on us. It's not the same kind of pressure. I mean, they don't have to worry about keeping the lights on. But it's pressure all the same. Pressure to be perfect. Pressure to be what everyone *thinks* they should be. Pressure to tick all the boxes.'

Jen thought about that. Anna was right. 'Alex was gay, but I never got to speak to her about that. I never brought it up with her because I always assumed she'd tell me when she was ready.' She dropped her chin onto her chest. 'Now I'll never get the chance.'

Anna nodded. 'She *would* have told you when she was ready.'

'Do you think that could be why...'

'No, I don't. When it comes to sexuality, there are a few dozen of those boxes to choose from now. That's the one thing my Pennie didn't struggle with.'

'Pennie is gay?'

Anna smiled and nodded. If Jen's grief wasn't taking up every inch of space inside her, she might have felt even more inadequate as a mother. This was a basic thing that she'd never talked to her daughter about. And yet, she claimed to know her well enough to be sure she wouldn't throw herself in the river.

'You're doing it again.' Anna cut through her dark thoughts. She reached over and took Jen's hand. She gave it a gentle squeeze. 'We can't know what they don't tell us. But you knew your daughter, Jen. You work your backside off for your family and you're a good mother.' She stood up. 'Now, I'd better get back. Pennie will be getting pissed off with one, if not all, of her half siblings by now and she'll be looking to come home. Can I drive you somewhere?'

Jen shook her head.

Anna nodded. 'Jen, before I leave, can I ask you something?'

'Of course.'

'You really believe that Alex didn't go in there of her own accord?'

Jen looked at the river again. 'I *know* she didn't.'

Anna nodded. 'Then I might know someone who can help. Give me a few days.'

Anna turned to go, and Jen broke down sobbing again. 'Thank you, Anna.'

'For what?'

'For believing me.'

Anna gave a small nod, then ambled slowly away.

# TWENTY-FOUR

## LIA

'She's lost the plot,' Jay said, standing by the sitting room window, looking out.

'Who has?' Lia asked, even though she didn't want to know. She didn't want to talk to him at all.

'Jen Blake. She's standing in her garden, looking like a homeless person. And she's just staring at our house. It'd be more in her line to get back to work.' He bobbed his head from side to side. 'Or not. If the bank takes the house off them, we might finally get some decent neighbours.' He turned away from the window with a smile on his face. Jay always took pleasure in seeing those around him being brought down a peg or two. Even if they were already close to the bottom rung. His smile vanished when he turned to look at Lia, who didn't appear her usual shiny self either. He came towards her, his demeanour changing again.

'What the hell is wrong with you?'

'N—'

'You listen to me...' He stepped in so close to her that she could feel his breath on her face. She pressed herself into the kitchen counter. 'I've been giving you too much leeway recently, and everything is going to shit because of it. Look at you.' He looked her over, disgusted by what he saw. Lia wrapped her arms around herself, but Jay pulled them away. 'You fat fucking slob. Have you even been going to the classes that *I've* been paying for? Are you just sitting around here, eating shit all day, while I'm out trying to build on our success?' He pressed his body against her, coming nose to nose with her. 'Or has that fucking nutcase' – he pointed towards the bay window – 'been getting in your head again?'

Lia lowered her eyes to the floor, fear and shame washing over her. 'I never see her, Jay. I—'

'Is that right? So why have you been cosying up to her at every basketball match then? You and her, huddled together at the railing, like old times?' His smile was filled with contempt. 'You don't think I hear about these things? You don't think I know what's been going on when you think I'm not watching?' He roughly tapped the side of her head. 'I am *always* watching.'

'Jay, I swear, I—' She sounded like a frightened child.

He grabbed what little flesh was around her waist painfully in both hands, making her inhale sharply. 'Don't you fucking swear to me. You may have apples, grapes and water for the rest of this week. Do you hear me?'

Lia nodded, tears welling in her eyes.

'You're an embarrassment.'

'I'm sorry,' she said hoarsely.

'I've been spoiling you rotten. A big house, designer clothes, a brand-new car under your arse and people who do everything for you. Your only job is to look good and make sure my daughter doesn't turn into the kind of whore *you* were when I first found you, and my son doesn't become a nancy boy. You don't think every other woman would give their left tit for your life? You don't think that sad bitch across the green would?'

*Don't cry. Don't cry.* But uncontrollable tears began to fall.

'Her daughter just died, Jay. That girl grew up with our children. She—'

'Don't talk back to me!' he shouted suddenly, and Lia flinched. 'She *wasn't* one of our children, was she? It wasn't *your* daughter who chucked herself in the river, so pull yourself together, woman!'

Lia's skin prickled as the air cooled around her. Jay's words had that effect sometimes. She was trembling all over and her stomach ached, as she fought for the courage to speak. Her voice had all but vanished. 'Jen thinks that Simon—'

'You shut your filthy mouth,' he hissed. 'That's our son you're talking about. *She's* the one responsible for Alex's death. *She's* the shitty parent, not us.' His tone was low and filled with menace. 'Now, I'm going to work. And when seven p.m. rolls around, you'd better be cleaned up and down at City Hall wearing the dress I've left out for you. Assuming it still fits. Do *not* embarrass me, Lia.' He turned and walked away, leaving her breathing heavily and unable to peel herself away from the counter, which was all but holding her up.

After Jay left, Lia stood frozen at the sink, watching her hands shake under the running water. The rage she never dared show him burst out suddenly – she grabbed the nearest cup and hurled it against the wall, then another, savouring the explosive sound of shattering porcelain. For a few precious seconds she let herself feel it all: the fury, the shame, the helplessness. Then she heard Muriel's car pulling up outside. Her cleaning lady couldn't see this. She couldn't know. Lia's fingers trembled as she gathered the broken pieces, methodically erasing the evidence of her momentary loss of control. Then from the kitchen she watched Muriel enviously through the open-plan space, as she sat in her parked car talking animatedly to someone on the phone through her Bluetooth system. Jay looked down his nose at people like Muriel. Heading towards retirement age, with grown-up children and still busting a gut just to break even. But Lia knew that, while Muriel might clean up their messes, she had joy in her life and personal freedom to wear and eat what she liked. As she stepped out of the car, Lia pulled her gaze away and hurried upstairs before Muriel had a chance to see her. She stopped outside Simon's closed bedroom door. He was at school now, but he'd been in his room for days. And she'd been listening at his door during that time, trying to bring herself to go inside. She needed to respect his privacy. That's what she told herself each time she walked away. But it was getting harder to silence the voice in her head. And the doubt that had been there even before Alex Blake's death. Her sweet little boy had become so cold and distant.

She opened Simon's bedroom door and went in, closing it quietly behind her. She was conscious of Muriel moving around downstairs now and she knew that she'd soon make her way up. She went and sat on his unmade bed and looked around. Then she inspected the bed under her and rubbed her hand across the rumpled sheet. She could see Alex sprawled exactly where Lia was sitting now. She saw Simon lying awkwardly on top of her. Lia brought her hand to her chest. She could almost feel the weight of Jay pressing down upon *her* for the first time, when she wasn't much older than Alex was. Not in a bed, but on the backseat of a car. She'd never felt the weight of a man on her before that night, and she was sure that Alex hadn't either. The difference, though, was that Lia had been looking forward to losing her virginity to Jay. She adored him, and she had her first time planned in detail. It was to involve rose petals, soft music and candles, and she planned for it to take place in a hotel room at the end of year dance. But Jay didn't want to wait that long. When she thought back to that night, she heard his voice as clear as anything, calling her a prick tease when she asked him to stop. Even now, the memory invoked pain in her lower back, where the sports bottle that had been discarded in the back of the car, dug into her. But that was nothing compared to the pain of his first thrust. She inhaled sharply and pulled herself up off the bed and back to the present.

She looked around the room again. Yesterday's clothes were strewn on the floor, his study desk was a mess, drawers were half open, and clothes spilled out over the top. His was a typical boy's room before she or Muriel got their hands on it. Lia went to his sock drawer. She started pushing the clothes back in so that the drawer would close properly. But she found herself rummaging through them instead. There was nothing in there. Just socks. She moved to the next drawer in the chest and did the same thing, with the same result.

'What are you doing?' she mumbled to herself.

But she still went and opened the drawer in his bedside locker. It was crammed with the usual stuff. Chargers, old phones and junk. She pulled the covers back on his bed and went about straightening them again. As she tucked the sheet under the mattress, she lifted it up and looked beneath. There was nothing there. Of course there wasn't. She smoothed down the bed and started picking his dirty clothes up off the floor. She felt the pockets of his jeans before putting them in the laundry basket in the corner of the room. Then she started tidying his desk, picking things up, leafing through books and straightening the surface. She was just tidying up, she told herself. She wasn't snooping. She opened the desk drawer on the left and placed some books inside. She pulled on the drawer on the right, but it was locked. Why would he lock a drawer in his homework desk? Was there even a key for this thing?

Lia pulled more forcefully on the drawer, and as she did, she got that prickly sensation up along her arms and down the back of her neck. She searched the desk, on top and underneath it, for a key, and before she could stop herself, she was rummaging through each of its other drawers, properly this time. She even felt around under the desk, thinking he might have taped the key to the bottom for some reason. She moved onto his wardrobe next and started pulling clothes out and searching through their pockets for the key.

'Mrs Higgins?' Muriel was at the door with a surprised look on her face. Lia jumped back with a start. Muriel pulled her earbuds out. She told Lia once that she liked to listen to audiobooks while she worked. The dark and twisted kind, she'd joked.

Lia caught herself. What must she look like? She took a step back from Simon's wardrobe. 'Muriel, hi.' She looked at the clothes on the floor, the clothes she'd pulled out like a woman possessed. 'I'm just cleaning up after my lazy teenager.' She smiled. 'This place is a sty. Don't you worry about doing in here. And actually, I'm about to take a shower, so you can leave our room for today as well.'

Muriel looked around, perplexed. 'Oh, are you sure? I can do the floors downstairs to give you some privacy and come back up here later, when you're done?'

Lia shook her head. 'No. That's okay. Have an easy day today, eh?' She smiled and stepped out of Simon's room, closing the door.

'Okay,' Muriel said, still looking uncertain. But when Lia didn't move, Muriel turned and went back towards the stairs. Before she headed down, she turned to Lia again. 'Are you sure you're okay, Lia?'

Lia swallowed and forced herself to smile. 'Of course.'

# TWENTY-FIVE

## JEN

'Did you go to work today?' Dale asked, when he came in and looked around the destroyed kitchen. He himself looked equally dishevelled. He hadn't showered in several days and his beard was wilder than ever.

Jen shook her head, but she didn't look at him. Her focus was on Alex's phone as she turned it over in her hands. She'd tried every code she could think of, but she hadn't been able to unlock it. Another of her failings as a mother was not insisting that she had access to the phone before handing one over to her teenage child. Apparently, *all* the mothers knew this one basic rule. But not her. She was too busy thinking about everything else. Everything other than her child's online safety.

Dale threw an envelope on the table. She glanced briefly at the word *Urgent* glaring at her through the plastic window. She pulled her eyes back to the fully charged, but locked phone.

'Jen, you have to—'

'What? What do I have to do?' she snapped. Her own phone buzzed with a message.

Dale turned and walked back out to the hall and upstairs. It was six weeks since Alex died and there were days when Jen was unable to get out of bed at all. But Dale worked. Then he went to bed. He worked, and he went to bed. He worked. That was it. He didn't ask *why* Alex had to die. He didn't wonder out loud, *What if?* He didn't ask if Jen was okay. He didn't cry with her, scream with her, lose his shit with her. Nothing. He just worked and slept and threw warning letters from the bank at her. Jen opened the unread message. It was from Anna Greene.

ANNA GREENE

Sorry I haven't come back to you before now, Jen, but I wanted to check with Holly first. Is it okay if I ring you now?

JEN BLAKE

Of course.

Jen had no idea why Anna thought she should have *come back* to her before now, but she'd somehow become the only person that Jen wanted to speak to. The phone buzzed in her hand and she answered on the first ring. 'Anna.'

'Hi, Jen. Listen, I wanted to run it by Holly before I said anything to you, but I spoke to her and she wants to take it on.'

Jen frowned. 'I'm sorry, Anna, but... who are you talking about? Holly who and take on what?'

Anna sighed. 'Christ, I'm sorry. Of course you wouldn't remember. You know I said that I might know someone who could help... you know, with finding out what might have happened?'

Jen sat up straighter. She hadn't really taken much notice of Anna when she said that. She was just glad the woman had believed her at the time. 'Oh.'

'I'll rewind. Sorry. You've heard of Holly Myer, yes?'

'As in, Holly Myer from Talk FM?'

'That's her. Well, Holly is my niece.'

Holly Myer was a researcher for a national radio station, Talk FM. More specifically, for their flagship morning show.

Over a few short years, she'd become more famous than the show's host for her investigatory skills. More stories broke on Talk FM than on any other media outlet, and it was all down to Holly Myer. 'You mean she's…'

'Paul's daughter. Yes.'

Jen placed Alex's phone on the table and gave her full attention to Anna.

'And I suppose you'll remember what Jay Higgins did to my brother, Paul.'

The memory came flooding back to Jen. 'I remember every detail of that night, Anna,' she said, surprising herself with the clarity with which it came back. 'Myself and Lia spent hours getting ready for that disco. I remember being even more excited than usual, because Jay was supposed to be away in Galway with his parents for his cousin's wedding, and I had my friend back for a night. I can't remember what I was wearing, but I remember what Lia had on.'

'Everyone remembers what Lia was wearing. Her outfit, apparently, was the reason my brother ended up in hospital.'

'Paul was a lovely guy,' Jen said. 'He came over to talk to us' – she closed her eyes, trying to remember – 'something about a comet that was due to pass over us that night.'

'He's still a lovely guy, thankfully. And still a science nerd.' Anna sounded like she was smiling.

'I remember Lia nudging me towards him. She was trying to set me up with Paul.'

'You?'

'Yeah. Then she leaned in and said, "Okay, I'll take him for a dance first. Then you."'

'I didn't know that.'

Jen nodded, with her head in her hand. 'She pulled Paul onto the dance floor, and then the music changed almost immediately to a slow song. Bryan Adams. I can remember it. And that's when Jay walked in.'

Anna was quiet for a moment.

'I'm sorry, Anna.'

'It wasn't your fault. Truth be told, it wasn't Lia's either. But after Paul was rushed to the hospital that night, my mother called the guards.'

Jen was nodding quietly, her lowered head still in her hand.

'But Lia told them that Jay left the disco early to walk her home. She told them that he wasn't even there when Paul was beaten to a pulp.'

'I know,' Jen whispered. She and Lia had their biggest falling out the day after that disco. When Lia asked Jen to back up her story, although she didn't tell Anna that. The guards hadn't been proactive enough to question Jen and all Jay's friends covered for him.

'Anyway.' Anna exhaled. 'Back to the reason I called. Holly.'

'Yes! Holly.'

'I hope you don't mind, but I told her what I know. Which is that Alex was being bullied at school, and about the fact that Simon Higgins was apparently behind it. I told her as well about how weird Simon is. I... I told her how terrified she was of water and that you don't believe for a minute that Alex, well, that she... I told her that you don't believe it was an accident.'

'And she believes it?'

'Holly is very black and white, Jen. She won't say yes or no to anything until she has all the facts.'

'But she must hate the Higginses.'

'If she does, you'd never know it. When it comes to her work, she's totally impartial. She has to be, and that's why she's as good as she is.'

Jen nodded, but a part of her hoped that in this case, Holly's family history with them would propel her towards the truth.

'Anyway, she's agreed to look into it, but you probably won't hear anything from Holly until she has something to tell you. That's the way it is with her.'

'Okay. Thank you, Anna.'

'Don't thank me yet. She might draw a blank.'

'Well, thank you anyway.'

'Call me anytime, okay?'

Anna ended the call and Jen sat there for a minute contemplating Holly Myer and wondering what she was thinking at this very moment. Her eyes were drawn again to the bright red lettering inside the windowed envelope resting on the table. She pushed back her chair and got up from the table.

Jen brought her own, and Alex's, phone with her up to Alex's room, which was where she spent most of her time now. She closed the door and sat on the bed helplessly. She'd tried all the obvious birthdays etc. She'd even Googled the dates associated with each of Alex's heroes who adorned her walls. She stared once more at the photo with creepy Simon in the background. Those kids spent so much time in Jen's house throughout their lives. Jen's thoughts turned to Willow. She sometimes glimpsed her heading off to school, her limp hair pulled into a low ponytail, dark circles under her eyes. The girl looked like she wanted to disappear into herself. As Willow walked through the estate, she'd keep glancing at the house, as if waiting for Alex to come out and join her, like she'd always done. She was a shadow of the girl she once was, and if Jen had it in her to worry about Willow, she would have.

But Simon. He'd gone in the opposite direction. The slightly chubby, awkward boy with the curly mop of hair, walked a foot taller these days. His hair was somewhat styled, and he'd adopted his father's swagger when he walked. What's more, he never gave so much as a cursory glance at the Blake house. Not anymore. Nothing to indicate that he knew them. That he'd apparently loved the girl who once lived there.

Love.

Jen looked at the photo again. But not at Simon this time. At Alex and Willow, laughing together like they always had. She brought the screen of Alex's phone back to life. When prompted, she entered the day and month of Willow Higgins' birthday. And there she was. Willow, smiling brightly up at her. Willow was Alex's screensaver. Alex had been in love. Jen hugged the phone to her chest and cried for the fact that, aside from her parents, the only love her child would ever know was the very worst kind of all. Unrequited.

# TWENTY-SIX
## JEN

JESS19

Was that really u Alex?

NEVVIENEV

Defo her! Id no dat a$$ anywhere

SMN69

I wud u mean

NIKKIV

Dats fake

ROYB

Ur fake

GAVIN

@ABlake Ur well able 2 take it!!

PENNIEG

Its fake, whoever did it is an idiot & whoever
believes it is a bigger 1

SMN69

Jealous much Greeners? Go have a puke 4
urself fat a$$

ROYB

Oh oh oh!! Greeners has entered the building!

SMN69

Hows de diet going Greeners?

*PennieG has left the chat.*

The group chat was named Class A3 – Alex's class, and ABlake was Alex Blake. This much she knew. The chat was an endless string of kids insulting each other, bullying and piling on. All deflecting attention onto others and away from themselves. Jen scanned through the chat until she came to anything mentioning Alex's name. This string was particularly jarring and as frantically as she searched, she couldn't find what they were talking about. What was fake? What was this thread about?

Jen cried out in frustration at her own ineptitude. The only social media platforms she knew her way around were Facebook and Instagram. Insofar as she knew how to scroll through them. She knew nothing about Snapchat or any other platform that the kids were on. She clicked open Alex's Snapchat, but she only seemed to have a handful of friends there and the photos made no sense for the most part. Extreme close-up selfies, random legs or arm shots, school bags, make-up purchases and some things that she couldn't make out. But nothing sinister. She went back over the WhatsApp messages again and again. Alex had several group chats going, but mostly very innocent. She had a three-way group with Willow and Simon Higgins, to which Simon contributed very little, while the girls exchanged general chat. But the most recent message between Alex and Willow was from Alex, asking if they could talk. The one before that was dated four days earlier and Willow hadn't responded to either. Had they had that talk? Was it about the posters on the walls, and why hadn't Willow replied to her? Surely her blame should have been directed at whoever put those pictures up there, and not at Alex. *Surely* she knew how painful that all would have been for her?

There was a basketball group, to which Alex contributed very little. Nor was she mentioned much, aside from a couple of queries as to why she wasn't at training. No one answered and the chat moved on. But the class group was venomous. Jen clicked on the icon beside the name PennieG. It was a cartoon figure of some sort. She opened a new chat and typed a message.

ABLAKE

Hi Pennie. It's Jen, Alex's mum. Can we talk?

Two blue ticks showed that Pennie had seen the message and her screen told Jen that she was responding.

PENNIEGREENE

Hi. I'm supposed to be asleep and mum will be in to take my phone any minute. Talk tomor?

Jen looked at the time. It was after nine and it dawned on her that she should have contacted Anna before messaging Pennie at this time of night. But she wasn't thinking about her own proper conduct. She was only thinking about Alex. She'd apologise to Anna tomorrow. Anna Greene was a better mother than Jen – going to her daughter's room and taking away her phone for the night. Why had she been so sure that her child was safe when she was alone in her room with her phone?

ABLAKE

Of course, sorry! Tomorrow please. I'll ask your mum if it's okay.

Pennie responded with a thumbs-up. A minute later she was offline. Jen stood up and went downstairs. She put on her coat and slipped Alex's phone into one pocket and her own in the other. She hadn't cared much about carrying her own phone until now. But while Holly Myer was looking into Alex's death, Jen wouldn't leave her phone out of her sight. Once again, she left the house. She'd been walking late into the night for the past few weeks. She couldn't bring herself to sleep having not tucked her child into bed. She couldn't bring herself to sit on the couch, without Alex beside her. She couldn't move around the kitchen, seeing Alex's favourite mug in the press, the yogurts she liked in the fridge, her various jackets and hoodies hanging on hooks and off the backs of chairs. The silence in their house now was too much to bear. Dale was falling apart, and Jen had, too, for a while. But that had to end. She couldn't afford to stay curled up in a ball for a moment longer. At least not until she found out what really happened to her child, and Holly's involvement gave her the energy she needed to make that happen.

Twenty minutes later, her own phone beeped with an incoming message, just as Blackrock Castle came into sight. She swiped open the message. It was from Anna Greene. Clearly she'd taken Pennie's phone to let the girl sleep. She'd done her due diligence.

ANNA GREENE

> Hi Jen. Why don't you pop over tomorrow? I'm home all day and Pennie will be here from 4.30 onwards. My kettle will be on. Pennie has a few things that she'd like to tell you.

# TWENTY-SEVEN

## JEN

Anna filled a teapot with boiling water and placed it on a coaster in the middle of the kitchen table. Jen had only ever been in Anna's house a handful of times, but she'd never sat and drank tea with the woman. It was always either to drop Pennie off, or to pick Alex up after a Lego-related carpool. Anna's was a small two-bedroomed terraced house, but it was warm and welcoming. She seemed like one of those mothers who knew exactly what to do in any crisis, and Jen imagined she probably had a full first aid kit, a light meal and a large supply of tissues and wipes in her handbag at any given time. Everything about her was calm and reassuring and Jen had the impression that she wasn't one for bullshit. Her own or other people's. That was rare these days. In Jen's world at least.

Anna poured tea into two cups and placed one in front of Jen. She sat down opposite her and clutched the hot mug in both hands. 'I won't ask how you're doing,' she said, with a warm but sad smile.

Jen lifted the corner of her mouth in appreciation. 'Thank you. I don't think I'd be able to tell you.'

Anna nodded. 'No words could describe it.'

Jen looked into her cup of milky tea. 'Anna, I'm sorry for messaging Pennie last night. I should have gone through you first.'

Anna held up her hand. 'That's alright. You've a lot to be thinking about. Pennie will be home soon, and you can have a chat with her then.' Anna looked into her cup for a few seconds as well, before tilting her head to make eye contact with Jen. 'She's doing well these days, thank God, but I never take that for granted.'

Jen looked up at her. She owed the woman that much after reading some awful, bullying messages about Pennie the night before. She wondered briefly if Anna had read them as well. She probably had, given that she paid proper attention. For the first time, Jen thought about how Anna was feeling. Jen felt a world of pain when she thought about how much her child had suffered at the hands of those bullies, and she'd been consumed with finding any clue as to how Alex ended up where she did. She hadn't considered the impact that St Brendan's was having on Anna's little family. What Pennie was going through was awful. First her father's rejection and then those assholes piling on her eating disorder.

'Pennie has battled with various eating disorders for a while now, but she's...' Anna's voice wavered, and she brought her hand to her forehead.

Jen reached across the table and took the woman's other hand in hers. Anna pulled herself together quickly and Jen guessed that she wasn't one to take sympathy from anyone, so she said nothing. Not that she had much sympathy to give. Not to anyone.

'I know how lucky I am to have my child here for me to worry about, Jen. Believe me, I do. I can't imagine what you must be feeling.'

'Is she still...'

Anna shook her head. 'She's been in recovery for a while now. She sees a therapist once a week. Twice if she's struggling, but she's doing well.'

'I'm so glad. I saw the messages,' Jen said softly.

Anna nodded. 'Kids can be very cruel. That was always the case, but at least we were able to leave it all behind at the school gate. Now it follows them home and into their bedrooms. They have no bloody escape from any of it.'

They both sat in silence for a while before Anna spoke again.

'Anyway, I don't normally bring my Pennie's struggles up in general conversation. But I just want you to know what she's dealing with. I know you need to speak with her, and I know why. I'd be doing the same thing in your situation. But please, be mindful when you speak to her. Can I ask you to do that, please?'

Jen nodded, tears pricking her eyes. When did it become so hard to be a kid? The front door opened and closed and after a brief kerfuffle in the hall, while Pennie dropped her bag and took off her coat, she came through the kitchen door. She seemed mildly surprised to see Jen sitting at the table.

'Hi, Mrs Blake,' she said with a watery smile. Then she went and gave her mother a kiss on the cheek. 'Hi, Mum.'

'Hiya, love. How'd your day go?'

'Grand,' Pennie replied, going to the sink and filling a glass of water from the tap.

'Grand,' Anna mouthed at Jen with a sceptical look on her face. But she didn't question Pennie any further. Not in front of Jen at least.

'Love, Mrs Blake would like to have a chat with you for a minute.' Anna stood up.

Pennie brought her water to the table and sat down. Jen had the impression that Anna and Pennie had already spoken about this.

'I'll give you a few minutes.' Anna left the kitchen, went into the sitting room and closed the door. Jen was surprised that she'd left them alone, but she appreciated it.

'Thanks for agreeing to see me, Pennie,' Jen said softly.

Pennie nodded, looking like she was barely holding her emotions in check.

'Are you alright?'

She shook her head. 'No. I'm so sorry about Alex, Mrs Blake.' A single tear rolled from each eye.

Jen reached out and took the girl's hand. 'I know you are, love. And call me Jen.'

Pennie used her other hand to wipe her face, nodding.

'I just... I can't understand.' Jen shook her head. Words were failing her suddenly.

'And you need to know what I know,' Pennie said, sounding wiser than her years. 'I'm not sure it'll do you any good, Mrs Blake. Everything I know is really all I've *ever* known. But it was new to Alex, I suppose.'

'What was?'

Pennie shrugged. 'Them.' She gestured towards the front door, like perhaps *they* were all standing out there, waiting for her.

'Tell me about them.'

She shook her head. 'One day you're completely invisible, the next, you're the punch line. And they're sharp.' She tapped the side of her head. 'If they get so much as a hint of your insecurities, they'll use them to destroy you.'

Hearing these words coming from Pennie caused a knot to form in Jen's stomach, and her temper to rise silently. 'And that's what happened with Alex?'

Pennie nodded.

'I saw some messages.'

Pennie dropped her eyes.

'Someone was asking if it was really Alex. What were they talking about?'

Pennie closed her eyes. 'I don't think you'll want to hear this.'

'I do, Pennie. I want to hear it.'

Pennie took a deep shaky breath and exhaled loudly. 'I don't know how they knew, because Alex hadn't come out yet as far as I was aware. But they must have figured it out. Then they decided that, because she was gay, then *of course* she must fancy Willow Higgins.' She shook her head in annoyance. 'Probably just because they spent so much time together. So whether Alex actually liked Willow or not, I don't know. But that doesn't matter to them. Alex is gay and Willow's a girl, and therefore Alex couldn't *possibly* see her as just a friend.' Pennie rolled her eyes at the ridiculousness of it.

Jen's chest ached for her child. And knowing that she couldn't go to her, and hug away her pain, was enough to break her. But she had to keep it together now. 'What did they do?' she asked instead.

Pennie shook her head. 'They got a picture of a' – she glanced towards the still-closed sitting room door – 'a naked model. You know... like, posing a bit provocatively.'

Jen closed her eyes.

'They blew it up really big, like, poster size, and they put Alex's head on it. They stuck it all across the entire bank of lockers one day. They had all these speech bubbles coming out of her mouth, about Willow.' Her voice was fading away. 'Then of course it was photographed and passed around online. All that kinda stuff. Some of the teachers got it taken down, but not before everyone saw it.'

Jen's bottom lip trembled, and she looked into her lap. 'Is that why Alex and Willow fell out?'

Pennie shrugged. 'I don't know. Willow Higgins doesn't talk to me. She never did, unless she had to.'

'But Alex did?'

'Yeah, she did. But she wouldn't have confided in me about Willow. They were best friends. Alex was only friends with me because of Lego club. But she hadn't been going to that.'

'Alex always spoke highly of you, Pennie,' she reassured the girl as best she could. And it was the truth. Alex liked her. Jen just didn't think they had a lot in common, outside of their interest in Lego.

'She was always nice to me,' Pennie confirmed.

If Jen could think about something other than her little girl, she would have felt immensely sorry for Pennie Greene. Like her mother, she was a sweet and kind person, who was overlooked by most.

'Who did it?' she asked instead.

Pennie shook her head. 'I don't know for sure.'

'Alex always said how clever you are, Pennie.' Her voice caught in her throat. 'So I'm guessing you have a theory.'

'Like I said, one day you're invisible, the next you're the butt of the joke. So when someone else was providing their entertainment, they stopped seeing me again. But that didn't mean that I stopped seeing them.'

Jen felt a glimmer of hope. 'And what did you see?'

'Nothing. But I heard something.'

Jen said nothing but continued to watch the girl as she battled with her emotions. Her own breathing sounded loud and ragged.

'Simon Higgins.'

'What about him?'

'At first, I didn't take any notice. Simon, Alex and Willow were a threesome. You rarely saw one without the other two. He and Alex were just talking, round the back of the gym one day. He shouldn't have been there. The class had gone swimming and Alex usually goes to the courts during class swim, but Simon should have been at the pool. I wasn't feeling well, so I was on my way home. But I saw them. Alex looked annoyed to see him there and she tried to move around him, but then Simon kind of shoved her against the wall and started raising his voice at her.'

'Saying what?' Jen's rage slowly burned.

'I couldn't hear at first. I was back by the trees. But I moved closer when I saw him shoving her. I heard him calling her a...' She lowered her eyes again.

'It's okay, Pennie. Just say it.'

'He called her a prick tease. He said she'd been leading him on all his life and who did she think she was?'

Jen's breathing became heavier.

'Alex pushed him back, but then he kind of pinned her to the wall. I... I heard him telling her that she'd be sorry.'

'She'd be sorry? He said that?'

Pennie nodded as Anna came back into the room.

'Everything okay?' she asked.

Pennie gave her a weak smile and nodded. Anna squeezed the girl's shoulders and went to where the kettle was, beside the cooker. 'Will I make a fresh pot, Jen?'

Jen shook her head. 'No, thank you, Anna.' She looked to Pennie again. 'Can I ask you one more thing, Pennie?'

'Sure.'

'Do you think Simon Higgins could have hurt Alex?'

Anna turned to face them, worry etched on her face.

Pennie shrugged, but it was Anna who answered. 'That boy thinks he has everyone fooled.'

'What do you mean?'

'He's always been *poor Simon*, the boy with no real friends. The quiet, shy, unassuming little Simon.' Her words were laced with venom. 'But I think that's nothing more than an act.'

'Why do you say that?' Jen agreed wholeheartedly, but she wanted to hear someone else say the words.

'Tell her, Pen.'

Jen looked to Pennie who was staring at her hands.

'I don't know how to explain it really. It's just the way he looks at people sometimes. Or he has this' – she waved her hand over her face – 'kind of a grin, that makes you think he's laughing at you. Or that he knows something that you don't want him to know.' She frowned then and shook her head again. 'That doesn't make sense, I know. It means nothing when you say it out loud. But he has a way of making you feel goose bumps on your skin, without so much as opening his mouth to you.'

'He gives Pennie the creeps. And not many people can do that,' Anna added as a matter of fact.

'He does,' Pennie agreed. 'And I know he gives other girls the creeps, too. As far as I know, Darina Hayes was putting pressure on Willow to cut him off. They didn't want him hanging around with them.'

'And did she?'

'Willow?' Pennie shrugged. 'She doesn't really hang around with Darina and Lucy anymore, so I'm guessing not.'

'Would you like to stay for dinner, Jen?' Anna asked, by way of getting Jen to wrap things up and leave.

She took the hint and shook her head. 'Thank you, Pennie.' She stood up. 'And you, too, Anna. I really appreciate you speaking with me.'

She pulled her coat off the back of the chair and walked out to the hall. Before opening the front door, she turned back to Pennie. 'Alex was right about you, Pennie. You're clever. Too clever for *them*.' She nodded towards the door, like Pennie had done earlier. 'In time, you'll fly higher than all of them put together. So don't let them stop you.'

Anna came and squeezed her arm as she opened the door.

'Listen, before you go, Holly wanted to know if she could access Alex's social media?'

'If she knows how, she can access anything she likes.'

'Oh, Holly knows how, alright.'

The women exchanged a teary half smile and then Jen left, feeling more sure than she had in years. Despite what people thought, including Dale, Jen was certain now that Alex hadn't taken her own life. Someone had taken it from her. And it was up to Jen, with the help of Holly Myer, to make them pay.

# TWENTY-EIGHT

## JEN

'I hear what you're saying,' said the Garda who'd introduced himself as Shane Walsh when he first took her to the quiet interview room, more than half an hour earlier. 'Bullying is a massive problem and while they are making moves in the right direction around cyber bullying etcetera, there's still a long way to go. We're up against it the whole time here and more often than not, our hands are tied. So, believe me when I say, Mrs Blake, that you're preaching to the choir.'

He'd been very kind to Jen since she arrived at the station, straight from Anna's house. But his kindness wasn't what she needed, and she could tell that she was losing him. He'd listened to her story and her theories, which, when spoken out loud, sounded paranoid even to her. He'd given her all the condolences he could, he'd insisted on making her a cup of tea and he'd told her in all the roundabout ways he could come up with, that Alex's death was a *tragic incident*. He'd referred to it as just that, twice. He didn't really believe that anyone else could be held accountable for Alex's death, but he felt too sorry for Jen to tell her that. Without saying it in so many words, however, he'd made it as clear as anyone could.

There was another officer with them, whose name Jen couldn't remember. He'd gone to check on *the details* twenty minutes earlier, and when he returned at that moment, Garda Walsh looked very pleased to see him. He took a seat opposite Jen and gave her another unhelpfully sad smile.

'So I've been through the coroner's report, Mrs Blake.' He held up a piece of paper. 'I gave their office a call as well, just to clarify things. There's no one answering there now, so I left a message for someone to call us back tomorrow.' His voice was low and solemn. 'Alex's cause of death is recorded as drowning, as you know. It seems she had no defensive wounds on her body and there were no signs that she might have been assaulted. Now, the coroner can only tell us what she sees on the body. That's to say, she wasn't there at the time your daughter went into that river. None of us were, unfortunately. But you say that Simon Higgins and your daughter had been friends for a long time and that he'd recently started bullying her because she rebuffed him. Is that right?'

She'd already told them this. She'd told them everything. 'Yes. Alex is dead because of him,' she replied, feeling the panic rising in her voice.

He nodded, still holding a piece of paper in both hands. 'Okay. So, do you really think she would have gone willingly to that river *with* him, knowing that he'd instigated the bullying campaign against her?'

'No, but...' She brought her hands to her temples.

'It's just that there's no evidence to indicate that Alex was handled with any kind of force...'

'His father has a history of violence and his mother, Lia, has a history of lying to cover it up,' she snapped. 'There's something very wrong with Simon Higgins.' She slapped the table with both hands. 'He did this!'

The officers both nodded. They'd already warned her about slandering Jay Higgins' name. He didn't have a criminal record, and Jen couldn't offer any kind of proof to go with her allegations. Both thanks to Lia.

She'd lost them completely now. She could tell by the way they looked at her. 'You don't think I have a leg to stand on, do you?' Her eyes filled up, but she roughly wiped them away before she cried. She was *not* the hysterical mother. And she was *not* imagining any of this.

The other one glanced at Shane, who took his cue. 'Jen.' He leaned across the table, looking like he was about to mansplain the situation to her. 'I believe every word you're saying. I believe that Alex was bullied, and I believe that what you're telling me about the Higgins boy may very well be the case. I've come across plenty of men like the kind you describe Jay Higgins to be.' He sat back then and held his hands out, palms up – *nothing we can do about that.* He paused to look at her, then he sat forward again, palms down and fingers splayed on the table.

'Then why won't you—'

'Because we have to tread very carefully here. It's extremely hard to prove that one person drove another person to suicide, because you essentially have to be able to prove what was happening in the victim's head at the time of the incident. And while all the stuff that went up online is vile and awful, none of it contains any threat of violence.' He tapped his finger on the table, making his main point. *It was too hard.* 'Now, if Alex had left a note implicating someone, or if you were able to capture any social media posts or messages between them – anything that might help, then maybe—'

'I'm not saying he *drove* her to kill herself,' Jen cried. 'I'm saying, she *didn't* kill herself.'

'But she *did* send a text message to Mrs Higgins, isn't that right?' the other one asked. 'Look, the last thing any of us want to do, is to add to your pain, Mrs Blake. But I'm sure you can see how that message to Lia Higgins could be perceived as a suicide note.'

They glanced at each other again. They wanted her gone now, but Garda Walsh was too nice to say so. The other one was not so delicate in his approach.

'Simon must have sent that from Alex's phone. It was found down by the quays,' she insisted. She could feel her legs start to shake. *They think I'm crazy.*

'Look, how about we go and speak with Simon Higgins tomorrow?' Garda Walsh offered at last in a conciliatory tone. 'We'll see what he can tell us.'

Jen nodded, her face still buried in her hands, though she didn't believe they would give him the grilling he deserved. *If they went to see him at all.*

As she walked out of the bustling station minutes later, a woman jogged confidently up the steps, heading in. She wore black leather trousers with Doc Martens and a red biker-style jacket. She glanced up and Jen recognised her instantly. Her picture had been on the side of a bus last summer after she'd won some award for Talk FM. Their eye contact was fleeting and the other woman nodded hello, but if Holly Myer recognised Jen, she didn't stop to chat. Instead, she let herself into the station with the ease of someone who'd done it a hundred times before, while Jen stood rooted to the spot watching her go.

# TWENTY-NINE

## LIA

Lia watched as Kevin, the 'man with a van', cleared the bed, lockers and the smashed-up study desk out of her son's room. Lia had the house to herself all morning, but she'd soon have to come up with a way to explain her sudden desire to upgrade Simon's sleeping quarters, which had only been redecorated last year. She'd probably lose access to their bank accounts again for a while, but she didn't care. Until such time as his new furniture arrived, which should be later that afternoon, all his stuff was piled neatly on the floor. Except for what she'd pulled from the locked drawer. There probably was a key for it, but clearly Simon didn't want her, or anyone else, to find it. A hammer worked just as well, but she'd lined up the replacement furniture and someone to remove the old stuff, before she took to smashing her way into that drawer. Usually, Jay was happy enough for her to spend money upgrading their home. But he could not know how or why this upgrade had come about. What she'd found in that desk made her feel sick, but Jay's response would make it so much worse. For her. Not for Simon. Jay would justify this perfectly for Simon and cement the path that her son was on. But Lia would be punished for the fact that it looked bad in the wake of Alex Blake's death.

There were dozens of photographs of Alex in there, which mightn't have been quite so alarming had his sister Willow not been crudely cut out of so many. Simon had cut himself out of some as well, but not from any in which he was standing close to, or had physical contact with, Alex. But to take things a step further towards incrimination, Alex's face had been scrawled out, or punched through, in every single photo. Lia had looked through all of them, several times, while she tried to make sense of what she was seeing. She tried to figure out how this damage could have occurred to these photographs. But she wasn't naive enough to believe any of the farfetched explanations her imagination threw at her. What she was looking at was her son's obsession. And the many scratched-out faces of a dead girl. Of course, Simon didn't kill her. But the likes of this would be enough to cast a lifetime of suspicion upon him.

'What the...' Simon appeared at the open front door with his school bag on his back. He watched the man load up his van with broken bits of furniture, which must have looked familiar to him, even in the state they were in. He glanced at Lia, who stood with her arms folded, looking back at him. He dropped his bag and ran up the stairs.

'What did you do?' he shouted, his voice cracked with shock.

Lia blanched and pins and needles pricked her entire body. Simon had never raised his voice to her.

'What did you do to my room?'

'It needed updating.' She picked up her phone as if checking something important, just to avoid looking at him as he glared down at her from the top step. 'Ah, your new bed is nearly here. Any minute.'

'What did you do with all my stuff?' His words were pushed

out through gritted teeth, as he stomped purposefully back downstairs.

She turned to face him now, seeing the panic on his face behind the thin veil of anger. 'You'll see it's all piled neatly on the floor up there. All awaiting their new homes.' She picked up her phone again and looked at it. 'I burned any junk you'd accumulated.'

He was silent now, and she studied his face carefully. He didn't know what to say. He was trying to gauge how much she thought she knew. What she might have seen. Whether or not she was clever enough to understand it. She blinked slowly and looked away from him.

Simon went out to the garden and stood in front of the fire pit. She watched him, trying to make out anything familiar, but there was nothing there. It was all gone up in smoke. Every last physical shred of his obsession.

'I'm making beef Bourguignon,' she said, taking a large bowl out of the fridge as Simon came wordlessly back into the kitchen. Large enough to hold two bottles of Burgundy, three bay leaves, a bunch of thyme and of course, the diced steak.

He looked at her for a moment, his face completely impassive now. Her boy was gone. 'From here on, I'd like you to stay out of my room,' he said, in a low voice.

Lia smiled and nodded. 'No problem. You'll need to keep it clean and tidy by yourself then.' She turned to look at him, still smiling. 'No more collecting rubbish and old, torn or damaged things.'

He gave her one last look, narrowing his eyes at her then turned and walked through the hall and out the front door, slamming it after himself.

# THIRTY

## JEN

Jen stood in the car park of St Brendan's at close to home time. It hurt so much to be there, knowing that, at any minute, Alex's friends were going to come bursting through the doors, all relishing their freedom, and she wouldn't be among them. She'd been waiting there for some time, chewing on what was left of her thumbnail. Finally, the first group of students came out and more emerged in their droves behind them. Jen straightened up and craned her neck to see. She was waiting for Willow Higgins.

In a second wave of kids, she saw Willow's perfect and fickle friends, Darina and Lucy. They were laughing and talking animatedly as if they hadn't a care in the world, not an ounce of grief apparent on either of their faces. Jen's stomach balled into a fist, thinking about how easily the rest of the world would go on without Alex. Her light, as bright as it was, had been extinguished. One of them spotted Jen standing there and nudged the other. Their laughter died and they fell into a hushed conversation. But they continued on their way, avoiding her completely. Jen craned her neck again, looking for Willow in the crowd. Eventually she saw her, walking alone out the doors and down the steps. The girl looked miserable. And exhausted. Jen waited until she came a little closer.

'Willow?' she called as gently as she could, but Willow didn't respond. 'Willow?' she called again.

The girl blinked and looked up. 'Oh, Jen. Hi,' she said. Immediately her bottom lip started to quiver, and she hurried over to hug Jen. The girl cried ferociously into Jen's shoulder.

Jen squeezed her eyes shut and hugged her back. *Thank you, Willow*, she thought, but she didn't say it. She could feel the girl's shoulder blades protruding through her uniform. Willow had always been athletically slender. But now she felt like a bag of bones, and when Jen stroked Willow's hair, long oily strands came away in her hand.

'I miss her so much,' Willow cried and Jen could feel her tears soaking through her shirt.

'I miss her, too. So much.'

They stood there like that for a few long minutes, both oblivious to the looks they were getting from groups of kids who were still hanging around. No doubt, this would become a dramatic schoolyard tale to be told and retold over the days to come. The grieving mother and the best friend, thrown together in a dramatic embrace.

'Willow, I need to talk to you,' Jen said softly, as she pulled back to arm's length.

'I know.' Willow turned and walked back towards the steps. She sat down heavily, as if her legs had given up. Jen followed and sat beside her. Willow sat there for a while, picking at some dry skin on the top of her finger and perhaps gathering her thoughts.

'What happened, Willow?' Jen asked, sensing that Willow didn't quite know where to start.

Willow shrugged. 'This place happened. It's like everything you say and everything you do is judged publicly here. And I mean everything. If you say good morning, without sounding ironic, you're a posh twat. If you wear the wrong top or speak to the wrong person or have the wrong opinion, or God forbid you make any kind of mistake!' She sounded a little hysterical now. 'You're torn apart in front of everyone. You can become a meme in a matter of seconds in this place.'

Jen rubbed her temples. Hadn't school always been a bit like that, minus the memes?

'You know once something gets posted to the internet about you, it's there, like, forever! Your phone buzzes all night long and it's all this shit, all the time! Your whole life becomes about being on the right side of it all. Nothing else matters.'

'The right side of... you mean, the right side of bullying?'

'Without becoming a bully yourself, yes.'

'And how do you do that?'

She cried softly again. 'By distancing yourself from anything that makes you a target.'

'And was Alex making you a target? Is that why you stopped hanging out with her?'

Willow lowered her head onto her knees and her whole body shook. It took everything Jen had to rub the girl's back. To offer consolation to her for turning her back on Alex when she needed her the most. But she knew that she'd get further with honey than with vinegar.

'It's okay, Willow. You can tell me,' she said instead.

'Darina is one of those people who can't do anything wrong. Do you know what I mean?'

Yes, she did. But she just nodded rather than reminding Willow who her mother was.

'If you're friends with her, then you're pretty much safe. Same with Lucy really, but that's by default. She and Darina have been friends since they were kids.'

'And did they tell you to back off from Alex?'

'They...' She glanced hesitantly at Jen and stopped.

'Willow, whatever you need to say, you can say it. Please. She's gone, and I just need to understand why.'

Willow gave a small nod and took a deep shaky breath. 'I just wish she'd told me, so I could have been prepared for...' She dropped her head again.

'Prepared for what?'

It took her a minute and some more back rubbing, before Willow lifted her head and continued. 'Darina heard that Alex had a crush on me. Then she started saying things like, you know, that Alex was only friends with me so she could perv on me during sleepovers...' She lowered her eyes, her cheeks flushing red. 'All that stupid kind of stuff.'

'If you knew it was stupid stuff, then why...'

'Because! When the whole school is jeering you about it, it's not so easy to laugh it off!' she cried, her face soaked with tears now.

'Were they jeering you, or Alex?' Jen asked more quietly.

Willow's shoulders shook again, and she brought her hands to her face. 'Alex,' she whispered. 'But my face was all over the place, too!' she added, with a hint of petulance.

Jen wanted to shake her. She wanted to shake the lot of them. More than that, she wanted to strike a match and burn this school to the ground, with all of them inside. 'I get it,' she said softly instead. 'I went to this school, too. I know how it goes.'

Willow looked at her more hopefully now. Like maybe Jen had her back.

'Willow. I need to ask you something.'

She nodded and wiped her eyes.

'I've been speaking to a few people since... well, you know. I'm trying so hard to understand this. To make some sense of it all. But, Willow, Simon's name has come up a lot.'

In truth, the only people who'd mentioned Simon were Anna and Pennie Greene, who also had good reason to dislike that family. And giving Pennie Greene the creeps wasn't a crime. But Jen's gut was crying out to her that he had something to do with Alex's death. That she'd missed something that had been right under her nose all these years.

Willow frowned and shook her head. 'Oh, I wouldn't be listening to that. That's just *them* adding arms and legs onto the sleepover stories.'

'What makes you so sure of that?' Jen kept her expression neutral. Like she'd heard this before.

'Because Alex did not sleep with my brother,' she said more firmly now, and Jen saw a hint of her mother's defiance in her suddenly.

'So why was he saying that she had?' She hazarded a guess, her stomach turning at the thought.

'He wouldn't have. Haven't you been listening? They take any scrap and use it against you. Obviously, they took the fact that Alex and Simon were friends and turned it into something else. Just like they did with Alex and me.'

Jen shook her head. 'But Simon...'

Willow stood up abruptly. 'My brother never said or did anything to hurt Alex. Anyone who says otherwise is lying. Now I need to get home. My mother will be wondering where I am.'

'Jen?' a male voice said softly, as Willow walked off.

Jen glanced back to see Larry Henderson coming down the steps towards her. He'd been a student at St Brendan's around the same time as Jen and Lia. Now he was the principal of the place. Jen closed her eyes and exhaled. She didn't want to see him now. His weak letters and unanswered phone calls since Alex's death piled high, but his show of strength against school bullies was paltry. He came and sat on the step close by, but not too near her.

'How are you, Jen?'

'What are you doing about this, Larry?' she asked, turning to look at him.

'The net is closing,' he said, sounding uncertain, if not nervous.

'Around who?'

'Well' – his head bobbed and his hands gestured, while he tried to come up with a politician's response, perhaps regretting the decision to come over to her – 'as you know, Jen, we've had several images taken down from various platforms. But kids can be quite tight-lipped when it comes to...'

'Their lips wouldn't be long loosening if you started doling out expulsions.'

He laughed uncomfortably. 'Well now, I mean, I can't just go expelling kids without hard evidence, but...'

'Jay Higgins makes some decent contributions to this school, doesn't he?'

Larry frowned and looked at his bent knees. 'Well, that's neither...'

'So is that the reason why you haven't taken a very close look at Simon Higgins?' She turned her whole body towards him then and made him look at her. 'Because, Larry, Simon Higgins doesn't have the kind of friends who will cover for him.' She stood up then. 'You're the principal of this school. *You're* the example to these kids. So, if you don't have the balls to ask the right questions, of the right people, then not only are you a spineless piece of shit, but you're complicit in my daughter's death. Stop kissing Higgins' ass for a minute and do your job.' Jen walked away from him, back to her car.

'Simon Higgins has been suspended,' he said.

Jen turned to look at him. He was standing now, too.

'That's what I was coming to tell you.'

'Suspended. Not expelled?'

'For now.' Larry nodded.

Something stirred in Jen then. Maybe it was hope, or

perhaps justification. Or maybe it was the fear that a couple of weeks off school would be the only punishment doled out for the loss of her child. She turned and watched Willow walking away in the distance. Whatever her reasons for not saying anything about Simon, Jen could see the Higginses' ranks firmly closing behind her.

# THIRTY-ONE

## JEN

'This is getting to be too much, Jen.'

These were the first words out of Dale's mouth when he arrived home from work that evening to find Jen, sitting at the cluttered kitchen table. They were also the first words he'd spoken to her for days and she didn't respond to them. Instead, she continued to scroll slowly through the images on her phone dating back to when Alex was about four years old. She was smiling in almost all of them. A big, wide, *nothing can stop me* smile.

'Jen? Did you hear me?'

'She wouldn't have gone to the river,' she said, more to herself, but Dale took it as his response and he heaved out a sigh.

'But she did,' he half whispered.

'Simon's been suspended from school.'

'Good.'

'Good? Is that all you can say?'

'Yes, good. He's a little prick who taunted my child. He deserves it.'

She turned in her chair to face him, her rage building again.

'He deserves a hell of a lot more than a few weeks off school, Dale.'

'He does, Jen. But I can't bring myself to give a flying fuck about Simon Higgins right now. None of that will bring *our* child back.'

'But he...!'

'She sent a suicide note.' His voice cracked and he looked like he wanted to lie down and curl up in a ball.

Jen felt her entire body sag. Their child was gone, and her husband was broken. They both were, and the void between them now seemed impossibly wide. 'You were there when she fell in that pool, Dale,' she couldn't help but add, her voice strangled. 'You remember the fear? Remember how much she panicked every time we tried to take her back to the water for the rest of that holiday? She hasn't been in a swimming pool since.'

'I know that, but...'

'And she hated the sea just as much. We had to drag her down to the shore for a paddle on any beach day we ever had, after Portugal.'

'You're not thinking, Jen,' he said, sounding exhausted.

'No, *you're* not. If you wanted to die, wouldn't you want to go as easily as you could? You would not want your last moments to be spent in absolute terror!'

'Well, you wouldn't be thinking about that, would you?'

Jen frowned at him. And he had the nerve to say that *she* wasn't thinking? 'Of course you would. It would literally be the one thing you'd think about.'

'How would you rather she did it?' His voice broke on the words, and Jen saw the tears he'd been holding back for days finally spill over.

The sight of his pain cracked something inside her. She wanted to go to him, to share this impossible weight between them. But his determination to accept their daughter's death as suicide felt like another betrayal.

'She didn't do it, Dale,' she whispered, her throat tight. 'How can you not feel it, too? How can you not know that our child would never...?' Her voice gave out completely.

'Why do you find it so easy to believe that she'd do this?' she whispered after a few laboured breaths.

Dale opened and slammed the fridge door, then turned to her again. 'You think I want this to be true? Do you think my heart isn't shattered into a million pieces?' His voice cracked. 'She sent a fucking note!'

Jen breathed heavily, calming herself. She lowered her voice and repeated with conviction, 'Alex did not jump into a fast-flowing, black, murky river. She'd jump off a cliff before she'd do that. Somewhere inside you, you must know that, too, Dale. You must.'

He said nothing as they stood there looking at each other, both breathing unsteadily. Both in their own private hell. 'We're about to lose our home,' Dale said, almost in a whisper now.

Jen blinked and turned away from him. 'Without our daughter, we don't have a home.'

Dale rubbed his face with both hands. 'Fine. I'll just continue to carry that one by myself then.' He walked out of the kitchen and went upstairs. Uber Eats would arrive soon carrying a meal for one, which Dale would eat in bed, and their new cycle would continue. But Jen wasn't giving up. She'd wasted too much time worrying about the faceless bullies at the bank while Alex was alive. Their constant threatening reminders about their mortgage arrears and the need for her and Dale to work more and more hours. They stole her away from her daughter while she was alive. They would not steal her attention away from her now.

Just then, Alex's phone vibrated with a message.

SMN69

Hey, u there?

Jen stared at it for a minute. Smn69 was Simon Higgins. Why was he messaging Alex's phone? Jen's fingers hovered over the keys for a while, before she responded.

ABLAKE

Hey Simon. It's Jen.

For the next few minutes the screen showed that Simon. was typing, then he wasn't. Then he was again, and then he wasn't. Jen's insides burned in anticipation of his response, until eventually, three torturous minutes later, it came.

SMN69

Sorry. Don't no y im msging. I no shes not there.

Jen pounced on the keys this time.

ABLAKE

That's ok. None of us knows what to do.

*You sick fuck*, she wanted to add, but she also wanted to keep him talking.

SMN69

Is nice 2 no im not the only 1

Jen frowned. From anyone else, she would have read that as a boy who wanted to know he wasn't alone in his grief. But Jen saw malice in Simon's every gesture.

ABLAKE

How could you be? We lost our beautiful daughter.

Nothing.

Four minutes passed before *Smn69 is typing* showed at the top of her screen. He stopped and started a few more times before:

**SMN69**

I don't know wat she told u but...

Jen sat up straight and stared at the phone, waiting for the rest. But what? Three excruciating minutes and she couldn't wait anymore.

**ABLAKE**

But what??

*Smn69 is offline.*
'No! Come back, you bastard!'

**ABLAKE**

But what Simon?

*Smn69 is online. Smn69 is typing.*
Jen shook the phone in her hand for all the minutes it took for him to type, delete, type, delete, type and delete until she was sure that he was doing it deliberately. Was he playing with her? Then finally:

**SMN69**

But, it was all good. Night Mrs B

*Smn69 is offline.*

# THIRTY-TWO

## JEN

Early the next morning, Jen found herself on Lia Higgins' doorstep. She didn't know why she was there, or what she planned to say when Lia opened the door. But as the morning sun rose after another sleepless night, it brought with it a fresh wave of helplessness. The only thing she knew for sure was that Alex didn't kill herself. She also knew that there were more answers at the Higginses' house than at her own. But for some reason, she wasn't prepared for Jay when it was he who answered the door.

'Jen.' He sounded exasperated, but still looked over her shoulder to see who might be watching.

'Where's Simon?' she asked, feeling a little unsure suddenly. Why was she here again?

Jay frowned. 'Simon? He's getting ready for school, Jen. Can I help you with something?'

Jen stood limply before him and laughed a humourless laugh. 'School? Haven't you heard? He's been suspended from school.' Her false bravado didn't last. *Had* he been suspended? Why would *she* know that, but his parents wouldn't?

A look of uncertainty passed very briefly over Jay's face, and it gave Jen a little more strength suddenly, He recovered himself almost instantly, but it was too late. 'Go home, Jen.'

'You can let me in, or we can do this on your doorstep,' Jen replied, her voice building with each word.

Jay's smile grew strained and his eyes bored into hers. But he stepped aside and opened the door wide for her. He waved to the postman and the woman next door, who'd come out to greet him. Both had paused their morning routine to watch.

'Jen, I know you're grieving so I'm going to forgive your hysterical outburst, but...'

'Go fuck yourself. I don't want your forgiveness. I want to speak to your son.'

Simon came to the top of the stairs. He was sneaking a peek down at her, but Jen saw him.

'Come on down, Simon.' She craned her neck to see him.

'Go back to your room, Simon,' Jay commanded, without taking his eyes off Jen.

'Jen?' Lia came jogging down the stairs, looking worriedly at the stand-off in the hall. She placed her hand on Jay's elbow and glanced at him. He blinked and then went into the sitting room and sat down. Lia nodded for Jen to follow her to the kitchen.

Lia closed the kitchen door, then went and closed the double doors leading to the sitting room, cocooning them inside, away from Jay and everyone else.

'Jen, I... I'm sorry. I've wanted to come and see you. To...'

'Why doesn't Jay know that Simon's been suspended from school?' she asked quizzically. Under normal circumstances, Jen would never have given Jay anything over Lia. They were no longer friends, but she still wouldn't give the man any more power than she believed he already had over her.

Lia froze, her features blank first, then something else. Fearful? Her eyes flitted towards the hall then back to Jen. She laughed nervously. 'Suspended? Why would Simon be suspended? You don't think the school would have informed us of something like that?'

Jen's own uncertainty flared again. Lia was right. How could he have been suspended without his parents knowing? Had spineless Larry Henderson just said that to appease her?

'I want to talk to Simon,' she said, moving on. But Principal Henderson was on her immediate to-do list.

Lia nodded, still shaken from the confidence Jen had when she spoke of Simon's suspension. 'I know. And I get it, Jen. I do. And you can speak to him. Of course you can. But I need you to calm down a little bit before you do.'

'Ever the politician's wife.' Jen sneered. 'So you want me to calm down?'

Lia closed her eyes and rubbed her forehead. 'I'm sorry. *Calm down* must be the most triggering phrase in the English language. It certainly sends me off the deep end.' She half smiled. Jen did not. Lia gestured towards the high stools at the kitchen island and, grudgingly, Jen did sit down. Lia was right. She did need to calm down. She wasn't going to get far by acting erratically, so she needed to think before she spoke. It seemed it was impossible to grieve and still be taken seriously, so she'd already blown it with the Gardaí. If Jen wanted to get anywhere, then she had to get a handle on herself.

'I'm sorry,' she forced herself to say. 'I know I *do* sound hysterical...'

'You're not hysterical,' Lia quickly responded, looking towards the closed doors to the sitting room. 'You've lost your child.' She lowered her voice dramatically. 'You're angry and you have every right to be. So don't listen to him.'

Jen was taken aback. Lia had never said anything to contradict Jay in her life. This was the first time she'd given any sign that she and Jay weren't completely and utterly on the same page. But her voice was so low that there was no way he could have heard it. Was she afraid of him? Jen suspected that, at times, she was.

There was silence in the seconds that followed, and Jen frowned. It was too silent. She stood up and went to the sitting room doors. She opened one and Jay was gone. Jen looked back at Lia, as she walked through to the sitting room window, just in time to see Jay's silent electric Lexus pulling out of the estate and onto the main road.

'Fuck you, Lia,' Jen hissed, marching towards the stairs and taking them two at a time to the top. 'Simon?' she called.

'Jen?' Lia called, hurrying up behind her.

'Is that why you brought me into the kitchen and closed the doors? So they could all leave without me seeing them?' She opened the door to Simon's room.

Their homes had the same layout, except the Higginses' had a costly extension at the back. So their kitchen was far bigger and brighter, and they had an extra bedroom upstairs. Simon's room smelled of *new*. New wardrobes, study desk and a fresh-looking sleigh bed. Sickeningly clean and tidy for a teenage boy's room.

'Jay had to get to work, Jen? He's just dropping the kids off at school on the way. Lia said, looking at her watch, probably knowing that they'd be at least a half hour early for school.

Jen opened the other doors, but of course, Willow and Simon were both gone. The door to the extra bedroom was open. There was a daybed against one wall that looked like it had been slept in. There was also a treadmill, a cross-trainer, a spin-bike, a pull-up bar, a rack of dumb-bells and lots of resistance bands hanging on a short rail. There was a wall of mirrors facing them. Lia moved past her and pulled the door closed.

'Please, Jen. Come downstairs.'

Jen gave her a look of disgust, then turned and walked slowly down.

'I'm sorry. I didn't know he was going to do that,' Lia said, when they reached the kitchen again. 'I didn't expect them to leave for a little while yet.'

'Sure you did,' Jen muttered.

Lia glanced at her and turned towards the coffee machine. She got a latte going for Jen, whether or not she would stay to drink it. 'You and I fighting about Jay. Feels like old times,' she said dryly.

'And you continue to do his bidding for him,' Jen retorted. 'It certainly does.'

'Jen, I really didn't know that he was going to do that. That's not why I brought you into the kitchen. I'm sorry if you don't believe that.'

Jen stared at the woman's back. She was wearing workout clothes and looked like she'd just rolled out of bed. Very unlike how Lia Higgins normally presented herself to the world. As she moved, Jen could see her sharp shoulder blades protruding through her T-shirt and the bumps of her long spine jutting out. She wasn't radiating health and beauty now. Not close up. Close up, she was painfully thin, her unwashed hair was limp, and she had dark circles under her eyes. Had she just rolled out of that day bed in the gym room upstairs? Did she work out round the clock to keep her husband happy? Jen always remembered the kind of remarks Jay made about women's bodies, and his constant praise for Lia's figure when they first met. It became an obsession for Lia before long. Maintaining a *perfect* figure for her *perfect* boyfriend. But Jen had left that argument behind years ago.

'Why won't Jay let me talk to Simon?' she asked, making an extra effort to keep her cool, as the word *hysterical* floated around inside her head.

'He will.' Lia placed a latte, served in an actual latte glass, in front of her.

Jen rolled her eyes at the perfection of it. 'And if he doesn't?'

'Then I will. When Jay isn't here.'

'Are you afraid of him?' she found herself asking. Having been there at the start of their relationship and seeing all the red flags he'd waved in front of her face, Jen sometimes wondered if she was the only one who knew what kind of man Jay Higgins really was. Then again, Lia was estranged from her whole family, so she guessed maybe they knew, too, but were powerless to do anything about it.

Lia smiled and shook her head. 'Of course I'm not afraid of him. He's my husband, Jen.'

'So?'

Lia's smile slipped, but she pulled it back and shook her head again. 'Why are we talking about Jay when...?' Her voice faded away.

'Well, it was you who brought up old times. I still see the same man that I saw back then. Scarier even. He's managed to fool so many people and I still wonder how you, my most intelligent friend, failed to see it.' She shouldn't be opening this old wound now, but she couldn't stop herself. She had scattered control over her emotions these days and she cared little for the words that came out of her mouth, despite knowing that she needed to. 'But can you see it now? The parallels, I mean.'

Lia turned her back and busied herself making her own black coffee. 'What?'

'I've been looking through so many photos of our kids over the past few weeks. Have you ever noticed how much Simon just kind of... loitered, in the background?'

'Simon didn't loiter, Jen. He...' A hint of defiance was back.

'Just like Jay used to follow you everywhere. Remember? When he first started pursuing you. Back when you were still Lia Carey and weren't making it easy for him. Remember how he used to turn up everywhere we went. Like he just happened to be there.'

'He was a romantic,' she replied, still with her back turned.

'And those photos he took of you. Remember those? Lia, Simon put those photos of Alex up all over school.'

'Anyone could have gotten those,' she said, defensively. 'They were on my Facebook page. I've taken them all down now.'

'How did Jay do it?'

Lia turned to face her now, her face drained of emotion. 'Do what?'

'How did he make you go from that, to…?' She looked Lia up and down.

'Neither of our lives are what we thought they'd be, are they, Jen?' she said, sounding accusatory suddenly.

'He raped you on your third date.'

Lia threw her cup at the sink, smashing it against the taps. 'He did not…'

'Then he love-bombed you for three weeks and that was all it took.'

'Is this why you came?' Lia's voice faded away, and her eyes filled with tears.

Jen lowered her head. 'Love-bombing wasn't a phrase back then, was it?' she said, in a much lower voice, filled with regret.' She looked at her again. 'I was sure you'd come to your senses. That you'd see him for what he really was. But then Paul Greene happened, and you lied to the police for him. You let him hurt you and then you watched him nearly kill a man. And you protected him at all costs. You're still protecting him.'

'Can we not do this, Jen? I know I lost your friendship, but I do wish I hadn't.'

'Prove it.'

'How?'

'Let me speak to Simon. Today.'

'What exactly is it that you think he knows?'

'My Alex did not jump in any river, Lia.'

Lia frowned and turned back to the coffee machine. She set

it going again, ignoring the shattered offering beside it. 'I know it seems impossible to imagine...'

'I can't imagine. Not in any circumstance could I imagine it. Alex had a mortal fear of water. She could never bring herself to stand near the edge of anything with a body of water beneath it. You know that.'

Lia was nodding slowly with her back still turned to Jen. 'But we saw...' She lowered her head, and her shoulders slumped. 'We were there when they...'

'When they pulled the body of my child from the river. Yes. I know. I *was* there. I saw it and I'll never unsee it. I'm not saying that my daughter didn't drown in the river, Lia. I'm saying she did not jump in.'

The coffee machine fell silent and the air in the room became heavy suddenly.

'And so how...?' Lia started, quietly.

'That's what I intend to find out. With or without your help.'

# THIRTY-THREE

## LIA

Lia stood facing the closed front door for some time after Jen left. Her shoulders rose and fell dramatically with her breathing and her teeth were clenched so tightly that her jaw hurt. When Jen Blake got an idea in her head, she grabbed a hold of it, like a dog with a bone. That side of her might have been lying dormant for a while, but Lia had no doubt that it was wide awake now. And once again, she'd set her sights on Lia and her family. She brought her phone to her ear. It rang three times, before Larry Henderson answered.

'Lia?'

'Why would you tell Jen Blake that Simon's been suspended?' she demanded.

'Wh... Lia, I sent a note home with him on Friday. Then I got that call from Jay... I mean, I...'

'Jay called you?'

'Yes! Obviously he wasn't very happy, but, Lia, we can't be seen to tolerate bullying at St Brendan's. I know you...'

Lia ended the call and stood there for another minute. If Jay knew that Simon had been suspended, there's no way he would have let it slide past Lia. He would have lost his shit, which left only one explanation.

'Simon,' she muttered. She turned away from the door and headed back towards the kitchen. He must have brought the note home, then pre-empted the phone call from the school by beating them to it. It seemed he'd become worryingly good at impersonating his father. Without warning, her stomach revolted, sending her hurtling towards the sink. Her diet of fruit and water left nothing behind to come up, but by the time she stopped heaving, bile covered the shattered cup in the sink. As she stood, hunched over the draining board, breathing heavily, she could feel her world starting to crumble. She pulled herself up straight and inhaled deeply through her nose. It was up to her to stop it.

Lia tore the house apart that day but found nothing. Not that she knew exactly what she was looking for, but when she put it all back together again, she still had enough time to get four fillet steaks cooked to perfection for when her family arrived home. It was Wednesday. Jay always came home at the same time as the kids on Wednesdays and it was "family dinner" day. The one day midweek when everyone sat at the dining room table and ate together. No phones. No distractions. No excuses. Lia was not looking forward to it.

By the time Jay arrived home, Lia had just set all four plates down on the table. Simon and Willow were already sitting.

'Hi, love.' Lia smiled, her throat tightening as Jay filled the doorway. Something in his controlled movements, the predatory gleam in his eyes, told her this would be one of those nights.

He didn't speak as he prowled into the dining room, his shoulders rigid under his perfectly tailored suit. The silence stretched thin as he circled the table, running his finger along the polished wood. When he reached the plates, a muscle twitched in his jaw. Without warning, he snatched up three of the steak dinners, his movements as precise as a surgeon's.

Lia flinched as he strode to the sink, her heart hammering against her ribs. The plates clattered as he dropped them in, sending water rushing over the perfectly cooked meat. He turned back, a cold smile playing at his lips, and took his seat in front of his own untouched dinner.

'So,' he said, voice silky smooth as he picked up his knife. 'How was everyone's day?' The blade caught the light as he cut into his steak, examining the pink centre.

Lia stood frozen, watching her children's faces drain of colour as they stared at their empty place mats. The only sound was Jay's knife against the china.

'Aren't you going to sit down, love?' His gentle tone carried an edge that made her stomach clench.

Lia returned a quivering smile and nodded. She went and sat at the opposite end of the table to Jay. He continued to eat his dinner, while his family sat in silence. Each of them had their eyes fixed somewhere between the table and their laps.

'Have you all gone deaf, or something? I asked, how was everyone's day?'

'Okay,' Willow muttered, barely glancing in his direction before lowering her eyes again. Her shoulders were high with tension and one of her legs bounced uncontrollably under the table.

'Fine,' Simon added, trying to sound like he actually was. Fine. But he, too, was stooped in his seat, making himself smaller than the man in charge.

'Good.' Lia smiled, hoping that it would hide her desperation, while her fingers wrung the life out of her cloth napkin.

Jay's eyes roamed over her. She'd dressed in a white wrap-around dress with red poppies on it. Her hair was washed and blow dried, and her make-up was done. She glanced at the napkin and placed it on the table. She began smoothing it out, avoiding his penetrating gaze.

'Why do you two sound so glum?' he chided the children.

Willow threw him a withering glare, as if he should know the answer. Which, of course, he should. Then her fingers found their way into her hair.

Jay dropped his fork with a loud clatter and glared back at her.

'You're just a bit tired, aren't you, Willow?' Lia answered brightly, stroking Willow's hair, before Jay had a chance to have a go at her.

Lia looked at the strands of hair that clung to her trembling hand when she took it away from Willow's head. Her fake smile faded, and she subtly lowered her hands under the table and pulled the hair off. Willow caught the action and moved her own hand away from her head. Lia could hear her heart beating, a loud whooshing sound in both ears, and she couldn't take her eyes off her daughter. Her narrow shoulders rising and falling fretfully, her eyes cast down and her face pale. Her beautiful girl was fading away and suddenly, Lia resented Simon whole-heartedly. He was pulling her attention away from Willow. *She* was the one who was struggling. Really struggling and it was becoming visibly clear now. Willow was physically fading, while Simon, it seemed, couldn't give less of a damn.

Although looking at him now, he looked every bit as terrified as the women in his life. Jay was the one person who never saw the other side of Simon. The boy was desperate for his approval, and now he sat, bolt upright, looking stoically straight ahead. He wanted his father to think that he was fine with the consequences being doled out by him. Maybe even that he *agreed* with them. But there was a sheen of sweat on his brow that showed Lia what was really going on behind those cold eyes of his. Even at a timid glance in his direction, she saw fear in its rawest form.

'Yes, I'm tired,' Willow replied robotically. 'Plus, my best friend is dead. So there's that.' Her voice wavered, but Willow fought her fear with defiance and Lia closed her eyes briefly. She admired her daughter's courage so much. But it was the courage of someone who never had a real reason to be fearful. Willow knew that one day she'd get to leave this house for the last time. And that knowledge was enough to push her on, despite the consequences.

Jay rolled his eyes. 'And what about you, Lia, my love?'

'Me? Oh, I'm fine.' Her hands automatically went for her cutlery, before remembering that she had no use for them. Busying herself was an automatic response.

'Are you? So you're not at all bothered by the fact that this family made me look like a fucking idiot today?'

It was as if the air was sucked out of the room and they each sat up straighter in their chairs. Simon's forehead shone a little more and his jaw tightened.

'I got an A on my English essay,' he said with a tight, delusional smile.

Lia looked hopelessly at him.

'Shut up, Simon,' Jay said, his tone level and his gaze still on his wife. 'I'd like to hear your mother explaining to me how you managed to get an A on your English essay when you were suspended from school. I'd like to hear her explain to me how she, a) allowed Larry fucking Henderson to do that, given what I have on him. And b)' – he was counting on his fingers – 'why she saw fit to let me find out about it from that nut job across the green, and c) why she watched me drive you to school this morning, knowing that you weren't expected to be there.'

Simon watched his father intently, while Willow lowered her head. Of course, she was probably aware that Simon had been suspended, but had kept it to herself. Lia didn't blame her for that. She already bore too much responsibility for her brother.

'Jay, I only found out this morning as well, when Jen came over. I was here, trying to appease her when you left...' She used her hands to gesture uselessly.

'It's your job to know!' he screamed, and they all startled.

Lia glanced at Simon, wondering if he would accept *any* responsibility for his actions here. If he would attempt to come to his mother's defence. But he continued to look fascinated by the exchange.

'He was suspended three days ago for plastering pictures of Alex *and me* all over the school,' Willow said, staring back at her father. 'He was suspended for starting a bullying campaign that has effectively ruined my life.'

Jay glared at Willow, then at Simon. 'Are you stupid, Simon?'

Simon's face reddened and he looked chastened at last.

'Hand me your phone. You, too,' he ordered Willow. 'To your rooms.'

Willow's face was a picture of rage and defiance. She shoved back her chair noisily and pulled her phone from her back pocket. She slapped it into his hand, shoved Simon out of her way, and stormed up the stairs as noisily as she could and then slammed her bedroom door shut.

Lia kept her eyes on the table, breathing as steadily as she could while she waited to see what came next. But before Simon reached the stairs, she forced herself to speak.

'Simon? I'd like you to leave your laptop here as well.'

'What? Why?'

Jay glared at her. Then, 'Go on away, Simon. You can keep your laptop.'

She had to tell Jay. Jen would keep digging and this would only get worse. Besides which, as much as Simon frightened her now, he was their son, and they needed to protect him. The time for doing that alone had passed.

'I was cleaning Simon's bedroom the other day and I came

across some... things that could be perceived in a certain light,' she said quietly. 'The photos that were used to bully Alex and more like it.'

Jay sat back, narrowing his eyes. But she had his attention. '*Bullying*,' he snorted, like it was such a ridiculous word.

'Jen Blake is adamant now that Simon knows something about what happened to Alex. The photographs that I found of her in Simon's room would have looked very, very wrong if anyone were to find them.' She was speaking too quickly, scared that he would stop her at any moment. Scared also that he wouldn't stop her, but would punish her afterwards.

'How could you have fucked up this badly?' he asked, placing his utensils methodically on either side of his plate. 'Bad enough you let him become a beard for that dyke, but you let him get suspended from school?! Have you any idea how it'll look for me if this gets out? *When* this gets out.' His voice was low and filled with menace.

'I only found out—'

'Show me the photos.'

'They're gone.'

'Gone where?'

'I burned them.'

'Hence the new bedroom furniture?'

Lia nodded.

'You're sure you got them all?'

She shook her head. 'That's why I want to see his laptop. Jen said something about a group chat and—'

'But you've been monitoring those, right?'

Her stomach dropped. She had been monitoring them, but then Alex Blake happened. 'After that thing with Alex, I just—'

He slammed his fist on the table. 'You're fucking useless, you know that? You *know* they'll be looking for all sorts of dirt on me soon. You don't think they'll find anything that our idiot son has put out there?' He shoved his chair back and came and stood over her. 'I mean it, Lia. If you don't get a handle on this shit... so help me.' He stormed out of the kitchen and up the stairs.

'Simon!' he roared.

Lia could hear Simon's footsteps overhead. He'd jumped off his bed and hurried to his bedroom door to let his father in. Not that he needed to let him in. Jay would make his own way in regardless.

Lia got up and started clearing up their ruined dinner. She pulled the destroyed fillet steaks out of the water-logged sink and shoved them into the waste-disposal unit. She turned on some soft music to drown out the urgent mutterings upstairs and thought about tomorrow's bake sale in aid of Pieta and suicide prevention. Raising awareness, in memory of Alex Blake. She would be expected to go to the school on time for elevenses, with a smile on her face, exquisitely fresh baked goods in her hands, and act as if everything was fine. The very thought of it made her want to scream and scream and scream. But instead, she'd make it some of her best culinary work yet.

# THIRTY-FOUR

## LIA

'Mm, Lia Higgins, how do you do it?' one of the other mother's, Helen, said as she bit a huge chunk out of a raspberry and white chocolate cupcake. She hadn't even taken the lid off her own Tupperware box yet and Lia had just begun setting up.

'Oh, they look fancier than they are.' Lia smiled, with her usual touch of self-deprecation, which they always appreciated. How she *did it*, was to get out of bed at half four in the morning, which she suspected Helen didn't do very often.

'Bloody hell...' She chomped, crumbs falling from her mouth and frosting clinging to her lips. 'That's my scones blown out of the water.' Helen dragged another table over and shoved it up against Lia's. She pulled the lid off her box and started piling lumpy and randomly shaped scones onto a plate.

'She's done it again.' Another small group of mums appeared, and all came to examine Lia's display before unloading their own. One of them was carrying four packets of iced buns from Aldi and a small stack of paper plates on which to display them. She was one of the martyrs, which is how Lia thought of the working mums. The ones who had time to attend these things only worked part-time at most, but they were forever complaining about *doing it all*. Or bragging, more like.

Lia had a display of cupcakes that wouldn't look out of place in any bakery. She had some chocolate orange, in addition to the raspberry and white chocolate. She had also made a fresh strawberry and cream roulade, a chocolate fudge cake and a smaller coffee cake, because Larry Henderson was a fan. Lia couldn't stand Larry Henderson. But she needed to bring him around today, beginning with sweetness and ending in whatever threats were necessary. Larry and Jay ran in the same circles during their school years and Jay had *something* on him. Lia wasn't privy to the exact details, but from the snippets she'd gleaned over the years, it had something to do with a party, cocaine and a girl called Grace.

'What, it's not enough for you to look absolutely stunning, Lia? You have to be Betty bloody Crocker as well?' another mum joked, as they all started displaying their messy and unimpressive looking offerings.

Lia laughed along with them, and responded with the usual, *Oh, I got these in the sales last year* crap. Really, she wanted to shout at them to shut up! To try getting up at half four in the morning to bake, when all you want to do is curl up under a rock. To panic when you step on the scales because you somehow haven't lost the two pounds you'd gained, despite starving yourself. At this moment in time, she would have traded places with any one of them. But her bed was well and truly made, and there was no getting out of it now.

Soon the teachers started to stroll into the school hall and the noise and chatter increased. Lia batted compliments and merriments back and forth with all of them, as she and her table were surrounded. During the quieter times she noticed, like she always did, that the other mums would gather in smaller groups to chat and gossip and laugh about whatever. But they never included Lia in those little gatherings. They all spoke to her, and they were nice to her. But they never went out of their way to include her. Jay said it was because they were intimidated by her, but Lia knew better. They had nothing in common with her, aside from the fact that their kids went to the same school. Maybe they thought she was too high maintenance, and they just couldn't be bothered. Either way, Lia kept smiling and dishing up cake until at last, Larry made his way over begrudgingly. She cut a thick slice of coffee cake, placed it on a napkin and held it towards him, still smiling.

'Larry! Here you go. Enjoy that.'

'Oh, is that coffee?' He grinned, despite his discomfort. He was with Ruth Terry, the science teacher.

Lia nodded happily. 'Oh, Jay and I met a friend of yours the other day.'

'Really?' he asked, taking a bite. 'Who was that?'

'You remember Grace? She said to say hello.' Lia was still smiling as she took Ruth Terry's five euro for her two cupcakes.

Larry stopped chewing and his stupid grin disappeared.

'Enjoy, Ruth,' Lia continued, happily.

Larry wrapped the remainder of his slice in the napkin, his appetite apparently gone. Ruth moved onto Helen's scones, while Larry stayed behind. The hall was emptying out at last.

'The board were looking to expel him,' he said quietly, through clenched teeth.

Lia continued to smile as if they were having pleasant chat.

'We all know he didn't act alone, Lia, but the other boys were happy to show the photos on their phones, and they all traced back to Simon's phone. His was the only name we were given, along with those photos. I had no choice, but really, it should have been much worse for him.'

'Yes, things could get so much worse for everyone, couldn't they, Larry?'

Larry stepped in closer and lowered his voice further. 'You should consider yourself lucky that your *wonderful* son will be back at school next week, and this will all be forgotten about soon after. And before you start threatening me, why don't you remind your husband that he's not the only one with a long memory?' He landed the tissue-wrapped coffee slice on Lia's table and walked away.

# THIRTY-FIVE

## LIA

After a punishing two hours at the gym following the bake sale, Lia arrived home just as Muriel was unpacking the grocery delivery. It was wrong to call Muriel their cleaner really, when she did so much more than clean their house.

'Hi, Muriel. Are the kids home?'

'They're both in their rooms,' she said, moving between the island and the fridge with her hands full. 'I hope you don't mind me saying this, Lia, but Willow doesn't look so good. She's struggling with everything that's happened, I think. And as for Simon...' She raised her eyebrows, blew out a breath and shook her head.

Lia didn't respond straight away. Muriel was right, but Lia's thoughts were scrambling around the idea that she'd made these observations, and that perhaps she might share them with other people. People outside of this family, if she hadn't already. The Higgins name was being bandied about too much as it was, and there were those who already begrudged their apparent success. Those who wanted to see Jay taken down a peg or two. And perhaps her as well. Not everyone appreciated the amount of time that Lia put into the outward appearance of their family.

She'd dedicated the past fifteen years of her life to being the perfect wife and mother. She could not allow the death of someone else's child to be the thing that negated it all. She needed to get back on top of all this. Back on top of her kids.

Lia went and took over unpacking the groceries. 'Thanks, Muriel. You're right. My children have lost their best friend and they're both struggling with that.' She placed some yogurts in the fridge and closed the door. 'I think you should take some time off, Muriel.'

Muriel stopped what she was doing and looked at her. 'Time off?'

'I think my kids could do with some privacy to grieve. And I could, too, if I'm honest. Alex was a part of our family.' She took a loaf of bread out of Muriel's hands and looked the woman defiantly in the eye. 'I think we need some time. I'll call you when we need you again.'

'Lia, I...' Muriel appeared confused. 'I'm sorry if I spoke out of turn. I just...'

'You didn't,' Lia said, turning away from her again and busying herself with the groceries. 'We just need to work through this as a family. I'm sure you understand.'

'Lia?' she said, more concern in her voice now as she reached out and touched Lia on the arm. 'Is everything okay? I mean...'

'Everything's fine, Muriel. And I know you'll remember your discretion while you're away. I know I don't have to worry about that.' She looked pointedly at her.

Muriel slowly withdrew her hand. 'Of course you don't,' she said quietly, more miffed now. She turned and picked up her coat and bag, and walked out the door, with her head held high in the air.

Lia put down the armful of vegetables she'd picked up and went upstairs. She knocked once on Simon's bedroom door and went inside. He was sitting at his new desk with his laptop open. Only it wasn't his laptop. His was a silver HP laptop that once belonged to Jay. The one he was looking at now was a black Apple MacBook. Lia frowned.

'Where did you get that?' she asked.

'Dad got it for me,' Simon replied, without turning to look at her.

'Mum?' Willow called from the next room.

Lia turned and left, leaving his door wide open. It slammed shut before she reached Willow's room. She squeezed her eyes shut and took a breath, before stepping inside. But that breath caught in her chest when she saw Willow, sitting on the floor with the scrapbook Alex had given to her for her birthday, open in her lap. Her face was streaked with mascara, and she looked waif-like. Her strong, athletic frame was shrinking and her once shiny hair was greasy and limp. Her child looked seriously ill.

'Willow? What is it?' Lia hurried over and dropped to her knees beside her.

'I don't know what to do.' She cried like a child, her voice small and pleading.

Lia looked at the book open to the back page. Written in rainbow ink in Alex's beautiful handwriting – *You're the best person in the world. I LOVE you, Willow – Alex xx*

'Oh, love,' she whispered, pulling Willow into a tight hug. 'Did you know?'

Willow squeezed her eyes shut, but couldn't control her crying. Finally she closed the book and pulled it away from Lia, who had her head tilted to see. She placed it gently on the floor like it was a rare and precious artefact and pulled her knees into her chest. 'What am I supposed to say? I don't know what I'm supposed to say!' She hugged her knees tightly. Her swollen eyes were wide and pleading with Lia to change something. To change everything.

'What you're supposed to say to who, love?'

'She was my best friend.' The words were strangled and the pain in Willow's voice was enough to break Lia's heart.

'I know,' Lia whispered, slumping lower. 'And you don't have to say anything. You're allowed to grieve in private, Willow.'

Willow looked up at her again. 'Tell the reporter that.'

Lia frowned. 'Reporter? What reporter?'

'Holly something. She was waiting for me when I came out of school today.' Her tears flowed again.

Lia's heart beat a little harder in her chest. 'Wh...' She cleared her throat. 'What did she want?'

'To know about Alex.'

Lia nodded. 'Oh, well...'

'And Simon.'

Lia's chest tightened and her breathing quickened. She brought her knuckles to her sternum and applied as much pressure as she could. 'Simon? What about Simon?' *Breathe.* She pressed the tip of her tongue to the roof of her mouth, like she'd been taught to do, and pushed whatever air was left in her lungs out. Then she inhaled deeply and too noisily for a count of four...

'She wanted to know why he posted those photos,' Willow continued, ignoring her mother's mounting panic. Or oblivious to it. 'And not just the ones on the lockers. She said she found stuff that he posted online. Pictures of Alex!' Her voice gained a little strength now and her words sounded more accusatory. 'She wanted to know how long he'd had a crush on Alex and if he's the kind of boy who takes rejection well!'

Lia reached out and took Willow by the chin, breathing exercises forgotten. She squeezed a little too tightly and lifted her head so that her daughter was looking at Lia. 'And what did you say?'

Willow yanked her head back and stood up. She paced

away from her mother, her anger rising. 'What do you think I said? I told her to fuck off.'

Lia nodded, feeling a hint of relief. But not enough to ease the tightness in her chest and the panic that rumbled through her.

'She asked me if he was ever violent at home.'

Lia frowned. 'What?'

Willow stepped closer to her again and lowered her voice. 'Or if Dad is.' She glared at Lia now.

'How would she...?' She cleared her throat painfully. It felt like it was seizing up. 'Why would that even come up? What is she hoping to hear from you?'

Willow's eyes widened. 'Um, the truth maybe? That my brother is a weird fucking perv and that my father hates us!' Her voice broke and she started crying again.

Lia slapped her across the face and instantly baulked at her actions. Willow's crying stopped immediately, and her hand shot to her reddening cheek. The shock on her face was devastating. Lia covered her mouth, and her own eyes went wide in horror. 'Willow, I...'

'Get out of my room.' Willow's voice shook with shock and rage.

'I'm sorry, Willow! I—'

'Get out!' she screamed. 'Get out, get out, GET OUT!'

Lia hurried from the room and the door slammed loudly behind her. She stood on the landing facing two locked doors. Her chest constricted, crushing her lungs as she fell to the floor and cried.

# THIRTY-SIX

## JEN

NIKKIV

Count me out if dat weirdo is going

NEVVIENEV

@Smn69 why u getn all da shade bro? 😵

ROYB

Sum ppl cant take a joke bro

NIKKIV

It wasn't funny. She fkn killed herself!!!!!!

NEVVIENEV

So why were u laughin so hard @NikkiV

NIKKIV

Count me out

ROYB

@Smn69 where u at bro? Defend urself frum the joke police! No1 going 2nite bcoz of u weirdo 😵 😵 😵

It was a gentle knocking at the door that pulled Jen out of the inane class group chat. She wondered if they could tell that she was there, stalking their senseless conversation? Did it say *online* beside Alex's name? She opened the Google app to check that, but before she had a chance to find out, there was another soft knock on her front door. She got up to open it.

'Hi. Is it okay that I'm here?' Anna Greene was standing uncertainly with one foot on the doorstep, the other ready to carry her quickly back to her car. In her hands was a freshly baked apple tart on a dinner plate.

Jen was caught off guard, but she didn't want to seem unwelcoming, particularly as Anna had shown her such kindness. 'Anna, of course. Come in.'

'I'm sorry.' Anna stepped hesitantly inside. 'I should have called first.'

'It's fine.' Jen glanced across at the Higgins house, like she always found herself doing. Then she closed the door gently and gestured for Anna to go through to the kitchen.

Anna stopped inside the kitchen door and looked towards the dining table. All of the chairs had clutter on them and so did the table. She placed the apple tart on the kitchen counter and cleared a seat for herself. Seeing her standing there, figuring out what to do, made Jen see her kitchen for what it had become since Alex died. The whole house, in fact, was a cluttered mess.

'I'm sorry for the—' She looked around.

'Don't be sorry.' Anna cut her off. 'The fact that you're still standing upright is what I'm in awe of, Jen. Now, sit down and let me make you a cup of tea.' Anna stood up again and went to fill the kettle.

Jen let her do it, and out of nowhere, she started crying. The woman's kindness was her undoing.

'Oh, Jen,' Anna said, switching on the kettle and going to put an arm around Jen's shoulders. She led her to the chair that she'd cleared for herself, and lowered Jen into it.

Anna didn't ask any questions about where anything was.

She just made do with what she could see. She washed two mugs that were sitting in the sink and dried them with the tea towel that hung on the oven door. She opened the tin marked *TEA*, and rather than looking for a teapot, she dropped the teabags into the freshly washed mugs and filled them up. She took milk from the fridge, seemingly without looking at the almost bare shelves inside, and she placed the carton on the table between them. She rinsed a knife and brought it to the table, presumably for the apple tart, which Jen couldn't imagine eating. Not because it didn't look and smell delicious. It did and she appreciated the effort that Anna had gone to. But food had lost all appeal for Jen. How could she want to eat something so nice, when her daughter couldn't?

'Drink.' Anna placed the mug in front of Jen and took a seat opposite her. 'And cry if that's what you need to do.'

'Thank you, Anna,' Jen said, in a whisper.

'Is Dale here?'

Jen shook her head. 'He's still at work.'

Anna nodded.

'I've been watching the classroom chat.' Jen held up Alex's phone.

'Ugh, it's like a viper's nest,' Anna replied with a shake of her head. 'Why are they so cruel to each other? What do they get out of it?'

Jen shrugged. 'Are you still monitoring that?'

'Not anymore. Pennie left the group so, thankfully, I don't have to witness any more of that tripe.'

Jen nodded, her eyes still on the phone. 'Clever girl.'

Anna nodded and looked into her cup. 'Does that Higgins boy have anything to say for himself on there?'

Jen shook her head, then she glanced up at Anna who was turning her cup round and round on the table. 'Do you know something, Anna?'

Anna smiled a humourless smile. 'I wouldn't claim to know any more than you do about the Higginses, Jen. But I know what Jay did to my brother.'

Jen closed her eyes at the memory. Paul Greene ended up missing almost a month of school following that beating and it was the talk of the school year. He never returned to St Brendan's, opting instead to travel to the other side of the city and back every day to finish out his secondary education. He left the county entirely for college, and as far as Jen knew, he never came back.

'The other thing I know is that Lia lied for him, and he got away with it.'

Jen nodded.

'You know she acted like she hardly knew me at the bake sale the other day.'

Jen said nothing, but she wasn't surprised.

'She just shows up in her fancy outfit, with her perfect cakes and acts like she's doing the world a great service.' She shook her head. 'I can't bring myself to believe a word that woman says. She'll always be a liar as far as I'm concerned. First for Jay. And now there's Simon.'

'I think he did something to Alex.' Jen finally blurted out the words.

Anna didn't look surprised when she slowly nodded.

'He was insinuating that something had happened between himself and Alex. In the group chat, at least.'

Anna nodded again. 'Pennie said that.'

'Pennie defended Alex. I saw that, too.' Jen gave the woman a weak smile.

Anna shrugged. 'Pennie's not quite the wallflower that I was, but she's not one of the St Brendan's pack either. She has her few friends over at St Mary's, and to be honest, I think she'll be moving there after this term. St Brendan's can say what they like about their success rate, but that bloody place is no better now than it was when we were there. Alex was always kind to Pennie, and Pennie is as loyal a friend as anyone could hope to have. So yes. She called bullshit on those photographs and all the stuff Simon was trying to get people to believe.'

Jen reached out and placed her hand on Anna's.

'Which brings me to why I'm here.' Anna exhaled. 'Holly would rather I didn't tell you all this yet. She likes to have all her ducks in a row before she opens her mouth about anything, but Auntie Anna has her ways when it comes to Holly.' She gave the slightest grin.

Jen was sitting up straighter now, afraid to speak and partially holding her breath.

'Holly has been piecing things together,' Anna said carefully. 'Kids talk – not to adults usually, but to each other. And Holly's good at following those threads, finding the digital footprints. She's uncovered a pattern of messages and posts from Simon about Alex. Screenshots that got passed around, things that went viral in their circles before being deleted.'

'And she has proof of all that?' Jen asked.

Anna nodded. 'There's more.' Anna reached out and took her hand. 'Jen, I'm telling you this because if it was my daughter, I'd want to know everything as it was emerging. Like I said, Holly would rather I keep my mouth shut.'

'Please tell me, Anna.'

'That Darina Hayes girl?'

Jen bit down on the inside of her lip and nodded.

'She posted messages claiming that something happened at the twins' birthday party.'

Jen pulled her hand back and used it to fidget with her jumper.

'The way Holly pieced it together, the party took place in the Higginses' back garden and Alex was sitting beside Simon. According to Darina, she looked uncomfortable. Then it sounds as if Alex went inside, and Darina makes out that it was because she wanted to get away from Simon. But – now again, this is according to message threads, so I don't know how reliable it all is – but Darina claims to have heard Alex saying *please stop* through the open upstairs window at the back of the house. Then apparently Alex went running from the house and didn't come back.'

Jen let out a loud sob and brought her hands to her face.

'Holly tried to speak to Darina about it, but that cheeky little mare told her where to go. Her friend, Lucy Nagle, was a bit more loose-lipped, however, when Holly told her that she already knew the whole story. Lucy put it pretty much the way I've just put it to you. Then when Holly spoke to Willow, she asked her about the party, but she said that Willow hesitated for far too long and became visibly upset. She eventually covered for her brother and said that Darina and Lucy were lying.'

'Anna, my baby,' Jen cried, wrapping her arms around her belly, which ached suddenly.

'I know, Jen.'

'I need to go to the guards,' Jen said. 'I need to make them listen.'

Anna nodded. 'You could. Of course, you could. But Holly has a thread between her fingers now, Jen, and she won't stop pulling until she's unravelled the lot. The other thing about Holly is that she has friends within the Garda ranks. She works closely with them, and you may be sure she's already taken this to them. What's more, she's asked them to look over the CCTV footage from the area around the quays on the evening when Alex went missing.'

Jen stopped crying and frowned deeply. She'd seen Holly at the Garda station looking as comfortable as anyone who worked there. 'And will they do that?'

'Ordinarily, no. Not when they believe it to be suicide. There's hundreds of hours of footage, between all the different businesses, warehouses, even the Port of Cork, and they mightn't find anything. So, from a manpower perspective, they wouldn't be keen to do that. Which is why Holly offered to do it for them. They know her. She has a proven track record of not going over the heads of the Gardaí, and she's always handed over everything she finds, in all the cases she's investigated. In truth, they're usually happy for her to do their work for them. They get to arrest the bad guy, and Holly gets to break the story. She's earned their trust and has built a win-win relationship with the Gardaí.'

'And that's what she's doing now?'

Anna nodded. 'She went to her Garda contacts, went through everything she knows and the reasons why she believed it might not have been a suicide, and...'

'She *believes* that?' Jen asked.

'I think she does, yes.'

Jen got out of her seat and went around the table. She hugged Anna as tightly as she'd ever hugged anyone. 'Thank you, Anna.' She cried into the woman's shoulder. 'When I didn't hear from Holly, I thought she'd moved onto something else.'

Anna stood up to hug her back. 'You might not hear from Holly until the very end of her investigation, when she has a result to offer either way. She doesn't like to be chased for updates either, but like I said – I'm Auntie Anna. And I would want to know.' She pulled back then and held Jen at arm's length. 'That family think they can bulldoze their way through the lives of anyone who stands in their way. But we won't let them.'

'Yeah, well.' Jen sobbed. 'I've lost the love of my life. I'll welcome the bulldozer, Anna. But by God, I'll take them down with me.'

Anna reached in her pocket and pulled out a folded slip of paper. She handed it to Jen, then gathered up her coat and bag.

*Holly Myer*
08543228761

'Try not to chase her too hard, if you can.' And with that, Anna stood up and left quietly, pulling the front door closed behind her.

# THIRTY-SEVEN

## JEN

Jen sat at her kitchen table the following day staring at the clock and chewing on her nails. It was almost midday. She'd called Holly Myer within an hour of Anna leaving and she'd been torturously counting the hours ever since.

Finally, there was a knock on the door. Jen stood up so quickly, she almost knocked over her chair. She straightened it up again and took one quick look around the kitchen. She'd tidied and cleaned it that morning. *Pull yourself together, Jen,* she told herself, taking a deep breath to steady her nerves.

'Mrs Blake? Hi.' Holly Myer smiled and held out her hand.

Jen shook it. 'Holly, thank you for coming.'

'No worries! And I take it my auntie Anna has been to visit as well?'

Jen tried to smile as she stepped aside and gestured for the woman to come in.

Holly stepped inside and closed the door behind her. Then she followed Jen to the kitchen. She carried herself through Jen's home with the easy demeanour of an old friend, and Jen felt herself relaxing. The ability to put people at ease clearly ran in their family. Jen put the kettle on to boil as the woman took a seat at the kitchen table. She removed her jacket and hung it on the back of the chair and Jen immediately felt a sense of gratitude towards her. She was here. And she was planning to stay a while.

She placed a teapot and two mugs on the table, along with Anna's apple tart, and sat down across from Holly.

'That was you, wasn't it? Coming out of the Garda station the other night?'

Jen nodded and forced another smile. 'It took everything I had not to follow you back in there.'

Holly returned a sympathetic smile. 'Can I begin by saying how sorry I am?' she said gently, as Jen poured.

Jen just nodded in reply. She didn't want another sorry. She wanted the truth. 'Paul Greene is your father?' she asked, after a quiet beat.

'He is.' She smiled knowingly. 'And I can see where you're going with this. I'm aware of my family's history with the Higginses, Jen. But that's not why I'm looking into this story. I'm looking into it because it's my job.'

Jen wrapped her hands around her mug. She sounded far more detached than Anna had.

'I'm sorry if that sounds cold,' she said. 'But that's how I have to approach it. If I become emotionally involved in a story, then I can't do my job the way I need to do it. You understand?'

'I do,' Jen conceded. 'I'm fully aware that if a woman finds herself in a situation where she becomes emotional, whether it's because she's angry, in pain, upset or, God forbid, grieving the loss of her child, then suddenly nothing she says is taken seriously anymore. Not until she's *in her right mind* again.'

Holly raised her eyebrows and nodded.

'And I am clearly very emotional at this time. My daughter died.' Her eyes filled with tears, but she roughly wiped them away. 'While I might have no control over my tears, there is absolutely nothing wrong with my mind. I know...' She blew out a shaky breath. 'I *knew* my daughter. It's true, she was a teenage girl, going through lots of changes, and I'm not naive enough to think that she told me everything. But I knew enough to say with absolute certainty that she would not have gone near, let alone into, that river. Not by day with a lifejacket on and certainly not in the pitch dark.'

Holly, like Jen, had her hands wrapped around her mug, but she'd only taken one sip so far. Her sharp eyes were on Jen, and she was intently watching and listening. Jen could almost see her thoughts turning over in her mind.

'When I say that,' Jen continued, 'I know what people think. *But she wasn't going for a swim. She wanted to kill herself.*' There was a short silence then, and Jen appreciated the fact that Holly didn't try to console her. Or to fill that brief silence before Jen was ready to continue. 'It's hard to imagine getting to a point where you want to end your own life, isn't it?' she said in the soft, reasonable tone of the woman she used to be. 'But if you were going to kill yourself... wouldn't you want it to be painless? Would anyone want to live their final moments immersed in the thing they feared the most?'

Holly took her time answering. She was waiting to see if Jen had more to add. When it became clear that she didn't, Holly nodded. 'I'd certainly agree with you there. I've spoken to Alex's teachers and to her basketball coach. Alex was excused from all activities involving the pool, is that right? She had a study period during the weekly swimming lesson that her class has had since first year.'

Jen nodded. 'Yes. She wouldn't go within ten feet of an open pool.' She inhaled deeply and exhaled a shaky breath.

'Take your time. I'm not in a hurry,' Holly said kindly. 'You told me on the phone that Alex was being bullied at school. I took a delve into her socials, and those of her peers. I hope you don't mind?'

Jen shook her head. 'No... I'm glad you have. I haven't known where to start...'

'Alex wasn't very active herself, but I've seen some of the images you talked about. Kids can be such assholes,' she said angrily. 'You're right about Simon Higgins, too. Or should I say, Smn69.'

Jen had to remind herself not to hold her breath while she listened to every word the woman had to say.

'All bravado and innuendo. Idiot teenage boy stuff, but he was very vocal about his relationship with Alex.'

'She would never have...'

Holly held up her hand. 'It wouldn't matter even if she had, Jen. What he was doing to her was horrific. No excuses. And Alex and Willow weren't a couple either, were they?'

Jen shook her head. 'No. I don't think they were.'

'Where did Simon fit into their friendship?'

'He didn't. Fit, I mean. But the Higgins twins came as a pair, so he was always with them.'

'From speaking with Willow, I'm not sure how much she enjoyed that either. She didn't say it in so many words, but I got the feeling his presence with them was at their parents' insistence, otherwise Simon would have been alone.'

'Willow is taking Alex's death hard. She's disappearing into herself, while Simon seems to have grown a foot taller. He couldn't care less, if you ask me. So perhaps they're not as close as I might have assumed.'

Holly looked down at the table now, thinking. 'Okay, so Alex was being bullied at school. She was being bullied online.' Holly counted out on her fingers. 'She was possibly in love with someone who didn't feel the same way as she did.'

'Willow,' Jen whispered.

Holly nodded.

'Alex wants Willow, Simon wants Alex...' Holly muttered, more to herself than to Jen.

'And now it's very easy to paint a picture of a child who couldn't take anymore, isn't it?' Jen said, her tone hardening slightly.

'It would be. If I hadn't spent so much time inside the heads of the other kids at their school.' She smiled resignedly then. 'I know Auntie Anna's told you exactly what I've been up to, and I can only assume that's why you called me yesterday. Plus' – she looked at the dinner plate on the table between them – 'I'd know her apple tarts anywhere.'

The two women sat looking at each other for a few seconds, before Holly spoke again.

'It's okay. She's a mum to her core. I get it. But when I first heard that part of the story, I didn't think suicide. I thought, how many women have died at the hands of a man who couldn't have what he wanted? And like you said, why go out in the most terrifying way possible?'

Jen exhaled loudly.

'Did you know that Lia dismissed her housekeeper?'

'Muriel?' Jen asked, surprised by the change of topic. Plus, Lia was not one to get her hands dusty and Muriel had been with them for years. 'No, I didn't know that.'

'Hmm. I went to see her the other day. She's not a fan.'

'Of Lia's?'

'Of any of them. She reckons they all look down on her, like she's beneath them.' Holly shook her head. 'Muriel probably has more disposable income than they do, thanks to her late husband. It seems to me that she worked there to stave off loneliness. Anyway, as you'd imagine, Muriel was privy to a few things, including some strange one-on-one time between Lia and Alex.'

'Strange? What did she mean, strange?'

'As in, Alex being over there, drinking coffee in the garden with Lia, while neither Willow or Simon were home.'

Jen frowned. 'Did she overhear what they were talking about?'

'She was working inside the kitchen, and they were in the garden, so she only caught snippets. But she said that Alex, who she described as a lovely, bubbly girl, seemed upset that day and she overheard Lia saying something along the lines of *what Simon did was wrong*. She said she also heard Lia telling her about men, and how they think they have the right to touch you... that kind of thing. She didn't have it word for word, but she had the gist of the conversation.'

Jen brought her hands to her face. 'I knew Simon did something,' she cried.

'Yeah, well, Muriel seemed to think so as well. It was really clear from speaking to her that she's a little creeped out by Simon. She also said,' Holly continued, not getting distracted by Jen's upset, 'that when she arrived to start work on the day she was let go, she found Willow on the bathroom floor, crying hysterically. She picked her up and held her, and she said that Willow cried, *We killed her, we killed her*, over and over.'

'Christ.' Jen's voice was high and strained as she rocked slightly in her chair.

'She didn't think the child meant it literally, but... when she told Lia that she was worried about Willow, Lia fired her on the spot.' Holly clicked her fingers. 'Just like that.'

Jen stopped rocking and looked up. 'She fired her? For being worried about Willow?'

'Weird, right? Most parents would want to know if there was something wrong with their child. Wouldn't they?'

'Unless they already knew,' Jen muttered.

'But they don't want anyone else to know,' Holly finished.

There was a moment of silence, before Holly tapped the table with both hands and got to her feet, indicating the end of their chat. 'Anyway,' she said, 'I've been looking for a reason to land on Jay Higgins' doorstep for a while. I'll see what else I can find out.'

'So, that *is* why you took this story?' Jen said, but it didn't matter to her. What mattered was that she was here.

Holly bobbed her head from side to side. 'I'm not going after him for what he did to my father. I wouldn't. It would be unprofessional. I want him because there's a chance this man could be given power over more people. They're so willing to drink the Kool-Aid he's offering without digging into the kind of man he actually is.'

Jen nodded. She really didn't mind what Holly's true motives were, but she asked anyway: 'Why haven't you been digging into him already then? Why wait until this close to the elections?'

'Why, indeed.' Holly raised her eyebrows. 'Talk FM's political reporter loves him.' She rolled her eyes. 'And politics isn't my bag anyway. But...' She tapped her nails against the table. 'Jen, I can't promise you anything at this stage. Only that I'm looking into it.'

Jen closed her eyes again and nodded. 'Thank you. And um...'

Holly looked at her as she turned to go.

'The CCTV?'

She smiled again and rolled her eyes. 'Cheers, Anna,' she muttered. 'Look, Jen, there's hundreds of hours of footage there. A friend of mine at Anglesea Street Garda Station is helping me look through it, but honestly, I wouldn't get my hopes up on finding anything. And even if we do, well... I have to warn you, you may not like what we find.'

Jen reached out and placed a hand on Holly's arm. 'Holly, if you find proof that my child jumped into the river of her own accord, then at least I'll know that much. Not knowing how or why is intolerable.'

'But I might not find proof of anything. That's what I'm

saying. I could get pulled off this story tomorrow, *or* I might find a smoking gun, so to speak. But more likely, I'll find absolutely nothing and you must be prepared for that, please.'

'I am,' she lied. Whatever hope Jen had left was pinned on the woman in front of her. 'So, can I ask what your plan is from here?'

Holly shrugged. 'I'm sorry, Jen, I don't work like that. I go where I go when I think to go there. And please, wait for *me* to contact *you*. I promise I will as soon as I have something solid to tell you.'

Jen stood at the door and watched her drive slowly out of the estate. Slower still past the Higginses' house. Then she stood there for a minute more, watching that house across the green. The perfectly manicured home and garden of the perfectly manicured family. Then, peeling her eyes away, she turned with a steely resolve, and closed the door on them.

# THIRTY-EIGHT

## LIA

It was after midnight when Jay arrived home from another dinner meeting. One that didn't require Lia to be shoehorned into a dress of his choosing, only to sit and quietly smile at the ridiculous men around him. Instead, when she wasn't nervously pacing the room, she was on the couch with her feet curled up under her, trying to look relaxed. She wished for fleece pyjamas and an open fire, but neither were permitted. Only slobs wore fleece pyjamas, and an open fire would blacken the cream bricks inside the ornamental fireplace. She wished for the opportunity to relax inside her own home, like she imagined other people doing. Instead, she lived on the edge of her nerve, with a ball of anxiety permanently resting in her gut. She tried to make herself throw up, sure that purging would bring a sense of relief, but there was nothing for her body to bring up. Her jaw hurt from clenching and muttering, as she rehearsed what she needed to say while she waited for him to come home. Then finally he did. She positioned herself primly on the couch when the lights from his car shone through the lowered blinds.

'Why are you still up?' he asked, taking off his coat and going to the kitchen.

Lia could hear him pouring a glass of red wine. One glass, not two. Her heart felt like it was flip-flopping around inside her chest and she desperately called upon her breathing exercises while she waited for him to come back in and sit on the opposite armchair.

'We need to talk about Simon,' she said, her voice slowly rising from her rehearsal mutters, to a more normal level.

'What about him?' He picked up the remote and turned off *Ten Things I Hate About You*. He didn't ask if she was enjoying it. He just put on, of all things, American football. A sport that neither of them could even pretend to understand. But Lia didn't care. She hadn't been watching TV. Her mind was fully occupied with this conversation.

'You know why, Jay. Why did you buy him a new laptop? What did you do with the old one?'

He blinked and looked at her. 'Hang on. You refurbished his whole room on a whim and now you're questioning *me* about buying him a new laptop?'

'I'm not questioning you buying...'

'Good. Because let's not forget who brings home the bacon here.'

Lia took a deep, quiet breath. She couldn't let him fluster her now. 'But we need to talk about *why* we had to get rid of all his old stuff and replace everything.'

Jay watched the American football and drank his wine, as if she were talking about the virtues of one cleaning product over another.

'What did you find on his laptop, Jay?' she asked, stilling the nerves in her voice.

He turned off the television at last and looked at her sharply. *Please not tonight.* She untucked her feet and sat up straighter.

'Why don't you cut to the chase, Lia? What is it that you're trying to accuse your own son of?'

Lia's scalp prickled. 'I'm not accusing him of anything. But there's something I didn't tell you.'

'I'd say there's *plenty* you didn't tell me.'

He normally said things like that when he was about to accuse her of flirting with one of the school dads, or one of his colleagues, or whatever man happened to engage her in conversation for longer than Jay deemed appropriate. Once upon a time, he would have beaten that man to a pulp. But he was more careful these days. Now it would be Lia who received the punishment. She took another deep breath. 'Remember that pizza night we had here for the kids' birthday?' She kept her tone as light as she could.

Jay stared at her blankly.

'I went upstairs to check on Alex, after I'd sent her to get some blankets.' She swallowed more air, but still felt like she was suffocating. 'I saw Simon...'

'You saw Simon, what?'

'He was forcing himself on her, Jay.' She spat out the words before she couldn't and then waited for whatever was to come.

Jay laughed. Whatever she was expecting, it wasn't laughter. 'Is that it?'

'Jay...'

His laughter died and he leaned threateningly towards her. 'I've watched that little tramp leading him on for years. And I've watched *him* taking it like an idiot.' He laughed again. 'Christ, I thought he was batting for the other side there for a while. I thought that I could finally start pushing him out there to get me the gay votes!'

He stood up and walked slowly over to the couch. Lia's body tensed as he hunkered down in front of her and pushed her knees apart. She tried to make herself relax. He didn't like it when her body didn't respond properly to him. He leaned against her, his smiling eyes never leaving hers as his hands moved slowly up along her thighs to her waist. He squeezed what little flesh he could grab, his way of telling her that it was still too much. She pulled in her tummy as tightly as she could, but he didn't linger there. Instead, his strong hands continued their slow journey towards her throat. One hand applied just enough pressure there to make her tense up again, while the other moved further up, cupping her face. 'Now, tell me again what you saw.'

# THIRTY-NINE

## LIA

Lia lay awake, staring at the ceiling all night. It hurt to move, and her racing mind refused to let her sleep, replaying the scene from the night before. Jay forcing himself into her on the couch. He hadn't let her lie down. He hadn't let her remove her underwear; instead, tearing the skin on her hip along with the expensive fabric. He'd punished her with every thrust for her betrayal of their family. And it *was* a betrayal to insinuate that their son was not of good character. While they had sex, she'd given Jay all the answers he continued to seek from her, while his hand wrapped itself tighter and tighter around her throat. What she'd seen was *not* their son forcing himself upon a girl. It was that girl seducing their inexperienced son. Yes, *the girl* was a bitch, like her mother. Yes, she'd been an attention-seeking whore. Yes, she'd thrown herself in the river because her own family didn't have time for her. Yes, Jay would make Lia a better mother.

She winced as she sat up and swung her legs slowly out of bed, desperately trying not to wake Jay. How had she ended up like this? The shame sat heavy in her stomach. She should have left him years ago. But yet, here she still was. She stayed there, bracing herself for a moment before standing up and walking slowly and quietly to the shower. It was exactly six am. She was always up, washed and groomed before everyone else. Then it would be the smell of a hot breakfast that roused them. That was how Jay's mother used to wake Jay and his father, and it was how Lia was taught to wake her family, too.

She'd just finished blow-drying her hair, when she saw a TALK FM Jeep pull up outside. She frowned and stood up from her dressing table. She moved to the side of the window and looked out to see what they were doing. Whose house were they looking for? Lia's dressing room was at the front of the house, separated from the bedrooms, so that she *could* get washed and groomed without waking anyone else. It looked directly down on their short driveway, so she could see the woman as she stepped down from the Jeep. She fixed her hair and continued whatever conversation she was having with the driver through her open door. Seconds later, he stepped out and came around to her side. They had a quick chat that looked like it was being delivered in bullet points before turning and walking towards Lia's front door. Lia's frown deepened. She moved back from the window and crept into their room.

'Jay,' she said softly.

He opened his eyes. Jay went from being in a dead sleep, to fully alert. He'd always been like that. There was no slow dawning for him. He was either fast asleep or wide awake.

'Were you expecting media here today?'

He sat up. 'What?'

The doorbell rang and he got quickly out of bed. He went to the window and moved the curtain just enough to see out. He frowned, too, but that was all the time he wasted. He went to the wardrobe and pulled on his Hilfiger jeans and a navy Ralph Lauren polo shirt.

The doorbell went again.

'Will I answer it?' Lia asked nervously.

'Wait,' he insisted, as he went to the en suite and splashed some water on his face. He ran his wet hands through his hair and rinsed his mouth with mouthwash. And that was it. That was all it took for Jay to look every inch the gorgeous, casual *I'm just like you* family man. Less than five minutes and he would appear in front of that camera, if there was one, and make whatever audience was on the other side of the lens either want him, or want to *be* him. But they would *all* trust him.

He looked her over from head to toe, paying special attention to her throat. He hadn't left much of a mark, and what evidence *was* there had already been covered up with make-up and freshly blow-dried hair. Lia knew she looked good. Her hair shone as well as it still could, her face was made-up, and she was wearing a floral wraparound dress that made her look like she belonged on the cover of *Good Housekeeping*.

'Come on,' he said, leaving the room and heading for the stairs with Lia behind him. 'Go to the kitchen,' he added quietly, when they reached the hall. 'And come out in one minute.'

She did as he said and went to the kitchen. She stood just out of sight of the front door as he opened it.

'Oh, hello!' she heard him say with his cheery smile. 'Wow, you lot are early.'

'Mr Higgins, my name is Holly Myer. I'm from the morning show on Talk FM – do you have a minute?'

Holly Myer. The whole city knew Holly Myer. She was the researcher for the country's most listened-to radio talk show. She was behind every big story that broke nationally and was known for her ability to turn ordinary people into whistle blowers. She wasn't on the political circuit, preferring instead to focus on breaking news. Lia knew all this. She also knew who her father was. But she wondered if Jay had copped any of it yet. She wondered, too, if Jay would even recognise the name

Paul Greene if he heard it, such was his consideration for what he'd done to the man.

It was time for Lia to appear by Jay's side. She went and opened the door a little wider, happy to let them see inside their gleaming home. 'Good morning.' She smiled.

Jay's arm moved around her waist in a display of affection, but his grip felt firm, which meant that he didn't like whatever the woman had just said to him. Lia hadn't heard what that was, but it seemed Jay was starting to realise that this wasn't about politics.

Lia glanced across the green to see Jen Blake watching them through an upstairs window. Was she smiling? Lia's insides turned cold. Holly glanced over her shoulder, to see what Lia was looking at, and Lia pulled her eyes away, just as Jay's grip tightened even more on her hip.

'I'm sorry. Did I catch you at a bad time?' Holly smiled, turning back to Lia again.

'Of course not,' Lia replied, as if she'd like nothing more than to spend the morning with this woman. 'I'm just not sure we're awake yet.' She half laughed, linking her arm through Jay's and pulling him lovingly closer, taking the pressure off her hip in the process. He leaned in and kissed the top of her head in response.

Holly was a short woman, young, with long shiny black hair and red lips. She wore skinny blue jeans with black utilitarian type boots. Jay despised that style on women, but Lia guessed that Holly's typical day could take her just about anywhere. As such, she looked like she was ready for anything. Lia wondered briefly what that might feel like.

'So, what brings you here this morning?' Lia asked brightly.

Holly brought her phone up close to her mouth as she was about to speak, and that's when Lia realised that she was recording the conversation. She brightened her smile, despite the fact that it was audio only. But it would come through in her voice. She knew that from experience.

'Mrs Higgins...'

'It's Lia, please.' Lia smiled.

'Lia. I'm recording our conversation, I hope that's alright.' She didn't wait for a response. 'We're speaking to people today about the tragic death of Alex Blake. I believe she was best friends with both of your children?'

Jay squeezed her arm a little tighter, but not so they'd notice. *Watch what you say*, he was telling her.

Lia's expressions never let her down. Her smile became less jovial and more sad. She nodded. 'Alex was the most beautiful soul, and yes, she was a friend to both of our children. As I'm sure you know, her family are also our neighbours, which is why I really don't feel like it's appropriate for me to discuss this with the media. It's just too close to home.' She looked lovingly at Jay and then leaned into him, upset now. He moved his arm around her shoulders and pulled her close. *Good girl.*

'I'm sorry. It's just been so upsetting,' he said.

'I understand,' said Holly, in a well-practiced tone. 'It was Alex's mother, Jen, who contacted us actually. We believe that Alex was the victim of some bullying prior to her death. Do you know anything about that?'

Lia frowned and let her tears fall. Jay responded accordingly by continuing to hold her close and looking even more pained. He shook his head and was about to answer, when the woman ploughed on.

'Is your son, Simon, home?'

Jay stiffened.

Lia straightened up but didn't try to hide her upset. She wasn't an ugly crier. She knew that. 'My son is grieving,' she said firmly, but without losing her genteel tone.

'Is it true that he spread rumours of a sexual nature about Alex?'

'I...'

'Is it true that he had images blown up and manipulated and spread throughout the school and online? Images of Alex Blake?'

Jay ushered Lia inside and took a protective stance outside their front door. 'I'm sorry, Holly, but—'

'Is it true that in the last weeks of Alex Blake's life, her torment was orchestrated by your son?'

'Is this supposed to be journalism?' Jay demanded, as annoyed about the fact that she'd cut him off, as what she was saying.

'Mr Higgins, Simon's peers have been providing us with some shocking information about his behaviour. For example, did your son sexually assault Alex on the evening of his sixteenth birthday?'

The atmosphere immediately soured, and Lia held her breath inside the door. There was a moment of silence while Jay formulated his response.

'You're trying to accuse an innocent child of hurting another child. A child who was his best friend. A child whose death he is currently grieving. Are *you* trying to bully a child to their death? Is that what this is about, Holly? Do your bosses know what you're doing?'

'Mr—'

'A professional journalist would know that you do not doorstep a family and accuse anyone, let alone a child, of something based on school yard gossip.'

Lia stood in the front room, near enough to the window that she could see them, without them seeing her. The woman lowered her phone and turned to the man with her. He'd been silently watching on and Jen wondered if Holly had brought him for back up. Or protection, maybe. He didn't seem to have another role here. They exchanged a look that caused Lia to worry some more. They had their own language, clearly. And they were not as impressed by Jay as he'd like them to be. That much was very clear.

'Look...' Jay's reasonable tone never wavered despite Holly's accusations. He would not give her what she wanted from him, which, no doubt, was to see the other side. Holly Myer wouldn't be here if she didn't already know that there was one. 'If you say that you were contacted by Jen, then I can only take your word for that,' Jay went on. 'Jen is our friend. She's our neighbour and she's not doing too well.' His tone was conspiratorial. Suddenly, *he* was the source this reporter should trust. Proof that he didn't know whose daughter Holly was and Lia wished he'd stop speaking. 'So I'm sure you'll understand that I can't comment on this until my wife and I have had a chance to speak with Dale and Jen. It's a very difficult time for them, and for us. Alex was like family to Lia and me, and there's a whole community of young people trying to come to terms with what's happened. With that in mind, I'll ask you to respect our privacy at this difficult time and give the Blake family some space to grieve.'

Lia watched the woman, watching Jay. Her face was impassive. She made no attempt to interrupt him, and Lia couldn't tell what she was thinking. There was a pause before she spoke again.

'Well, Mr Higgins, questions are being asked about what led to Alex Blake's death. Her family believe that there is more to it than what they've been told.'

'Really? Her *whole* family? Or just Jen? I can almost promise you, Holly, that if you speak with Dale Blake, he'll be...' Jay exhaled and shook his head sadly. 'Let's just say, they're *both* grieving. But as a mother, poor Jen is having a hard time accepting what's happened. And who can blame her?' He oozed empathy now. An emotion Lia was sure he'd never known firsthand.

Holly paused before responding again. Lia noticed she did

that a lot and imagined that the woman measured her words with care, only using ones that would make an impact.

'Well, grieving or not, accepting or not, she tells a compelling story. One that I'm inclined to believe.' She took a small step closer to Jay, invading his personal space, but only briefly. Her point was made when she smiled at him. 'And if there's a thread to be pulled, Mr Higgins, then I intend to keep pulling.' She stepped back again and turned to go. 'Have a good day, you two.'

Jay stood on the doorstep watching her go and it wasn't until their Jeep pulled away that he went back inside and closed the door.

'You have one job today, Lia,' he said in a low, menacing voice.

Lia walked away from the window and out to the kitchen. She knew he didn't mean breakfast, but she went about preparing it anyway.

'You'd better get Jen Blake to wind her bloody neck in. You hear me? I don't care how you do it, but sort this shit out.'

Jen could see Lia coming from the time she left her house. She and Jay were nothing if not predictable and they honestly thought that everyone bought the whole *I'm just like you* bullshit that they churned out when they wanted something from people. Whether it was votes, or to have the dogs called off. But Jay was born with a silver spoon in his mouth and an enormous sense of entitlement. He felt he was entitled to hold office and to maintain power over people's lives. Just like he'd felt *entitled* to young Lia Carey. To pull her from her no-frills life and crush her into a shape that suited him better. That's what Jay Higgins did. He crushed those he thought were beneath him. Some, like Lia, were happy to let him. Growing up with poverty and unemployment meant that she'd always been desperate to change her circumstances. But up until Jay came along, she'd planned to do it with a college degree. Turned out she was happy to sell her soul in order to climb the social ladder and now here she was, coming to do his bidding once more — convinced, somehow, that their world was the only one that mattered.

Holly hadn't told Jen that she'd be calling to their house. In fact, she hadn't heard from Holly since she'd sat in Jen's kitchen, promising her nothing, nearly a week ago. But she did see the Talk FM Jeep pulling up just after Dale left for work. She'd been glued to the window ever since. As Lia stepped onto Jen's driveway, Jen went and opened the door. She just stood there waiting, but she didn't say anything.

'Jen, hi.' Lia gave a sad smile, which she'd probably practiced in front of a mirror before leaving the house. In her hand was an oven dish with a silicone lid on top.

Jen opened the door for her to come in. She still hadn't said anything, but she was interested to hear what Lia had to say. To hear what tactic she'd use to get Jen to back off. She and Lia didn't *act* like two people filled with resentment towards each other. They hadn't for a long time, not since the kids came along. They treated each other like old acquaintances forced back together by those very same kids. That was no longer the case, but nevertheless, Jen wanted information from the woman and so she invited her inside. No doubt Lia felt the same way. She wouldn't be there otherwise.

The kitchen was still clean and tidy in preparation for Holly Myer, who Jen hoped might turn up with some news at any time. But still, even at its best, it was nothing like Lia's showroom-worthy kitchen. Jen didn't care, though. She gestured towards a kitchen chair and Lia went and sat down.

'What can I do for you, Lia?'

Lia placed the oven dish on the table. 'It's only a lasagne. Nothing fancy, but I thought it might save you cooking for a night.'

Jen ignored the weak offering and kept her eyes on Lia.

'How have you been?' Lia asked.

'You know how I've been. So why are you here?'

Lia looked at the dish and shook her head. 'I'm sorry, Jen. I know I've been a terrible friend to you, and—'

'You haven't been my friend since we were eighteen years

old. Ever since Jay stopped allowing you to have friends. Remember?'

Lia stood up again, her own anger making a rare appearance now. 'Do we have to start this again?' Her voice trembled, but Jen couldn't bring herself to feel anything for her.

'I'm not starting anything. But don't come over here talking about being a bad friend. You were my *best* friend until you chose not to be. But we're grown women now, Lia. Let's just accept that we're a long way past pretence, okay? You chose your life, and I chose mine, so just tell me what you want.'

Lia's anger evaporated and her face fell, but only slightly. The Botox saw to that. She sat back down. 'You're right.'

There was silence for a minute, but Jen's guard stayed up. Lia would have made a great actress.

'We can forget about you and me, if that's what you want. But our kids were best friends, Jen. Willow loved Alex so much.' She shook her head now, seeming genuinely sad for the first time. But for *her* daughter, not for Jen's.

'And Simon?'

Lia shook her head. 'Yes! And Simon. What, Jen? They've been best friends all their lives! You think he underwent a personality transplant in the past few weeks or something?'

Jen didn't respond. Instead, she let an uncomfortable silence settle upon them, knowing that Lia would feel the need to fill it eventually.

'He's—'

'Did Jay send you over here?' Jen cut her off before she could start making excuses.

'No, he...'

'You know what kind of man Jay is. You know better than anyone, and yet you still—'

'Jay is a good man, Jen, and—'

'Yeah? Tell Paul Greene that.'

Lia frowned. 'Paul Greene?'

Jen raised her eyebrows. Standing face to face with Lia like this, minus the pretence of their daily existence, she felt some of her old strength return. 'Have you actually forgotten about Paul Greene? Because I haven't. I remember quite plainly the beating Jay gave him. And I remember *very* clearly how easily you lied to protect him. *Again.* You lied when he raped you, too, remember? You called *me* a liar, then you sat back and let him spread all sorts of rumours about me.' She looked her up and down, making no effort to hide her disgust. 'You always put on such a great show for everyone. The perfect wife. The perfect mother. But you're a liar, Lia. So, when you stand there, telling me how *good* your husband is, and how *good* your son is, and that your family had nothing to do with my daughter's death' – she stepped in closer – 'remember who you're speaking to. I *know* you. I know *him*. So your words hold no water with me.'

Lia's breathing became heavier now and Jen could feel her own body trembling. She knew she had her. She had come here to get Jen to call off Holly Myer. But now she was lost, and she couldn't see a way to get to her desired destination. And Jen had no intentions of making it easy for her.

'Jay sent you over here to tell me to back off. Am I right? But you know that Holly is Paul Greene's daughter, yeah? Good luck getting *her* to back off. And I'm not backing off either, so you can relay that back to your loving husband. You might be afraid of him, Lia. But I'm not.'

Lia ignored the fresh jibe about Jay as she recovered herself from Jen's list of harsh truths. 'My son didn't do anything,' she said defiantly. 'This is bullying, Jen. That woman wants to push my son—'

'Like he pushed Alex?'

Lia flinched, but she recovered herself quickly and stood up again. She stepped closer to Jen, her own pretence gone now, too. 'You're not coping, Jen. You're not thinking rationally, so I'll forgive you for that. But come after my family and I swear to God, it'll be the last thing you ever do.'

'Ah.' Jen smiled bitterly. 'There she is. The real Lia Higgins. Where have you been?'

Lia turned and walked away, and Jen stood watching her go. As the front door slammed shut, Jen picked up her phone. It was answered on the first ring.

'Hello?'

'Holly? It's Jen. You've rattled the cage.'

# FORTY-ONE

## LIA

Alone in her kitchen as she so often was, Lia felt the walls slowly closing in, the weight of the deafening silence pushing against them. Jay was so used to getting people to do exactly what he wanted. But he didn't know Jen Blake. Not like she did. Jen was one of the most dogged people she knew. If she believed there'd been a wrongdoing, then she would not shut up about it. She certainly wouldn't *pull her neck in*, regardless of what Jay wanted. He underestimated her, but Lia did not. Not anymore.

Now, having stood in her shabby kitchen, she could see just how far the woman had fallen. Jen Blake had nothing left to lose, and that made her incredibly dangerous. But Jay would never hear that. He refused to see anyone as a threat, especially not a grieving woman in worn-out clothes.

Lia brought her hand to her chest. It felt painfully tight, like she was headed for a heart attack, which of course she couldn't be. She worked out and ate too healthily for that. But something was definitely happening to her. The room was spinning, her mind was racing, her skin felt uncomfortably hot and prickly. Jen would do everything she could to bring them down. She'd been looking for a way to do that for years. But up until now, she couldn't. Not without hurting her own daughter. Then a thought occurred to Lia. She looked sharply at her phone, which was sitting face down on the table. Still rubbing her chest with the heel of her hand, she hurried over and picked it up. She opened her Snapchat and scrolled until she found the text message thread she was looking for. Lia saved all chats, just in case. Her chest tightened a little more, and heat spread through her entire body. She pressed her thumb against the screen to highlight, then pressed delete. She repeated the action for several messages then she stood there for a while longer, staring at the phone.

Lia paid attention to the apps her kids used. One of her jobs was to be central to their lives, so she knew that if she deleted a Snapchat that she had saved, it would delete for the other person as well. She started deleting.

She hurried upstairs in search of her laptop, her mind racing through all the things that could be held against them. Before the machine had a chance to boot up, Lia's mind raced off ahead of her, sending her to her wardrobe where she started tearing clothes out onto the floor. She pulled her dark blue jeans out and threw them on the bed, then she kept rooting until she found the pink cashmere sweater that Jay had bought for her in Milan. She threw that on top of the jeans. What else was she wearing on the night when the whole city searched for Alex Blake? Which of her belongings carried the stench of the murky river? Because that was all she could smell now. She went to where her jackets were hung and started rooting through those as well. But then she closed her eyes, thinking. No. No jacket. She shoved the jeans and jumper into a bag and brought them out of the room with her.

She moved to Simon's room next and started pulling clothes out of his wardrobe. She fell to her knees and fought to keep breathing, sure now that she *was* having a heart attack. She tried to start her breathing exercises, but there was no air passing in *or* out. She was suffocating. She could hear a ringing phone, and she crawled towards the door, but the ringing stopped before she got there. It started up again immediately and the front door opened downstairs.

'Mum?'

'Willow,' Lia tried to call, but her voice wouldn't carry.

Willow came upstairs anyway. 'Mum!' She ran to Lia and dropped to her knees beside her. She glanced over her shoulder into Simon's room and the pile of clothes in the middle of the floor. She frowned, her face pale and blotchy. 'I'll call Dad.' Willow stood up.

'No,' Lia said, pulling herself into a sitting position. 'Don't call Dad.'

Willow's arrival brought with it the fresh air that Lia's lungs had been crying out for. The pain in her chest began to ease and her breathing, though still rough and loud, was calming.

'Mum?' Willow started to cry, though she looked like she hadn't ever stopped.

Lia reached out and caught her arm. 'I'm okay, Willow. I'm okay.' She made herself smile at the girl, who looked as bad as Lia felt. She took another minute to breathe as deeply as she could, then accepted Willow's help to stand. 'What are you doing home?' she asked, when she could. It was less than halfway through the school day.

Willow shook her head. 'I can't be there, Mum.' She leaned against the wall and slid to the floor, tears and snot flowing down her face suddenly.

Lia looked at her, then lowered herself shakily back down beside her, relieved to be off her weakened legs again. Her mind was all over the place. It was on her phone content. It was on Simon's. It was on Jen Blake and the panic attack she'd just had. She knew that's what it was now, because it had happened before. Several times, and each time she was convinced she would die. But of course, she didn't. She'd learned exercises to help quell them and sometimes they worked. Just not today. But now, she needed to bring her focus back to Willow. It's like her beautiful, rebellious daughter was disappearing before her eyes and was being replaced by this shell of a girl. Lia's full focus should have been on Willow all along, and suddenly she resented both Jay and Simon for taking up all the space in her head.

'What's going on?' she asked as softly and as steadily as she could.

'I just can't be there,' she cried. 'I didn't just lose my best friend, Mum. I've lost the ability to *make* friends. All because I'm twins with *him*.' She waved a hand towards Simon's room.

Lia recoiled slightly.

'He doesn't like girls, and they don't like him. Alex was the only one of my friends who didn't stop hanging out with me, because of Simon.'

'What do you mean, he doesn't like girls?' Lia's breath caught in her chest. Willow didn't respond, but her crying had stopped, and her shoulders rose, juddered and fell with her own erratic breathing.

Lia took a moment to get her thoughts in line, while she breathed deeply, counting her inhales and her exhales. 'I hope you haven't said that to anyone else, Willow,' she said after a while.

Willow glared at her then, her eyes narrowed in disgust. 'He's my brother,' she hissed.

Lia nodded and pulled her closer. After a few seconds, she said, 'But you didn't answer my question.'

Willow pulled back from her. 'What did you find in there that made you rip his whole room apart?' She gestured again towards Simon's open bedroom door.

Lia shrugged. 'Nothing. I just got tired of how it looked.'

Willow's face said that she didn't believe her. 'So how come you're going through it again then? What are you looking for?'

'That's *his* mess,' Lia lied. 'I was about to tidy it up. Like I'm not busy enough.'

'With what?'

'I always have things to do.' Lia struggled to her feet again. 'Don't tell your dad you bunked off from school.' She went into Simon's room and started folding his clothes and placing them back in the wardrobe. In the pile she found his black padded school jacket. She looked at it for a second, then balled it up and put it in the bag with her own clothes. When she finished in his room, she closed his door and left, exuding a calmness now that she did not feel.

Willow was still sitting on the floor on the landing. She followed her mother with her eyes, but Lia avoided her stare. Willow was never very good at hiding her feelings. Even without ever saying a word, the way she looked at Lia, and the way she went out of her way to antagonise Jay, made it very clear what she thought about them both. It was the only thing that gave Lia any hope now. Hope that Willow might build a life for herself that was as far removed from Lia's as it could get. But first Lia had to somehow untie the girl from her brother.

Lia went downstairs and let herself out into the back garden. She opened the wheelie bin, which was three quarters full and pulled out two bags. She placed the bag of clothes inside and replaced the other two bags on top. The bins would go out tonight and then everything would be gone by tomorrow.

# FORTY-TWO
## SIMON

They weren't subtle. But he supposed idiots never were, so he could see them all whispering in closed circles about him when he returned after his two-week suspension. Nudging each other and talking wide-eyed whenever he walked by. Or falling silent when he entered a room, which was just as bad. He fucking hated this school and everyone in it. He didn't want to go here, but as usual, he wasn't given a choice. Simon had seen pictures of his parents from when they attended St Brendan's, so he knew how fit and good-looking his father had always been. He was the kind of guy that all the girls wanted and all the boys wanted to be. Those were the words *he'd* used to describe his time there, back when Simon's choice of secondary school was being made *for* him. His father was still that kind of man, and for some reason, he expected Simon to become that as well. Even now. And as for his mother, well, she was just a younger version of herself. Pretty, but thick. If his dad wasn't the switched-on man that he was, then Simon would have thought she'd slept with someone else to get pregnant with him. It was the only way to explain the fact that he was fat and ugly, despite their gene pool. But his dad would have known if she did that, and he wouldn't have let it slide. He certainly wouldn't be raising Simon as his own. Only a fool would do that, and his father was no fool.

He shoved his books into his locker, ignoring them all, and then he turned and walked towards the door. He could hear Alex's name being whispered. It's all anyone talked about now. You'd swear they fucking liked her or something.

He walked away from the school and in the opposite direction to home. He wasn't ready to go there yet. He couldn't stand to be around his mother, ever since she found those photos in his desk. She thought he was some kind of weirdo or something and she wanted him to feel like shit about it. Like *she* knew anything about anything. He didn't want to be around Willow either. She acted like he was contagious. Like she was so much better than him. She could be such a bitch sometimes, but she was falling apart and strangely, no one else seemed to notice. Or give a shit. Willow, the social butterfly, the perfect princess, was fading in front of everyone's eyes, and no one cared. She hadn't eaten in weeks, she'd lost too much weight, her hair was falling out and Simon had seen her examining their mother's Xanax bottle a bit too closely last week. But no one else appeared to see a thing and he wondered how popular Willow was feeling now. Simon was starting to think that women in general were just bitches. His father had told him as much when he was taking away his laptop. Even the ones who were supposed to care about you by default. His mother, his *twin* sister, the girls at school. Alex.

He'd given her nothing but love since as far back as he could remember. He'd spent hours looking up random shit about female *trailblazers* and outspoken bitches, for her. He'd gone to the weird movies that Willow didn't want to sit through, with her. He sliced his finger open trying to fix her bike when her waster of a father couldn't free himself up to do it for her. She'd laughed, cried and done everything with him. With *him*. She'd been leading him on his whole life.

'Bitch,' he muttered to himself, feeling his anger rise.

'Hey, Simon?'

He turned when he heard the voice. It was Nevin, or NevvieNev as he idiotically called himself online.

'Oh, hey, Nev.'

'You ditching, too, bro?'

Simon smiled and nodded. He could feel his face flushing red and he hated that he was so fucking awkward. Talking was easy. So why was he so bad at it?

'Come on,' Nev said, bobbing his head towards the rugby pitch.

Simon nodded and walked behind him. The clubhouse was locked up when they got there, as they knew it would be, so they went round the back and sat at the bar's outdoor seating.

'Here, mental what's going on, isn't it?' Nev said, lighting up a cigarette and offering one to Simon.

Simon looked at the pack. Smoking made him feel physically sick, but he found himself taking one anyway. 'Yeah. Mental.'

'And now that reporter is sniffing around as well.' He nudged Simon and grinned. 'Don't worry, bro. I won't hang you out.'

Simon squinted at him. What did *that* mean? But instead of having the balls to ask, he just took baby puffs of his cigarette, while Nev sat back inhaling deeply on his.

'It must be weird for you, though. Having a girl that you were actually with, topping herself.'

Simon just nodded, feeling his insides tighten.

'So, like, was it just a one-time thing with you and her, or what?'

Simon knew exactly what was going on here. Nev was gathering information. Information that he would use to stoke the fires and put himself front and centre to the drama.

'Well?' Nev nudged him.

Yet Simon craved his approval. He shrugged. 'Friends with benefits,' he said. He enjoyed the smile that came to his lips when he said it. He enjoyed the idea that people would believe that he'd been able to *have* Alex whenever he wanted her.

Nev raised his eyebrows and chuckled out a long stream of smoke. 'Nice. And Willow?'

Simon's smile melted away. Willow. Miss Popular. Miss *How Is He Your Twin?* Willow. 'Don't be daft,' he said.

'I'm only saying what I heard, bro. Still, though, must feel a bit weird now. What exactly happened, do you know? The way that reporter is going on, it's like she thinks she was pushed or something.'

Simon's fleeting smile was long gone now, and he shrugged. 'I only know what you know. That she chucked herself in the river. Who'd be bothered to push her?'

Nev hissed and nodded slowly. 'You must feel a bit shit about the posters now, though.'

Simon looked sharply at him. 'You printed them!'

Nev laughed. 'Only because you gave them to me, bro. It was all your idea, remember?'

Why the fuck did he have to send those pictures? He knew they'd use them. Maybe that's why he sent them. Maybe *he* wanted to be at the centre of something for once. Maybe it was time Willow and Alex were the ones being laughed at, instead of him, for a change.

'Obviously she couldn't take a joke,' Nev said, as if it was a perfectly normal thing to say.

Simon got up. 'Anyway, see ya.'

'Where you off to?'

'Home.'

'Won't your parents kick your ass for ditching school?'

Simon looked at his watch. It was after two. 'Nah. My mother will be at the gym and my dad will be at work.'

Nev laughed quietly. 'I hope you don't mind me saying this, bro. But your mother...' He shook his head. 'I totally would.'

Simon forced a smile and a nod, then he walked away.

He hated when people said things like that about his mother. But worse was how much *she* loved it. It was her job to look good for his father. *Not* for the rest of the city. She flaunted herself any chance she got, and she was teaching Willow to do the same. That's why she wore half nothing whenever she left the house now. Or, at least, she did. It was all for attention from men. That was how they trapped them.

Simon did like women, though. He liked looking at them. He thought about them a lot and lost control of himself within minutes of letting his imagination go where it wanted to go. Seconds sometimes, which he knew would be embarrassing when an actual woman became involved in those moments. That's why Alex wouldn't let him do it. That's why she turned into a bitch. That's why, when he *did* get to do it with a woman, it would be with someone who couldn't make him feel that embarrassment. Someone who didn't *get* to say no.

# FORTY-THREE

## JEN

HOLLY MYER

Can we meet?

JEN BLAKE

Where and when?

HOLLY MYER

The café at Blackrock Castle Observatory? I'm there now.

JEN BLAKE

I'm on the way.

Jen was already halfway to the car by the time she sent the last message to Holly. Another week had passed since she'd doorstepped Lia and Jay, and Jen still hadn't heard a peep from her. She'd had to stop herself from calling or texting Holly incessantly since the day she first met her. She guessed that it would be the quickest way to put the woman off. When she did call her to say that she'd rattled Lia's cage, she got the distinct impression that Holly didn't appreciate Jen's intrusion into her investigation. Jen knew now that Holly didn't need the running commentary, or pats on the back. She certainly wouldn't enjoy having Jen hounding her for answers, so despite her own impatience, she forced herself to leave Holly alone. But now it was Holly calling Jen and so she drove a little too fast to get to Blackrock Castle. To say that she was keen to find out what Holly had to say, was an understatement.

Jen used to love Blackrock Castle, but the place was shrouded in darkness for her now. When she got there, Holly was at a table at the back corner of the café, beside the window. In front of her was a steaming coffee and beside it, a cup that had already been drunk.

'Thanks for calling,' Jen said, gratefully, sitting down opposite her.

'Sorry for the short notice.' Holly smiled, sticking her hand in the air to get the waiter's attention. 'I tend to work on a minute-by-minute basis.'

'You can call me anytime.'

'What can I get you?' A smiling teenager arrived at the table.

'An Americano, please,' Jen answered, keeping her eyes on Holly. She didn't particularly want coffee, but requesting some was the quickest way to get rid of the boy. She desperately wanted to hear what Holly had to say.

'Okay, so I don't have anything yet that would stand up in court, but... what was Alex's relationship to Lia Higgins?'

Jen frowned. 'Lia?'

'Yeah. It's just that something's come up that made me wonder. So I went back over all the stuff I've gathered from Alex's phone and socials etcetera, as well as what I've gathered from the kids at St Brendan's. We have a whole heap of stuff linking Simon Higgins to the bullying campaign against Alex and some very weird comments he's made about her. Enough to paint a pretty dark picture of Simon. But there seemed to be a lot of back and forth between Alex and Lia as well. Nothing sinister. All pretty normal stuff really, but would that have been usual for them?'

'What do you mean?'

'WhatsApp and Snapchat mostly. Mind you, the Snapchat ones have since been deleted.' She raised her eyebrows then. 'Which is strange in itself. They were all innocent enough messages, so I thought nothing of them when I first read them a few weeks ago. And they'd been saved. So why delete them now?' She looked questioningly at Jen, like she should know the answer.

'What kind of messages?' Jen stared at her, wondering if she'd seen some that Jen hadn't. She had seen messages between Alex and Lia, but only the usual stuff. Nothing worrying. Jen messaged Willow sometimes, too. Good luck with this, well done on that, making arrangements for drop-offs and pick-ups. That sort of thing. She hadn't paid any attention to the message threads with Lia, because like that, it wasn't unusual. But what had Holly seen? Or what else had *come up?*

'She didn't mention Simon or anything like that. But on the day before Alex died, they were messaging each other on Snapchat. Lia messaged Alex, asking if she was okay. Alex responded, *Not really*, and Lia told her to come over.'

Jen frowned again.

'All innocent enough. Your kids were best friends, they were in each other's lives, and it's got a motherly kind of vibe to it, right? Could it be that Lia knew about the bullying and was concerned for Alex? Even though her son was the bully?'

Jen thought about that for a second, doing her best to keep her fragile ego at bay. 'Well, Willow would have cried on *my* shoulder from time to time when they were younger. Not so much since Dale lost his job and I became so much busier, but... it wouldn't be outlandish to think that Alex might have cried on Lia's shoulder at times, too, I suppose.'

Holly nodded. 'But would she have confided in Lia if Simon was the one who was bothering her?'

Jen was assailed by jealousy now. She was never home. Lia was never anywhere *but* home and she was the cool fucking mom. But she was also Simon's mom.

'Honestly, Jen – the last person a teenager wants to confide in, is their own parent.' Holly must have sensed her ridiculous insecurity. 'Lia Higgins seems to put herself in the middle of her kids' lives. Cool mom, right? So, would Alex have confided in her?'

Jen nodded, her lip trembling with emotion. 'She might have,' she admitted. 'But she was *Simon's* mother. Surely Alex would have known that Lia would side with him?'

'Maybe that wasn't the impression Lia gave her? Either way, by the looks of things, Lia invited Alex over the day before she died. And then there was this...' Holly turned her phone towards Jen. She tilted her head and read the message.

> **ABLAKE**
>
> I have to tell my mum, but can you come with me when I do? She won't freak out if you're there. I'm at the courts. We have to fix this.

'Alex sent this to Lia Higgins at a quarter to six on the day she disappeared, and then she saved it.'

Jen closed her eyes, thinking. She frowned deeply and shook her head. 'What did she need to tell me?' The words crawled slowly out, weighed down with sadness and regret.

'I don't know. But Lia does.'

Jen stared wide-eyed at Holly. 'Surely the guards will see this for what it is?'

'She didn't tell you about this message, did she?'

'The only message Lia told me about was Alex's...' She brought her hand to her mouth. 'Her...'

'Suicide note?' Holly offered gently.

'But why wouldn't she tell me about this? She knew I was looking for her – wondering why she hadn't come home. Why would she just say nothing when she knew how worried I was?'

Holly sat looking thoughtfully at her for a moment. Then she asked, 'What time did you first contact Lia that day?'

Jen shrugged and shook her head. 'About seven, I think.'

'And was Simon there when you spoke to her?'

'I don't know. But I spoke to him first. Around six o'clock, or maybe a little later. He was outside, on his way home.'

'At six? So Alex was last seen running from the school at home time. That was around three. Obviously, she didn't go straight home, but she texted Lia at a quarter to six saying that she wanted to tell you something.' She looked away, thinking. 'Did Simon say where he'd been until six o'clock? Or you said it might have been a little later?'

Jen shook her head. 'Only that Alex was acting strangely.'

'Nothing about the locker prank that sent her running from the school? Only that *she* was acting weird?'

Jen's face darkened at the memory and anger flared in her again.

'So, is it possible that Lia received that message from Alex and went out looking for her herself? If Alex had been confiding in her about Simon, and he hadn't come home from school by that time either – she might have felt that need.'

Jen didn't respond. Hairs pricked on the back of her neck and her mind was racing.

'Okay, so I'm working backwards, joining the dots that I can see,' Holly continued. 'We can only assume that Lia went to try to find Alex after receiving that message, which would make either Lia, if she found her, or Simon Higgins the last person to see Alex before she died.'

Jen's eyes filled with tears again. 'But why wouldn't Lia say something? Why would she leave me like this – not knowing? I sent her off to school that morning and I never got to see her again.' Tears dripped off the end of her chin. 'Lia knows that. So why...'

'She received the second message hours later. The one that they're calling her suicide note.'

'Does that mean she didn't find her?' Jen asked, desperate for the pieces to connect and start making sense. 'That Simon... that he...'

Holly opened her laptop, tapped some keys and then motioned for Jen to move over to her side of the table. Her face was impassive to Jen's emotion, but she had a determined look. Like Jen had just confirmed something for her.

'Come here,' she said quietly, when Jen failed to pick up on her head movements.

Jen moved haltingly around the table to sit alongside Holly, who twisted her laptop so that Jen could see whatever she was about to show her. A night-time image of a section of the quays filled the screen.

'What's this?'

'It's CCTV. The way the tide was that night, rescuers believe that Alex didn't enter the water down here. Experience tells them that she went in closer to town and that the current carried her to where she was found. This footage is from the Port of Cork building, further up along the quays.'

Jen studied the footage. A few cars drove by, heading towards the city. Workers heading home for the evening. Then there was nothing for a while. Jen had her eyes peeled for Alex and she must have radiated desperation.

'You won't see Alex, Jen. I'm sorry. I should have said that before now.'

Jen sat back. 'Then what am I looking at?'

'I know he's too young to have a licence or even to legally drive, but does Simon know *how* to drive?'

Jen shook her head and shrugged.

'There!' Holly pointed to the screen.

Whatever Holly had seen, Jen missed it. Holly hit a couple of keys, and the footage played in reverse. A car moved backwards across the screen, then she made it move forward again. A dark coloured car.

'So? What am I looking at?' Jen asked, feeling a little impatient now.

'Look closely at the car, Jen. Do you recognise it?' She rewound the footage again and played it at a slower speed this time. 'It's a dark blue Tesla. Doesn't Lia Higgins drive a dark blue Tesla?'

Jen bolted upright and leaned closer to the screen again. Jay and Lia changed their cars so often that most of the time, Jen had no idea what they were driving. But Holly was right. The blue Tesla had turned up a week before the kids went back to school. 'Go back.'

Holly did and Jen's eyes were glued to the screen now as the 2025 registered navy-blue Tesla moved across the screen in slow motion.

'Can you zoom in?' she asked, desperately.

'I can't. Not on this. But the guards would be able to. Could it have been Simon driving that car?'

'I... I don't know. Maybe?' Jen answered uncertainly. 'Is there more? I mean, other cameras? Can we follow that car?'

'Well, this isn't an episode of *Law and Order*, Jen. We've spent a combined total of nearly a hundred hours looking through CCTV before we found this, and it was purely by chance that I recognised the Tesla. But my Garda contact is coming under pressure to call a halt to us taking up their space, which is why I wanted to work backwards through everything I've found, look at it in a new light and speak to you, before asking for a little more leeway from them. Maybe even get them to help us, now that we have something. But it's tenuous at best, so don't get your hopes up.'

Holly hit another key and the screen froze. 'But... whoever was driving that car, assuming it *is* the Higginses' Tesla, on the night your daughter died... we now know that she was messaging with Lia Higgins at a quarter to six and the time stamp on that footage tells us that, about two and a half hours later, someone drove an identical car to Lia's down along the quays, past the Port of Cork building – we need more footage, but it certainly looks like her car, doesn't it? This would all coincide with the length of time they believe Alex was in the water before she was found a few hours later.'

Jen brought both hands to her mouth, squeezed her eyes shut and more tears poured down her cheeks.

Holly placed her hand on Jen's shoulder. 'Jen,' she said softly, 'I'll be very honest and say that I really battled with myself about whether or not to bring this to you. I mean, it really doesn't prove anything. It means nothing just now.'

'What do you mean, it doesn't prove anything?' Jen snapped. 'I knew it. Why did I take no for an answer from the guards?'

'Because they weren't listening,' Holly replied sadly. 'And they wouldn't have, because everything about Alex's death looks like a teenage suicide, including the awful bullying that she endured in the run up. Even with this' – she gestured towards her laptop – 'it still means nothing. But...'

Jen lifted her head to look at her.

'I think it might be enough to take to my Garda contacts and *maybe* pique their interest. At least enough to let us continue examining the CCTV, now that we know what we're looking for and where.'

'Make sure they know that Lia has a history of covering for those she loves, Holly, regardless of the consequences. You know that. So, if Simon pushed Alex into that river, then all he'd have to do is call his mother, and she'd cover for him until her dying breath. She'd somehow make it all go away.' Jen's mouth turned down in anger and disgust. 'Then she'd look me in the eye and smile, while holding a fucking bake sale in my honour.'

'You really think she's capable of all that?'

'I know she is.'

Holly nodded slowly and looked away, thinking.

'Holly?' Jen forced herself to be calm and remove some of the bitterness from her voice. 'I know this is a job for you. I know that I'm a grieving mother and as such, I must appear quite unreliable. Even I can see that.' She forced half a smile into her voice and Holly turned to look at her again. 'I also see what you're saying – the messages, the footage – none of it means anything on its own. But take me out of the equation. Take away my emotional investment in all of this. You could be the one to uncover a murder, where no one else was even looking. Please, talk to your police friends. Show them what you have and tell them – make them understand that Alex Blake had big plans for her life. That she had a mortal fear of water. That she would not have chosen to end her life, and she especially wouldn't have chosen to end it like that. Please. Make them understand that. Then show them what you have. After that – it's your story. You can tell the world what you did for our family.'

Holly closed her eyes. 'I think maybe you're—'

'I'm not.' She grabbed Holly's hand and made the woman look at her. 'Holly, I'm not. You're an excellent reporter, but you're an even better investigator. If I'm right, then you can help me... but if I'm wrong, you'll discover that, too. *That* will help me, too. And we can all move on,' she lied.

Jen watched the woman getting her thoughts in order. 'Okay,' she said finally. 'I'm not promising you anything. Like I said, this all means nothing...'

'Unless it means *something*.'

Holly nodded and closed her laptop. 'I'll be in touch soon.' She drained her second cup of coffee and stood up, shoving her laptop into her shoulder bag. She squeezed her way out around the table. Then she paused before leaving. 'For what it's worth, I do believe you,' she said softly. 'I just don't like to say things like that, and then be proven wrong.'

Jen closed her eyes and cried again, as Holly left.

# FORTY-FOUR

## LIA

'Lia, hi!' Holly smiled, pulling her backside away from the bonnet of Lia's car, where it appeared to have been resting for some time.

Lia paused momentarily as she walked out of the gym following a Bikram yoga class. Caught off guard, she was hot and sweaty, despite having showered inside. She hated Bikram yoga. But Jay had signed her up for ten classes and she still had another two to endure. The last thing she needed was to find someone waiting for her when she came out. And Holly Myer *was* waiting for her. That much was clear. Her car was parked right beside Lia's, despite the car park being mostly empty. But still she had the gall to sit on Lia's bonnet and not her own.

'Hi... Holly, isn't it?' Lia recovered herself quickly and smiled at the woman. She continued past her, to avoid looking at her for as long as she could. She opened her back door and threw her kitbag onto the seat, then closed it and opened her driver's door. She stood behind it, as if about to get in, keeping the door between her and Holly. Her mind raced through all the stupid things her son might have done to make Holly Myer believe she had a reason to be here.

'Do you mind if I ask you a couple of questions, Lia?'

'I'm sorry, but if it's about my husband's campaign, then I'm afraid you'd be better off speaking with him.' She knew it wasn't about Jay, but Lia did *not* want to speak to this woman. She'd say the wrong thing, her words would get twisted and Jay, along with the rest of the city, would hear Holly's version of this conversation.

'Oh, I'm not here about your husband. I'm here about your son, Simon.'

Lia folded her arms across her chest and dropped the smile. She stared at the woman momentarily, then she looked away and sat in her car, her insides turning soft suddenly.

'Why were you on the quays on the night Alex died, Lia?'

Lia froze, her finger on the ignition switch.

'Was Simon down there? Did he bring Alex there?' she asked, her voice getting slightly louder. 'Did he call you to come get him? Is that what happened, Lia?'

Lia jumped out of the car again. 'If you insist on going after my child like this, I'll have you in court so fast, your head will spin. Do you hear me?'

Holly gave an understanding smile. 'I get it. You'll do what you have to do to protect your child.'

'What would you know about that?' She looked the girl up and down. Holly was in her mid-twenties, single and childless as far as anyone knew.

Holly shrugged. 'Can you remember what your car was doing on the quays that night? Were you driving it?'

Lia got back into her car. 'I was there, searching for Alex Blake. Same as everyone else.'

'Yes, but I mean *earlier* that evening. Around the time Alex went into the water. Do you remember why you were there at *that* time? Or was Simon driving the car? Or maybe it was your husband? You'd been messaging with Alex earlier in the evening, isn't that right?' She faked a confused look. 'Were you the last person to see Alex Blake alive? You know, after she sent you that message saying that she was planning to tell her mum?'

Lia felt sick. She pulled the door closed and employed a white-knuckle grip on the steering wheel. Had she not been driving a silent Tesla, she would have revved and left tire marks on the tarmac as she pulled away. She watched the girl in her rear-view mirror, leaning casually against her own car now, watching Lia go. She had a smile on her face and a part of Lia wanted to knock the car into reverse and run the self-righteous little bitch over.

# FORTY-FIVE
## JEN

Jen had taken to walking the quays all the way to Blackrock Castle most nights now. She didn't care about the dangers of walking by herself in such a lonely area at night. She didn't care about anyone lurking in the shadows. Nothing compared to the darkness that lived with her ever since Alex died. So once again, she got in her car and drove towards town. Tonight she parked up near the Port of Cork building and got out of the car. She stood there for a while, watching the river flowing past her towards the mouth of the harbour, wondering what secrets it was taking with it. She pulled her zip up to her chin and buried her hands in her pockets. Then she turned and started walking.

Usually, Jen kept her eyes on the river while she walked, but tonight, she was looking up. For the first time she noticed the sheer number of CCTV cameras all along the quays. Just about all of the many buildings and warehouses had them. She'd walked by these buildings countless times in her life, and never noticed any of them. But thankfully Holly Myer was more in tune with her surroundings than Jen was. Apparently, those cameras were dotted all around the city, watching everything, and most people were lucky enough never to have to think about them. But Jen wasn't so lucky. Instead, she looked at every camera and wondered, did *this* one see Alex that night? If so, did she look scared? Was she crying? Did she look cold? Was she thinking about Jen and wondering why she wasn't there with her? Why she was *never* there with her?

A wave of anger, upset and deep, deep regret bubbled up through her and came out in a loud, heaving sob. Why *her* child? Why Alex? Jen roughly wiped her eyes with the heels of her hands and started walking again. She continued along the path, her eyes scanning the river sprinting alongside her, hoping that it would tell her exactly where it swallowed up her child. The sun had set now, and it was a windy evening. There was no one else around and the thought of jumping in there herself briefly entered Jen's mind. As her eyes scanned further along the path, she stopped in her tracks when she saw the silhouette of a woman up ahead. She was standing at the edge looking down into the river, her arms limp by her sides. All of Jen's senses heightened and suddenly she was on high alert. She looked around again. There was no one else here. She started moving slowly towards the woman and only when she got so close that she could reach out and touch her, did Jen realise that it wasn't a woman at all. It was a girl. It was Willow Higgins.

# FORTY-SIX

## JEN

Whether or not Willow knew she wasn't alone, Jen didn't know. The girl never looked around. She never moved or gave any indication that she knew she was being watched. She just stood there like a limp, scrawny statue. That is, until she leaned forward and let herself fall, into the rushing river below.

'Willow!' The name burst from Jen as she lunged to grab her. But she was too late. Willow was gone. Swallowed up by the river.

Without thinking, Jen ran and dived in. The shock of hitting the icy water paralysed her momentarily. It felt like dozens of knives stabbing her repeatedly, and as she sank beneath the surface there was nothing but blackness all around her. Everything Jen thought she knew about swimming was forgotten, and she panicked, as the river overpowered her and pulled her away from the shore. Within seconds, she'd become completely disorientated and had no idea which way was up. She felt sure she was going to die. But finally, her legs started to respond. They kicked wildly, and her arms pulled at the wall of water above her head, clawing their way through until eventually she broke the surface and heaved air into her lungs. She looked all around her, but she couldn't get her bearings. And she couldn't see Willow.

'W...' She heaved and coughed. 'Willow!' she called as loud as she could, her voice cracking and breaking as she spun herself around and searched frantically for the girl. She was being pulled downriver and Jen had to fight hard to keep her head above the surface. 'Willow!' she screamed. Had she imagined her?

But then she saw an arm waving in the air and then disappearing under the surface. A head bobbed up and then under again.

'Willow!' She tried to swim, but her body was frozen and rigid, her clothes heavy with water. She forced her legs to move and kick and the river propelled her forward. But it also pulled Willow along. 'Willow!' she screamed again, and this time foul-tasting water rushed into her mouth. The violent river seemed determined to claim them both. To swallow them whole like it had Alex. The air in her lungs was replaced with water and they burned, as she coughed and spluttered and sank beneath the surface again. But this time she wasn't alone in the darkness. Alex was there. Her presence was so clear that Jen reached out her hand to touch her. Alex smiled her beautiful smile, then turned and glided away, like she was on a leisurely swim. Something she'd never had the chance to do in life.

Jen mustered all the strength she could, and she kicked and pulled until she broke the surface again and she coughed and cried and begged the air around her to fill her up. Someone else gasped and choked on water nearby. She looked around frantically.

'Alex!' she called.

She saw the head sinking below the surface again.

Jen kicked and splashed and pulled herself towards where she saw her going under. 'Alex!' she cried again, reaching under the water and grabbing a fistful of hair. She pulled until the girl broke through and the weight of her pushed Jen under. But she clutched her to her chest. Willow. Jen held her breath and squeezed her eyes shut and begged Alex to help her. With that she was above the water again and her legs were pumping hard.

'Kick, Willow! Kick!' She coughed and gasped.

Willow was crying out, screaming and flailing, and she was driving Jen underwater again. Jen could feel whatever strength she had leaving her. She couldn't keep going. She couldn't hold on, and she couldn't swim anymore.

Her head bumped against the wall before she could orientate herself and her hand searched for something, anything to grab onto as relief washed over her. Her other arm tightened again around Willow's chest and Willow was clutching it back. Neither of them noticed the blue lights flashing in the darkness further back. Neither of them noticed anything other than their own desperation to survive.

'Willow, grab onto something,' Jen begged the girl. 'Help!' she tried to shout, when she heard people, somewhere nearby, calling out. But she was too weak to project her voice.

Willow was trying to grab onto the bank. She twisted her body and stretched her arms out in all directions. Jen sank beneath her again, but she somehow managed to hold her breath this time and push Willow off her, towards the wall, pinning her to it. Suddenly the weight of Willow lifted, and Jen felt light again. But weak. So weak.

'Grab on!' a voice shouted, and a life ring landed beside her, just as she was going under again.

Jen reached for it and gripped with both hands. Willow was being pulled up onto the bank. She was out. Jen held on tight as the ring started to move, being pulled by a man, while another was helping Willow to sit up. They were firefighters, who looked like they were ready to enter the water themselves.

'Willow,' Jen cried, as she clawed at the mucky bank, before hands grabbed her and started pulling.

Willow coughed and cried, and Jen had never seen such fear in another human being. As she was pulled up the bank, she reached out her hand and grabbed Willow's knee.

'It's okay. We're okay,' she said, her voice hoarse and shaking as violently as her body was. Willow's lips were tinged blue, and her skin was ghostly pale. Jen knew she must look the same. She was numb and yet her bones ached like nothing she'd ever felt.

'It's my fault,' Willow cried loudly, coughing and heaving and sounding like she wanted to die. 'Alex is dead and it's all because of me.'

'You're okay.' The man who'd pulled Jen out let go of the rope and rolled her onto her back. He helped her to sit up. She didn't have the strength to do that for herself. 'There's an ambulance on the way. You're okay,' he continued reassuringly as two Gardaí arrived behind him.

'Did you say Alex?' one of them asked. 'Alex Blake?'

Jen's loud gasping breaths stopped, and she turned her head to looked at him.

'Mrs Blake?' It was the guard who'd sat and half listened to her at the station that day. The one who made her tea, but didn't believe her story. Garda Walsh.

Jen nodded.

He frowned and crouched down between Jen and Willow. 'And are you Willow Higgins, pet?'

Willow just cried. 'I'm sorry,' she keened, shaking her head from side to side. 'I'm s... so s... sorry.'

'H... h... how d... did you kn... know where to f... find us?' Jen asked, hardly able to speak, let alone process what Willow was saying. That Alex was dead because of her. Moments ago, Jen was certain that they were both about to die. She saw Alex. So how, in the blink of an eye, were they on land and surrounded by people?

'Someone saw you going in and they called 999. I just

happened to be on duty.' He took his phone out of his pocket and started texting someone.

Jen cried again and willed her brain to wake up. She wanted to ask if he was taking in what Willow was saying because she could hardly take any of it in herself. Not well enough to come up with any kind of a response. But then she remembered Alex's beautiful face, smiling at her through the darkness. Jen had tasted just a morsel of the fear that her child would have felt in the last minutes of her life. She pulled herself together and forced her thoughts into line.

'This is W... Willow Higgins,' she sobbed finally, pulling her hand slowly away from Willow's knee and turning to look at the girl. 'And she's going to t... tell you what h... happened to my child. She's going to tell us a... all how Alex d... died.'

# FORTY-SEVEN

## JEN

Jen hadn't really slept. Not since Alex died and not that night either. Yet, it was close to lunchtime now and she was still lying there, looking up at the ceiling. She couldn't bring herself to get up today. She couldn't bring herself to do anything, including answering the door when the bell chimed.

A loud knock quickly followed the bell, and Jen was tempted to go on ignoring it. But instead, she pulled herself into a sitting position and leaned towards the window. Holly Myer was out there, impatiently looking for signs that Jen was at home. Jen jumped up and knocked on the window. She held up two fingers, asking the woman to wait. She pulled on the tracksuit bottoms she'd discarded on the floor the night before, and her hoodie that was bundled on the chair in the corner of the room. She finished dressing while hurrying down the stairs. When she opened the front door, Holly came inside without waiting to be invited and she walked ahead of Jen to the kitchen. Jen eagerly followed her.

'I wanted to be the one to tell you,' she said, clearly trying to control her excitement.

'Tell me what?' Jen asked, breathlessly. 'You've been ignoring my calls for two weeks.'

'I wasn't ignoring your calls, Jen. I was choosing not to answer until I had something to tell you.' There was a hint of annoyance in her voice now. 'And here I am, by the way.'

'No one will talk to me, Holly. I've been calling the police station every day. Willow admitted that Alex was dead because of her, but then they stuck an oxygen mask on her, Jay and Lia rocked up and that was the end of it!' Her voice rose in frustration. It had been two weeks since she and Willow were pulled from the river. Two weeks since she'd eaten anything substantial and a lot more than two weeks since she'd slept. It was as if she'd ceased to exist when her feet left the shore that night.

Holly's smile was gone. 'I'm here now, Jen,' she said reassuringly. 'I'll tell you what I know. Actually, let's sit in here.' She nodded towards the sitting room and the couch near the window. She sat in a way that she could look across at the Higginses' house, while she spoke to Jen. 'You're right. Willow clammed up as soon as Jay and Lia arrived at the hospital. They wouldn't let her speak to anyone. But Shane Walsh, the guard who was there when you two were pulled from the river, was aware that my contact, Cillian Twomey, was looking into Alex's death. Building on the CCTV footage that we found, Alex's message to Lia, and everything else that cast shade on Simon Higgins, he decided to take a look. Shane messaged him as soon as he saw the two of you that night. He *did* take in Willow's apologies, and whatever else she was saying before she clammed up. Cillian got some company, and they looked a little harder at the whole thing. That's all I know for sure,' she said, no longer able to keep the smile from her face. 'That, and the fact that the Gardaí are on the way to the Higginses' house and as far as I know, they're coming with an arrest warrant.'

Jen fell into a chair. 'Wh...' She shook her head. 'For who?'

'That's the bit I'm not sure about. My contact wouldn't tell me. He said his head would roll if it got out. But he did say that an arrest was imminent, and that they're confident they have enough evidence to send to the DPP.'

'What evidence?' Jen asked, holding her stomach tightly. It was empty and churning and creeping upwards.

'My guess is that the CCTV from the quays eventually came up trumps, or Willow spilled her guts. Or both. But something happened and... they're coming.'

'So... it wasn't suicide?' Jen asked almost in a whisper.

Holly shook her head.

Jen doubled over and cried loud, heaving sobs. Her arms wrapped more tightly around herself, as her head fell onto her lap.

'Jen?' Holly said, her phone in her hand. 'This is because of you. *You* never gave up.'

Jen could hardly breathe with crying, and her chest was as tight as a fist.

'Will I call Dale?'

Jen looked up and nodded. Suddenly she wanted him here. She hated him for not believing her. For believing so easily that Alex had died by choice. But he loved Alex more than life itself. He deserved to know this, too.

As Holly moved away with her eyes fixed on the phone, Jen's peripheral vision picked up a twirling blue light outside the sitting room window. She straightened slightly to see a squad car pulling into the estate and heading towards Lia Higgins' house.

'Holly!' Jen dragged herself to her feet and stumbled towards the door. She fought with the latch until Holly opened it for her and she all but fell out onto the driveway. The police car crawled along the road, checking house numbers. Jen stumbled onto the green, Holly's steadying hand on her shoulder. Time seemed to slow.

At the Higginses' door, Lia stood with her phone pressed to

her ear, face draining of colour as she watched the car approach. She knew. Of course she knew. Jay's car screeched into the estate seconds later, as if summoned. Behind Lia, Willow appeared, then Simon at the upstairs window – he turned and moved away the moment the squad car stopped at the end of their driveway.

Jen's hands curled into fists as the Gardaí approached Lia. One reached for her phone, but she jerked away, still frantically speaking to Jay. He abandoned his car half across someone else's driveway and went running toward them.

'Jay!' Lia's voice carried across the green. She tried shoving her children back inside with one hand while holding the other out toward the guards like a shield. Simon's face was pure terror behind Lia now. Willow looked shell-shocked. Finally, Lia's eyes found Jen's. Their gazes locked and something crumbled in Lia's expression. She started to cry, and Jen's knees gave out. This woman had covered up Alex's death, had watched Jen and Dale spiral into madness with grief, had protected the monsters in her family just like she'd always done.

Hot lava bubbled up inside her and a blind rage took over. She got to her feet and half stumbled, half ran at the woman.

'Jen!' Holly called after her, but Jen ignored her.

Both Gardaí turned to look at her. One of them left his colleague and hurried towards Jen, while the other one tussled with both Jay and Lia now.

'They killed my baby!' Jen cried out, as the Garda reached her and held his arms out to stop her from going any further. She screamed over his shoulder, pushing against him.

He was trying his best not to manhandle her, as neighbours appeared at their doors. 'Leave it. She'll get what's coming to her,' the Garda said softly to her.

His voice was so full of conviction that Jen did stop pushing. 'She?' Her voice cracked. Willow? Alex's best friend? The love of her life? Or was it Lia herself? Jen squeezed her eyes shut and her heart broke all over again.

The guard placed both hands on her shoulders and squeezed gently as Jen dropped her head against his chest. She cried until she lost her breath, and it was only when several pairs of arms reached around her, that the Garda took a step back. Her neighbours. People she hardly knew because she'd spent so much time at work. People who thought she'd lost her mind, along with her child. People in disbelief that this could have happened in their quiet little cul-de-sac.

She should have taken solace in the fact that her fears had been vindicated. In seeing the real Higgins family on display for the world to see. Jay was feral, going nose to nose with the guards, roaring at them, sticking his finger in their faces and threatening their jobs. Neither of them lost their cool in return, but when their colleagues arrived and manhandled Jay into his house, the Garda who'd comforted Jen gave her a small nod, before pulling handcuffs from his belt.

Jen's memory of that day would always be hazy. She remembered the panic on Lia's face and the rage on Jay's. The resignation on Willow's face and the blankness of Simon's. She vaguely remembered the Garda cars leaving with the rest of the Higginses scrambling into Lia's car and following on. The sudden and loud chatter that rang out around her, as neighbours cried out in disbelief. But what she would remember most vividly was how in that moment, standing on the green, she felt more bereft than ever. Her fears, her paranoia, her grief-induced madness had all been vindicated. Now all that remained was the gaping hole in her life, where Alex had once been. She turned to look towards home, a place she desperately wanted to leave now and never return to. Standing there, with his hands cupping his mouth, was Dale. He looked like the ghost of himself and when his eyes met hers, she saw a flicker of the man she once loved. As Jen walked towards him, leaving her shocked neighbours behind on the green, where no doubt they would start the discussion of the decade, Dale seemed to disintegrate. His body sagged and his tears fell, while he vomited on the ground.

# FORTY-EIGHT

## LIA

It was during her sixth hour of silently ignoring their questions, when the woman detective – the one who looked like the fictitious Mrs Trunchbull – threw the question that would change everything. Up until then, Lia had almost convinced herself that, if she just kept her mouth shut, Jay would sort it all out. He'd come along with Graham Dunleavy, or one of the firm's other heavy hitters, and they'd get her out of there.

'Did you know that your husband has left the county, Mrs Higgins?'

Lia frowned. 'What?'

'Mm. He's gone up West, I believe.' Trunchbull nodded and then directed her next question to her colleague. 'I wonder if she knows about his twenty-two-year-old intern. You know, the pregnant one?'

Lia's frown deepened. She was confused momentarily – not taking in what the detective had said about the intern, as she tried to get her head around the fact that Jay had left. They were mistaken. They had to be.

'Did he tell you about her?' the woman continued. 'Aisling.

She's been working on his campaign as part of her college degree.'

Lia cleared her throat. 'What?' she said, her first word in six whole hours with a shake of her head. 'So?'

'It seems your husband's boss' – she leafed through the pages of her notebook – 'a Mr Dunleavy, is currently dealing with a sexual misconduct case against your husband. Did you know about that? They're not overly pleased with him at the moment, Mrs Higgins, and that was *before* his wife was arrested for murder.'

A blade of ice cut through Lia's insides as Trunchbull's colleague took over, a man who'd introduced himself as Garda Twomey. She remembered his name. But not Trunchbull's. Maybe because he had a kind face, and she didn't.

'You should know that your husband's firm, Dunleavy and Co, are no longer backing your husband's campaign.'

'I want to speak to my husband,' she said, shaking her head. They were lying. They had to be. 'I want my lawyer.'

Twomey nodded. 'Very wise. But it seems Dunleavy and Co are declining to get involved, given their current case against your husband. They feel it would be a conflict for them. But, by all means, let us know who else we can contact for you. I believe your husband is somewhere up around Galway. I'm assuming that's his way of telling you that you're on your own. But we're certainly doing our best to get hold of him.'

'Call my husband.' Lia's chest tightened and her voice sounded like it was coming from somewhere far away.

'We've *been* calling him, Mrs Higgins, and he's not picking up. Our colleagues up West are tracking him down,' Trunchbull said, matter of fact. She leaned across the table. 'But you should take it that he's not coming to rescue you. He's too busy distancing himself. Covering his own arse, if you will.' She paused then leaned a little closer. 'He's leaving you swinging in the wind, Lia. Now, while you sit there and convince yourself that your husband will somehow make this all go away, let me tell you what will happen. This isn't a TV cop series. You sitting there mute won't lead to you being released without charge. You *are* being charged with the murder of Alex Blake, and I'll tell you why.'

Lia pressed her tongue into the roof of her mouth and started her breathing exercises. She was cold, even though a bead of sweat ran from the base of her neck, down her spine. It pooled with the others near the waistband of her royal blue trousers.

'Why don't you tell her, Cillian?' She turned to her colleague and then sat back, as if it was her time to relax. Like her words weren't shattering someone's life.

Lia kept her eyes trained on the table. Her knee bounced uncontrollably under it and her breathing exercises were faltering. The pain increased in her chest, as her heart tried to break out through it.

'We have CCTV footage of you, driving your car past the Port of Cork building, and further down along the quays,' Twomey said, his face grave. His hands were clasped together on the table in front of him and he looked straight at her. No need for notes. 'Another camera picks you up where you parked your car, and we have lovely clear footage of you stepping out and pulling a black kitbag over your shoulder.' He looked to Trunchbull then, and she had the audacity to smile, like they were recalling some shared, happy memory.

'What's the bet that if we zoom in, we'll see the St Brendan's logo on that kitbag?' she said.

He nodded, but he didn't smile. He just kept his eyes on Lia. She could feel them burning into the top of her head, but she refused to look up as the walls of the small, airless room closed in around her.

'Anyway,' Trunchbull continued, 'while you're busy slinging Alex's kitbag over your shoulder, we see Alex Blake getting out of your passenger seat.' They both stared at her then, letting a heavy silence bear down, crushing Lia where she sat. But still, she refused to meet their eyes, her mind still reeling over the insinuation that Jay had abandoned her.

'That's the thing,' Trunchbull said. 'You literally can't go anywhere these days without leaving a trace. And in your case, it's all come together like a home movie.' She lost her smile then and her face turned vicious. She slammed her hands down on the table, making Lia jump and look at her at last. She scraped her chair right into the table and left as little space between her face and Lia's as she could. 'We *see* you placing an arm around Alex.' Her voice was low, but very clear. 'We *see* you pulling that kitbag off your shoulder and slinging it over the child's neck. We *see* you shoving her – a child who knew you all her life – a child who trusted you. A child who *you* knew had a mortal fear of water. We *see* you pushing her to a most terrifying death and then...' She paused and breathed heavily through her nose. 'And then running away, like the coward you are.'

Lia's insides slackened as she relived the scene they were setting out before her. Alex assuring her that it would all be okay. Alex. Assuring *her*. Lia remembered feeling the tremble in the girl's shoulders when she placed her arm around her. She could almost smell her fear as she glanced towards the fast-moving river that snaked alongside them. Alex hadn't spotted her kitbag on Lia's opposite shoulder, and even if she had, she would never have considered why it was really there.

*My mum will know what to do.* Lia could still hear the conviction in her voice. And the naivety. *It's all going to be okay.* The bag felt heavy as the rough strap dug through the cashmere of her jumper. She knew it would sink her. Even if Alex *could* swim – but she couldn't.

'We have the messages between Alex and you, which you tried to delete,' Twomey continued, pulling Lia back into the room. 'Those, and the fact that you carried the kitbag' – he paused – 'show premeditation. You *planned* this, Lia.' He said it like he desperately wanted to understand it all. And suddenly she *wanted* him to. 'You *planned* to kill a fifteen-year-old girl. Your daughter's best friend.' He frowned sadly and shook his head. 'Why?'

'So, you see, you *are* being charged with murder, Mrs Higgins,' Trunchbull said, not giving her a chance to respond. 'You can either tell us what happened – your side of the story, or we can paint our own picture with the evidence that we have. And it's a compelling bloody picture that will see you going away for a very long time.'

'Why did you do it?' Twomey asked again, in the same confused tone, which was in direct contrast to Trunchbull's accusatory one.

'Because she's a callous bitch.' Trunchbull answered his question.

'Did you fear for your life?' Twomey asked, his eyes still on Lia like maybe he *did* understand.

'From a fifteen-year-old girl?' Trunchbull trilled, incredulous.

'From your husband,' Twomey said in the same level tone, never taking his eyes off her.

Lia's deep breathing stopped momentarily, his words sinking into her brain.

'Because you know the judge will take everything into account,' he continued. 'She had something on your family, didn't she? Something your husband wouldn't want to get out. Did he threaten you, is that it?'

Lia's tears started to fall, and her shoulders shook. She brought her trembling hands to her face.

'She was fifteen years old,' Trunchbull said, her voice soft, almost pleading suddenly.

'She was going to tell,' Lia said, too softly to be heard.

'I'm sorry?' Twomey asked.

Lia squeezed her eyes shut and thought about her family. Her children. Simon. They were right. She did kill Alex, and they had all the proof they needed to put her away. But anyone else's version of what happened might place her son under a microscope. This was her last chance to protect her boy. She inhaled loudly through her nose and straightened herself up in her seat. She was ready at last to tell her story. 'She saw,' she said, as clearly as she could. 'Alex saw him. And she was going to tell.'

# FORTY-NINE

## LIA

'She saw?' Twomey asked. His tone was soft. Gentle even and Lia much preferred him to Trunchbull. 'She saw who? What did she see, Mrs Blake?'

Lia picked painfully at the skin around her manicured thumbnail and rocked slightly in her chair. She couldn't look at them while she spoke. She couldn't. She had to concentrate. She had to line up her thoughts because it was over for her. A strange sense of relief passed over her when she thought about what that meant. It. Was. Over. All of it. It was time, at last, to tell the truth. Or at least, *most* of it.

'She saw Jay,' she whispered.

She sensed a subtle shift in the atmosphere as the two Gardaí glanced at each other.

'Go on,' Trunchbull nudged gently.

'Alex had been... struggling. At school. Her parents have their own problems and so she turned to me.'

They didn't scream at her that Simon was the reason she was struggling, but she sensed that they wanted to. 'My son can be a bit misguided at times,' she said, knowing that she couldn't avoid it entirely. 'He did some stupid things, which he's sorry for, but yes...' She glanced up at them, feeling some of her old resolve returning. 'It did affect her. But that's not why this happened.'

The guards sat silently listening and neither one of them moved. Lia placed her hands on the table. They'd stopped shaking. Her tears still flowed, but they were silent, and her breathing had somehow regulated. Despite where she was and what she was saying, Lia felt a sense of freedom. Something she hadn't felt in more than twenty years.

'Alex messaged me, to say that she needed to tell her mum about the bullying. She asked for my help.' She inhaled and breathed out until her lungs emptied. 'I went to meet her. To see if I could help. And that *was* my intention. That *was* what I planned to do.'

'Where was she?'

'At the school, near the basketball courts. She got in my car, and I brought her home to my house.'

'To your house? Not her own?'

*Can you take me home, Lia?*

'Jen was frantic by then. It would have been the wrong time to tell her anything. I know her, you see, and she would have gone nuclear, so I offered to take Alex to my house so we could decide how best to tell her.'

'So what time was that?'

'About seven forty-five.'

'Go on,' Twomey nudged.

'The kids had gone out again. Willow went to watch a basketball match at the school, and Simon was... out, too. Probably at the same match. Jay wasn't supposed to be home until after nine. But then his car pulled into the driveway.' She looked to the ceiling and took a few more breaths. 'This is the first time I've ever said any of this out loud,' she said, almost in a whisper.

'It's okay,' Twomey assured her. 'Take your time.'

'My husband has controlled me for most of my life. I won't bore you with the details, only to say that, when he's unhappy with something we've done, his punishments are severe.'

'In what way?'

Lia shrugged, her bottom lip trembling now. 'He'd starve us, take away access to money, beatings, emotional torture...' She waved her hand and laughed a frightened laugh. 'You know, that kind of thing. Anyway – I couldn't let him find out that Alex was struggling so much with what Simon had done. Or that she was planning to tell her parents. I was supposed to have it under control, you see. I was supposed to have sorted it all out. So, when his car pulled into the driveway, I ushered Alex into the kitchen and told her to hide.' She lowered her eyes. 'I could tell she was confused. Maybe even frightened. She would never have seen that side of me. The *scared* side.' She forced a laugh again at the ridiculousness of it. Of *her*. 'I'm the one who always has her shit together, you know?'

Twomey nodded. 'So what happened next?' It seemed Trunchbull only spoke when she had something to growl about.

'He came in and asked why I wasn't over at the match, cheering on the Bulldogs. He thought it looked bad if we weren't front and centre of everything and those are the kinds of things that set him off.' Her hands found each other under the table and started fidgeting. 'It wasn't even Willow's team, but that didn't matter. Next thing I knew, his hand was around my throat. He shoved me into the front room and onto the floor. I...' She cleared her throat, her knees starting to bounce again. But she forced herself to look up. To keep going. 'I saw Alex, watching through the crack in the door. She heard the names that he called me. Useless bitch. Whore. The usual. She heard him asking how much I'd had to eat that day. My food was severely rationed. Then she saw him kicking me in the ribs and the back, telling me how disgusting I am.' Shame radiated from her as she looked past them, into the middle distance. 'I saw the fear in her eyes.'

'Did he know she was there?' Trunchbull asked, her aggression halved.

Lia shook her head. 'He couldn't know. He would have killed me for letting anyone see him for who he really is.'

'How did Alex get out of there without him seeing?'

'When he was finished with me, he went upstairs to have his shower. I pulled myself off the floor and went to her. She was crying. Terrified. Like she'd just realised that everything she thought she knew, was a lie.' Alex had vomited on herself as well, but Lia didn't tell them that. 'I begged Alex to be quiet,' she continued. 'And we left as soon as the bathroom door closed and the shower went on.'

'Is that when you drove her to the quays?'

'She was such an incredible girl.' Her voice was a whisper again. 'Brave. Like only a child can be.' She smiled, remembering, 'She wanted to bring me and Willow home to their house. She said that Jen would help us. That we could all go together to the guards and report Jay. Tell them what he was really like.' Her smile quivered and fell. Alex had wanted to report Simon, too. Both of them, but this true story was all about Jay with her son's chapters redacted. Jay had abandoned her, so her children were her priority now. 'She said that Willow and I could stay with them until he was taken away.' She shook and lowered her head again. 'She wanted to save me.' She lost her voice on the last syllable. 'And Willow. She wanted to save us both and she was so sure that she could. She was sure that it was just *that* simple.'

'But you didn't think it was?' Trunchbull asked.

'I *know* it's not. This whole city think they know my husband, detective. The handsome, decent, family man who serves food to the homeless and uses the law to fight injustice. And if his persona didn't save him, then he's with one of the most powerful law firms in the county. And what am I? I haven't one true friend. No one who *actually* likes me. Who would believe me?' She smiled a bitter smile. 'He'd get off and then he'd kill me for humiliating him.'

A moment of tense silence passed before Trunchbull asked, 'So, you drove to the quays?'

Lia nodded slowly, then looked at her hands. 'Yes. We drove to the quays. I let Alex talk all the way and I just knew. I knew that she'd never understand.'

'Understand…?' Trunchbull again.

'She wouldn't understand that outing Jay would mean destroying my family. If I'm dead, which I would be, then my kids would have no one to protect them from *him*.'

'So you killed Alex to keep her quiet.'

'I had to.' She looked at them frowning, her hands splayed on the table now. They had to understand. 'No matter how I explained it to her, I know Alex Blake. She's her mother's daughter.' Her strength slowly returned now that the worst part of the story was told. This was why she *had* to kill Alex. She didn't want to. But she didn't have a choice. She knew that, even now.

'What does that mean – she was her mother's daughter?' Twomey asked.

'Jen Blake has a self-righteous and totally unrealistic sense of right and wrong. Black and white, and she brought her daughter up the same way. They're oblivious to the *thousands* of shades of grey all around them.' She closed her eyes. 'I *knew* Alex Blake. She would tell. And my children's lives would be ruined.' Even as she said the words, she could see the irony. The guards could, too, but they kindly didn't say anything.

The three of them sat there in silence for a few long minutes before Lia spoke again. 'She was so scared.' Her voice was low and filled with sorrow and regret. She looked up at the guards, who were watching and listening intently. 'When we walked away from the car. She was so scared... just being that close to the river. That's why I put my arm around her.'

More silence enveloped them, aside from Lia's loud breathing, as a slow-motion reel played in her mind's eye. She heard herself asking Alex, as they walked like mother and daughter along the path, if they could wait before they told anyone. She saw the confusion on Alex's face and something like disappointment, too. Lia remembered the certainty with which she knew that it was no use. Then her hands moved of their own accord and the bag was off her shoulder and slung around Alex's neck. In the split second between then, and the push, Alex looked questioningly at the bag. Then at Lia. 'She was so clever,' she said, her voice hoarse and cracked. She closed her eyes and saw the realisation dawn on Alex's face. Something bad was about to happen, but before that thought could fully form, and before she could react in any way, her body was floating through the air, away from Lia and into the black river. Now whenever Lia thought about Alex Blake, which would be every minute of every day for the rest of her life, the years of smiles and laughter would be erased and her features would be forever frozen in that mask of terror, as she floated away from her. And away from the big life she might have gone on to have.

'You slung the bag around her neck to weigh her down.' Another long pause. 'Why the river? When it terrified her so much. Why...?' Trunchbull asked, sounding genuinely curious now. Like she needed to know that one detail, for herself.

Lia sniffed loudly and wiped her eyes, which continued to pour. She shook her head and cast her gaze all around the soulless room. 'It was the only way...' she sobbed. 'The only way I could be sure...'

'That she would actually die,' Twomey finished for her, sounding like he'd never been in the presence of something so disgusting in his entire life.

Lia saw her true self reflected in his expression and her skin tingled and crawled. She was a killer. A *disgusting* child killer. It was all true, and suddenly she thought about what that *really* meant. She was going to prison. She looked to the ceiling and slowly exhaled. Soon her life as she knew it would be a distant memory. She'd be a fat, unkempt, perhaps foul-mouthed prisoner. Her eyes dried up and her shoulders fell. Soon, she would finally be free.

# EPILOGUE



*Six months later*

The sight of Lia Higgins made Jen's breath catch in her chest. It was the first time she'd seen her since her arrest, and she looked like a completely different person. Her once long and shiny blonde hair had been hacked into a rough bob. She had dark circles under her eyes, and she almost filled the oversized grey tracksuit that had been issued to her. She sat hunched at the metal table, prison grey drowning what was left of her former elegance. She barely looked up when Jen entered. 'I didn't think you'd come.'

Jen's hands trembled as she lowered herself into the chair. She'd imagined this moment for months – facing the woman who'd killed her child. Now that she was here, the rage threatened to choke her. 'Neither did I.'

'You look good.' Lia's eyes flickered over Jen's new pixie cut, with the auburn tint. A ghost of her old appraising gaze.

'You don't.' The words came out like ice.

Lia laughed – a hollow sound that echoed off the concrete walls. 'I deserve that.'

'You deserve to rot.' Jen's voice shook. 'You watched us search for her. You stood there, with your arm around me, while they pulled her body from the water. You came to her funeral.'

'I hear you and Dale split up.' Lia's deflection carried a hint of her old manipulative skill. 'I'm sorry to hear that.'

Jen took her time responding. She had no idea how she was going to react to coming face to face with the woman who killed her child. But more than a year had passed since Alex's death, and Jen had come a long way. In honour of her daughter, she would not crumble in front of Lia now. She wouldn't give her that satisfaction. She nodded in response to Lia's question. 'We did.'

'You don't look too upset about it.'

Jen shrugged, barely holding herself in check. 'I'm not. And neither is Dale.' She made herself smile then. 'He was my best friend, once upon a time. After you disappeared from our world and before any of the kids came along. Dale was my person. Unfortunately, we lost sight of all that after he lost his job and life got hard. But now...' She shrugged again. 'I have my friend back.'

Lia's smile faded and died. Her bottom lip wavered, and she nodded. 'That's good. I'm happy for you.'

'I hear Jay moved on.' She couldn't help herself.

Lia lowered her eyes to her fidgeting hands and that's when Jen saw the raw cuts on her scalp. It looked like Lia had been tearing her hair out. Literally. Or maybe someone else was doing it for her. She was a child killer after all. But she couldn't bring herself to feel anything more than hatred for her.

'Why did you ask me to come, Lia?' Her voice shook and her stomach remained in a tight ball. It had been like that since she woke up.

'Why do you think?'

Jen shrugged again. 'For absolution?'

'For killing a child?' Lia shook her head and finally looked up from the table. Her eyes were wet with tears. 'There is no absolution for that.'

'For killing my child, *and* for leading me to believe she killed herself. You sent that text from her phone, didn't you? The suicide note.'

Lia nodded with her eyes on the table. 'I had to. She wanted to tell you what Jay had done. You could have gone to the police and Jay would've...'

Jen held her palm up to stop her. 'The first sign of you justifying any of your actions or asking for forgiveness and I'm leaving.'

'Jay would've killed me.'

'You could have told the guards that you were afraid of him. You could have gotten help. *I* would have helped you. I'd been offering for twenty fucking years.' She paused to catch her breath. 'But you killed Alex instead.'

'I'm not asking you for forgiveness.'

'So, what then?'

'Did you know that Willow had to be admitted for residential psychiatric care?'

Jen nodded. 'I did.'

'Course you did. I believe she's involved with you now.' There was a trace of bitterness in Lia's voice then and she roughly wiped her eyes.

'So you know about what we do?' She could see Lia's humiliation but had no interest in rubbing the woman's face in it. She had no time for pettiness now.

Lia shrugged. 'Not really. But I get the gist of it, I think.'

'Anna Greene started a GoFundMe for my family after you were arrested. Did you know that?'

Lia shook her head.

'She knew we were broke.' Jen looked Lia in the eye, letting her know that she was no longer embarrassed to admit that. 'She wanted to ease our financial pressure,' she continued, 'and provide for Alex's funeral. And for myself and Dale to have some counselling. As embarrassing as it was at the time – we needed the help.'

'But I'm guessing you got more than that.' Lia's response was snide, and her expression matched it. Her face had filled out dramatically and while it still held traces of her beauty, minus the permanent smile and the make-up, she looked *real*. Like someone who *thought* and *felt* and *reacted* in a way that made sense.

'That fund raised more than two hundred thousand euro. So, we used it, not just for counselling for ourselves, but for kids like Alex.'

'Hence the name.'

'That's right. The Alex Blake foundation.'

'And what's Willow's part in all this?'

She could have used this as her cue to taunt Lia with the fact that Willow had yet to visit her. Or that she was refusing to take her calls. But she didn't. She was stronger than that now. Instead, she wanted Lia to see how well her daughter was doing, *despite* her.

'Well, to begin with, we set up a hotline with trained counsellors on the other end. Me and Anna travelled around to schools, first around Cork and now further afield, talking about bullying – the different types of bullying, how easy it is for otherwise nice kids to pile on and get caught up in it. And of course, the consequences. We're making sure every school kid in the country has our number and let me tell you, Lia, those phones ring nonstop. And on the other end are kids like mine. And kids like yours.'

Lia raised her eyebrows and blew out a breath as she nodded, her eyes full again.

'So, to answer your question, Willow accompanies me from

time to time when I'm visiting schools. Her story is powerful' – Jen leaned across the table – 'and so is she.'

Lia brought her hand to her face and her shoulders shook as her tears fell. 'Why are you being kind to us?' The words were muffled behind her cupped hands.

Jen frowned and her lip curled in disgust. 'I'm not doing anything for *you*. Willow was Alex's best friend. She loved her. We *love* her. And she was as much a victim in all this as anyone else.'

Lia sniffed loudly and wiped her eyes. She smiled again, and Jen noticed how stained her teeth were now. Those teeth that were permanently bleached and perfect were now the clearest sign of how far the woman had fallen. Or how far she'd jumped. 'You sound like you spend a lot of time around those counsellors.'

'I'm training to become one. So is Anna. We're in the process of getting government funding for the foundation and lots more donors are on board.' Jen smiled then. A one-upmanship smile, despite telling herself not to. 'My daughter has left quite the legacy,' she added proudly.

'I'm sorry,' Lia choked, lifting her head and looking Jen in the eye for the first time since she sat down.

Jen didn't answer. The room began to spin. *Just breathe*, she told herself. *Just breathe*.

'For all of it. I'm sorry. I'm sorry that I ever chose Jay,' she said bitterly. 'But then I wouldn't have had my Willow.' She sobbed.

'Or Simon,' Jen added.

Lia lowered her head again.

'He's gone to stay with Jay's sister in Galway, hasn't he?'

'Leave him alone, Jen. Please.' Lia searched her eyes pleadingly.

'I have no intention of harming your son, Lia. As much as I'd like to. But I will be keeping track of him. As will my friend

Holly. Thanks to your husband, there's no shortage of people who'd like to see either one of them step out of line again.'

'Getting fired was a bigger punishment than you can imagine for Jay.'

Jen shook her head. 'Do *you* think it was punishment enough?'

'No,' Lia answered, pulling herself up straighter in her seat. Her honesty caught Jen off guard.

'Which is why you finally made a complaint against him. Presumably that was at the behest of your defence solicitor?'

'For all the good it'll do. I never "documented"' – she used air quotes – 'any of my injuries. I have no physical proof that he was ever anything but sweet to me.'

'But you have Willow.'

Lia nodded and her tears came again. 'She was always so much braver than me. She stood up to him every chance she got.'

'It's just a pity there was no one to stand up for her,' Jen said, bringing a silence crashing down upon them. She let it sit for a minute before continuing, 'She's willing to take the stand against him. But Lia, you cannot lose your nerve when you're faced with him. If you do, you'll leave your daughter hanging. Again.'

Lia roughly wiped her face and looked angrier now. 'Is this why you agreed to come? To remind me what a shit mother I am?'

Jen shook her head. 'I came here because Willow asked me to.'

Lia frowned. 'To aid my defence?'

Jen huffed out an incredulous laugh. 'Absolutely not. You're not getting away with killing my child, Lia. But that bastard played a part in it, too. He needs to be held to account. So, if you feel yourself faltering, and clearly your children aren't incentive enough for you, just think of the other woman he's playing happy families with, while you're locked up in here.'

'You told Willow that I contacted you?' She ignored Jen's sharp instructions.

Jen nodded.

'So you're, like, her replacement mother now?' She sounded sad at last.

'No. Your sister is taking really good care of her.'

Lia nodded and a spiteful look crossed her face again. 'Saint Alice,' she muttered. 'She always hated me.'

'She always hated Jay. As far as she's concerned, she lost her sister to a monster. I can't say I disagree with her there.'

Lia just continued nodding, her eyes on the table and her hands fidgeting with each other. Jen could almost see the conspiracies floating around behind her eyes.

'I wasn't going to come,' Jen said honestly. 'But Willow wanted me to remind you of' – she waved her hands around – 'what I just said. If Willow is asked to give evidence, it will be by video link. But it still won't be an easy thing for her to do. And I know you'll agree that she's been through enough. So wear your big girl pants, Lia, and tell the truth about your husband. For once in your life.'

Lia continued to nod, eyes still fixed on her hands.

Jen stood up to go.

'I am sorry, Jen. For all of it.' Lia stood shakily to her feet.

'I don't want your apologies, Lia.' Jen pulled her bag onto her shoulder. 'I don't want anything from you.' She turned and walked away towards the door.


Jen stepped out of the prison into the sharp winter air. Soon another teenager would call their hotline, voice trembling because they trusted the wrong person, or were unknowingly filmed with the person who said they loved them, or simply because their world had turned against them. Another parent would reach out, desperate to protect their child. And thanks to the strength which passed from Alex to Jen in the river that night, Jen would be there, armed with her daughter's truth. With everything she'd learned from the bravest girl who ever lived. Her darling Alex Blake.

Dear reader,

Thank you for reading *A Good Mother*. If you would like to join other readers in keeping in touch, stay in the loop with my new releases by signing up to my email newsletter here.

www.stormpublishing.co/michelle-dunne

If you enjoyed it and could spare a few moments to leave a review, that would be hugely appreciated. Even a short review can make all the difference in encouraging a reader to discover my books for the first time. Thank you so much!

This book was inspired by all the amazing mothers I know. And of course, by being one myself. Our worst nightmares revolve around the safety of our children. That constant worry that something bad might happen to them – something outside of our control. Or God forbid, something we missed. We're learning all the time about the challenges they face, online and off. We know that we can no longer assume that they are safe, even when they're alone in their rooms. In turn, mothers are expected to juggle far more than ever before, excelling in all areas. And to never, EVER, drop the ball.

With every story of schoolyard bullying and awful headline about a young life lost, we find ourselves asking: What would I do if that was my child? What would I do if my child was bullied to death? What would I do if my child *bullied* someone to death? It doesn't bear thinking about. But...

Enter Jen Blake and Lia Higgins...

On that note, with the daily bombardment of Instagrammably perfect people, we have to remind ourselves from time to time that a mother is just a person. She's not perfect. But she's someone who does whatever it takes to keep her child's world turning. She works as hard as she needs to. She puts everyone's needs before her own and she juggles as best she can. She takes on the expectations of the world around her and the judgement that must feel constant at times.

But she loves fiercely, and with every inch of her heart. That much a good mother *does* know.

Michelle x

 facebook.com/MichelleDunneAuthor

 x.com/NotDunneYet

 instagram.com/michelledunneauthor

# ACKNOWLEDGEMENTS

I must once again thank the incredible team at Storm Publishing for their expert guidance and their passion for what they do. Claire, you're exactly the kind of editor that any writer would hope to have. Thank you, Alexandra, Elke and the entire team, for your attention to detail and for being generally fabulous to work with!

And to my lovely agent/therapist/guidance counsellor/friend, Nicky Lovick – thank you, from the bottom of my heart. With you, Madeline, and the powerhouse team at WGM Atlantic, I always feel like I'm in very safe hands.

I dedicated this book to mothers everywhere, because I feel it's the least I owe them. Before becoming one myself, I was one of the many people who underestimated what it is that mothers do. And what do they do? Everything. They do EVERYTHING! To my own mum, Ann. My best friends (and other mothers to my child), Yolanda, Louise and Annemarie. To the school-gate mums who support and encourage each other through each step and every crazy phase. You're all amazing!

To the beautiful girl who calls me Mum – Emily. Right now, you'll be marketing this book all over the playground and asking me when you'll be allowed to read it. You're the funniest, kindest and most loving person I know, and I'm so proud to be your mum.

Finally, a heartfelt thank-you to the incredible booksellers, readers, reviewers and bloggers who carry our work out into the world. By spreading the word about the books you enjoy, you're keeping us authors going. Without you, there'd be no point. Thank you, thank you, thank you.